THE GHOSTWRITER

THE GHOSTWRITER

ALESSANDRA TORRE

ISBN: 978-1-940941-94-3

Editors: Madison Seidler, Susan Barnes, and Perla Calas
Cover Design: © Sofie Hartley of Hart & Bailey Design Co
Proofreader: Janice Owen
Formatting: Erik Gevers

A gentle pull on my hand. I resist, turning away, and smile when I feel the tiny fingers pushing aside my bangs, the soft weight of a body against mine.

"Mommy." A huff of breath against my cheek. "Mommmmmy."

"Mommy's asleep," Simon whispers. "If we don't wake her up, we can eat all of the delicious chocolate chip pancakes ourselves."

I growl, and clamp a hand over his, which is sneaking under the edge of my sleepshirt. I open my eyes and look up into his face, those handsome features dusted by flour and a smear of chocolate. "Easy," I warn him, pulling on his wrist and dragging him onto the mattress, my movements quick as I wiggle out of the covers and atop his waist. "You know the monster is grouchy when she is awoken."

"Let me, let me!" Bethany scrambles before me, straddling his chest and gripping the front of his shirt, looking back at me with a smile.

"Ah..." I crow. "My monster keeper and I have got you captured, Mr. Pancake Man!" I shift atop him and he gives me a look, the sort of look that—years ago—led to naked events that create babies. I smile at him and wrap my arms around my child. "What should we make Mr. Pancake Man do, Princess Bethany?"

"He should feed the monster!" She announces, and raises both hands in the air to exclamation point the phrase.

"AND... do the dishes!" I raise my own hands in the air and Simon groans in protest. Bucking up his hips, he deposits us both onto the mattress, giving Bethany a quick tickle, and me a deep kiss.

"Come, Monster," he commands. "Come and let me fill that big belly."

I come, I eat, and afterward, while Bethany draws and I settle into the recliner to write, he does the dishes.

A perfect morning. A perfect husband. A perfect daughter. A perfect lie.

I'm dying. It's a grim start to any story, but I think the news should be delivered in the same manner as a ripped band-aid. Short and blunt, a stab that burns for a moment, then is gone, the moment over. My doctor tip-toed around the news, showing me test results and citing blood cell counts, CEA numbers, and an MRI that showed a tumor the size of a small lemon. He drew out what could have been accomplished in two short sentences. *You're terminal. You have three months left.*

I should be sad. I should be emotional, my fingers shaking as they press cell phone buttons and make depressingly bleak phone calls to all of my friends and family. Only, I don't have friends. And my family… I have no family. I have only this countdown, a dark ominous chant of days, sunrises and sunsets before my body gives up and my mind shuts down.

It's not really a terrible diagnosis—not for me. I've been waiting four years for something like this to happen, a guillotine to fall, an escape door to appear. I'd be almost cheerful about it, if it weren't for the book. The story. The truth, which I've avoided for the last four years.

I step into my office and flip on the light. Moving forward, I reach out, my hand trailing over the corkboard wall, hovering over the tacked up photos, the pages of abandoned ideas, jotted notes of a hundred sleepless nights, sparks of inspiration—some that led nowhere, some that now sit on bookshelves all over the world.

My husband made me this board. His hands held the wood frame in place, cut the cork, and nailed the pieces into place. He kept me out of the office all day to do it, my insistence at entering thwarted by the lock, my knocks on the door ignored. I remember sitting back in this same chair, my hands on my belly, and seeing the final product. I had stared up at the blank board and thought of all the stories I would build on it, the words already itching for their place. It had become everything I thought it would.

I stop at the page I've read countless times, its paper worn more than the others, the edges not obscured with clippings or neighboring photos. It's the synopsis for a novel. Right now, it's just one paragraph in length, the type of copy that might one day be embossed on the back cover of the book. I've written fifteen novels, but this one terrifies me. I fear that I won't have the right words, the right arc, that I will aim too high, hit too hard, and still not properly affect the reader. I fear that I'll tell everything, and still no one will understand.

It's a book I had planned to write decades from now, once my skills had grown, my writing sharpened, talents perfected. It is a book I planned to spend years on, everything else pushed aside, my world closing in on the one thing that mattered, nothing else moving until it was finished, until it was perfect.

Now, I don't have decades.

I don't have years.

I don't have the level of skill.

I don't have *anything.*

It doesn't matter. I pull at the tack that holds it in place, and set the page carefully on the center of my clean desk.

Three months. The deadline is the tightest I've ever faced. There will be no frantic calls to my agent, no negotiation for more time.

Three months to write a story that deserves years.

Is it even possible?

When I meet him, the night is singed with the smell of funnel cakes and cigarette smoke. He smiles and something inside of me shifts, a crack in between the vertebrae, my heart beating a little bit harder than it ever has.

Boys like him don't go for girls like me, they don't follow me with their eyes, or listen when I speak. They don't lean closer or want more.

He is different than all the others. He doesn't laugh. He doesn't step away. Our eyes meet, his mouth curves, and my world changes.

Writing the first chapter burns. Maybe it's the new drugs, maybe it's the memories, but I feel hot with the effort, my shirt damp against the small of my back, my chest tight and achy by the time I finish the story of our meeting and our first date. It was a night where he won my mother over with one easy smile, and won me over with tacos and Mexican beer, his fingers looping through mine as we walked out to the car. He had kissed me against that car, my mouth hesitant, his strong and sure, my nerves dissolving in the first confident dive of his tongue.

I had been such a young twenty-year-old—one that had never been on a date, never been pursued, never *cared* about boys and romance, outside of the pages of my novels.

But everything had been different after that night. Simon swept into my life and turned it into something fiery and wild, my days beginning with an excited fervor, my nights ending with thoughts of love and of a future—one of travel and passion, of his eyes and his touch, of being desired for something other than my words.

It had been love. From the very beginning. Wild. Crazy. Senseless. Love.

I save my work and close the laptop, feeling nauseous.

At precisely 2:24 on Wednesday afternoon, I stop typing. Moving the laptop aside, I clear off the top of my desk, moving my phone into the center of the space, a fresh notepad pulled from the drawer, a pen uncapped and placed on its white lined surface.

In the next two minutes, I settle back against the chair and extend my arms over my head, closing my eyes and stretching my chest.

At precisely 2:30, the phone rings. I sit up, grabbing the phone and lifting it to my ear. "Hey Kate."

"Good afternoon, Helena." There is a hitch in her voice, as if she's run to the phone, as if she hasn't had all week to prepare for this call and set aside this time. Irritation blooms in my chest, a common occurrence on these calls. "I have four things to discuss."

It took years for me to properly train Kate, to curb the agent's tendencies for mindless chit-chat and pleasantries. In the beginning, she was more resistant to my expectations, but the first advance, the first bestseller, the first commission—that made her more pliable. It's amazing what money will do to a person, the level of control it can establish. It's made Kate my monkey. It made Simon my pet—the sort who doesn't clean up his messes, the sort who marks his territory, the sort who bares his teeth and will attack your child if you don't keep him on a tight enough leash.

Kate brings up a foreign offer first, my pen scratching out the terms under a neat heading with today's date. I accept the terms, and we move on to the second item—a third reprinting of *Hope's Ferry*. Wahoo. I sigh, and manage to make it through the third and fourth topic. She falls silent and I consider my next words, choosing ones designed to cause as little a reaction as possible.

"I'll need you to close any open action items. I'm retiring." Retiring, I decided over breakfast, would be the best way to put it. It's sort of the same thing as death, as far as Kate is concerned. Both mean that my book production will stop. Both mean that I won't be able to meet any outstanding deadlines.

There is a long silence, the sort that stretches over canyons, the kind that causes someone to pull the phone away from their ear and check the connection. When she finally responds, it is decidedly unimaginative, and I sigh at her predictability.

KATE

"Retiring?" Kate says dumbly. She spent the greater part of the last ten seconds trying to find a better response, one that Helena would appreciate, but the thought is so… absurd, that she can only repeat it. There is no way Helena Ross is *retiring*. Not when Marka Vantly is churning out a fresh bestseller every four months. Helena will write until her fingers fall off purely out of competitive spite for her rival. Besides, who *retires* at thirty-two?

"Yes," Helena snaps. "It's when people stop working."

"I'm familiar with the term." She pushes against the desk, her office chair spinning, the room a soothing blur of pale pinks and cream. "Why?" She closes her eyes when she asks the question, knowing—even as she utters the word—that it isn't allowed. Rule #4 on Helena's Rules for Kate is to Not Ask Personal Questions. A rule she's broken before, the results always disastrous. She steels herself for the click of the receiver, the sharp cut of Helena's voice, the dreaded ding of an incoming email—one full of stern admonishments about their agent/client relationship and its boundaries.

Instead, Helena only sighs, the lack of reaction as odd as her retirement announcement. "I need you to reach out to the publisher about *Broken* and let them know I won't be delivering it."

Kate's eyes snap open, her teeth baring in the inhuman act of not repeating the woman's words. She sits upright, pulling herself closer to the desk, using the moment to flip the calendar open, her fingers skimming over the dates until she gets to the neatly written words. *Broken Due.* A little over a month from now. Last week, when they spoke, Helena had been eighty percent done, and confident about her delivery. In their thirteen years together, Kate could count the number of times that Helena had missed a deadline on one hand. Her requested extensions had never been for more than a week or two, her personal rules as strict as the ones she had for everyone else.

But now, she isn't asking for an extension. She is telling Kate that she wants to walk away from a publishing commitment, a book that has already been announced, pre-marketing in place, half of her seven-figure advance already in the bank, Kate's commission way past spent. Non-delivery is a rare event in the publishing industry. For Helena Ross, it's inconceivable.

She stands, every muscle tightening in preparation for battle. "Helena," she says carefully. "What's happened?"

"Stop being dramatic, Kate." Helena's voice is brisk, one that an elder would use with a child, despite Kate's ten-year jump on her. "Call the publisher, wrap up my other obligations. If you can't handle that task, I'll find another agent who will."

There is something else. Kate can feel it coming, something even bigger than the *Broken* news, a tsunami moving calmly toward the shore, preparation useless, her feet rooted in place, disaster eminent. She swallows, leaning against the edge of the desk for support, her fingers tugging at the double strand of pearls at her neck, fighting the urge to reach higher and pick at her lips. "I can do it." Maybe she's wrong, maybe there isn't something else. Between retirement of her biggest client, and cancellation of a contract—maybe the bloodletting is over.

"There's something else." Three words Kate doesn't want to hear.

She drops her head and exhales. Whatever it is, she can handle it. She hasn't survived thirteen years with Helena without becoming strong. The woman is a freakin' wrecking ball of high-maintenance unpredictability.

"I'm going to write a new book. I'd like Tricia Pridgen to edit it."

Of course she does. Tricia Pridgen is the hottest editor in publishing. When she wants a book, she gets it. And everything she publishes turns to editorial gold. #1 Bestseller, multi-print-runs, foreign explosions. But Tricia Pridgen won't take a new Helena Ross. She doesn't *do* romance novels. Hell, she barely does fiction. Her last novel was a collection of OJ Simpson interviews, perfectly packaged and still dominating the bestseller lists. Helena should know this, Helena *has* to know this.

"You want to walk from *Broken*, *and* retire, *and* write a new book to sell to Tricia Pridgen?" It is a bad math problem, the variables not adding up.

"Yes."

Kate closes the calendar and tries to think, to work through the steps in this impossible equation. "Do you have an outline?"

"No outline."

A relief, something to buy her a few weeks of time. "How long will it take you to finish one?"

"I'm not submitting an outline. Or a synopsis."

She sighs. If Helena were anyone else, she'd think she was bluffing, that this entire conversation is a joke, a camera hidden in her bookshelf, her coworkers giggling in their offices. But Helena doesn't, outside her novels, have a sense of humor. She doesn't believe in *anything* that wastes time. There is no way she would spend—Kate glances at the clock—twenty-four minutes, on something that isn't vitally important. "I can't pitch without an outline. *Especially* without a synopsis. You know that. I could get away with that with Jackie, but not with Tricia Pridgen, who—by the way—doesn't take romance submissions."

"I know what Tricia Pridgen is interested in, *Kate*." The words are a whip, one that paints the words NOT WORTHY in red blood across her face. Not Worthy to handle the Great Helena Ross's submissions. Not Worthy to be the agent of romance's hottest star. Not Worthy to ask personal questions, or to call on any day except for Wednesdays at 2:30 pm, or to issue opinions about Helena's novels. Not Worthy to do anything except keep her mouth shut and *obey.*

"Then, please explain to me how you'd like me to sell this book without knowing a thing about it." Kate uses her nicest voice, the one she reserves for when Helena is at her most difficult, a voice that—had she used it on her ex-husband—he might have stayed around a little longer.

"I don't want you to sell it now. I want you to sell it in a few months. Once I… retire." There is something funny about the way she says *retire*, as if she hasn't grown used to the word quite yet.

A few months. Once I retire. A few months is too soon. Too sudden. The tsunami grows closer, and the foreboding feeling mounts. "How much will be done by then? How much will I have to use?"

"All of it." She says the words with quiet finality, as if she's tired of talking, her mind distracted by something else. "I've got to go."

Helena can't hang up. Not now, not when she just dumped a mountain of work on Kate. "Wait," Kate says wildly, searching through all of the questions she still needs to ask. "Talk to you next Wednesday?" A huge waste of a question, their Wednesday phone date so regular she could set her ovulation schedule to it.

"Wednesday?" Helena says faintly. "Yeah. Maybe."

There is the click of the receiver, and Kate's worry blooms into full-fledged panic.

My rules for visitors are simple, printed clearly in size 16 font, laminated and nailed to the center of the door, in an impossible to miss spot. The first rule, as always, is the most important.

1. Do not ring the doorbell.
2. Do not park in the driveway.
3. If you are a solicitor, leave.
4. If you are a religious or political advocate, quietly place your collateral materials underneath the mat.
5. If you are here on a social call, go away.
6. If you are here for business or legal purposes, please contact my agent or attorney.
7. Package deliveries—you have my authorization to leave packages without a signature.

I check the peephole, then crack open my front door and glare at the doorbell ringer, a young woman foolish enough to ignore my sign. She's probably the nanny of those kids, the ones who have shrieked in the street for almost two hours now. I had incorrectly assumed, three years ago, when I bought every other cul-de-sac lot, that I would be guaranteeing myself exclusive use of the giant round space. Apparently, that isn't the case, my complaints to the homeowners association met with stubborn denials. "Yes?"

"Helena Parks?" I almost flinch at the use of my married name, one so rarely used. "My name is Charlotte Blanton. I'd like to ask you a few questions."

I'd like to ask you a few questions. The police officer, his eyes grim, the smell of October in the air. *I have just a few questions.* The mortician, his thin fingers, the tap of them against a display of coffins.

I stay hidden behind the door and watch the movement of her throat as she swallows, her hands flexing around a stack of papers.

"*Are* you Helena Parks?" She is less sure of herself, and I enjoy the unease. Maybe she's a fan, a reader who hunted past publishing records and marriage licenses. It's happened before. The last one required the police. This woman, her thin shoulders jutting through a cardigan, I can probably handle.

"I'm not interested in visitors." My words are scratchy, and I clear my throat.

"It will only take a moment."

"No." I start to shut the door and she places her palm on it. I pause, and I really need to amend the rules and add *Visitors will not touch the door.* Then again, this girl obviously has no regard for authority, her eyes skipping right past my laminated list in her ring of the bell.

"Please," she says. "It's about your husband."

My husband. I hate those words falling from another person's lips. They are so bland, so weak for everything that he was. My fingers tighten on the knob. I made my statements to the police, answered hundreds of their questions. I had passed that test. To go through it again *now*, with this new woman, isn't something I am interested in. Especially not today, the giggle of children still scraping on my nerves.

I say nothing, avoiding her eyes as I close the door and flip the deadbolt, the click satisfying as it locks her outside.

I turn away from the door, hurrying toward the stairs, intent on getting away, to my office where I can shut the door, turn up my music, and drown out the sound of her intrusion.

She knocks, a rap-rap-rap that stabs at my psyche, my breath coming hard as I attempt to jog up the stairs, my muscles resisting, my body's weakness showing.

Over four years since that day. What loose thread could this woman have found?

My oncologist has prescribed me fourteen different medications, a mountain of orange pill bottles that cover every symptom my body could think of producing. Not one of them treats the pain in the ass which I currently battle. Marka Vantly: International Bestselling Author. She sucks, and in more than just the biblical sense. I inhale deeply, and stare at her latest email.

> Helena,
>
> I just had the displeasure of reading *Drumbeat.* It's interesting what passes for successful literature in this day and age. I'm so sorry about your *Publisher's Weekly* review, though I certainly understand their opinions on the novel. Congratulations on your release!
>
> Marka

The bitch. This email has taken longer to come than the others, two months passing since my pub date. Marka had probably been too distracted by gangbangs and shopping sprees to bother with something like reading. In her last interview, she'd been stretched out naked on a pile of her paperbacks, her blonde hair tumbling over their covers. For an author, she doesn't have a spare ounce of fat, no dark roots showing, her eyes lazy and seductive as they'd stared up into the camera. It had been disgusting. *So* disgusting that I'd called *The New Yorker* and cancelled my subscription. Writers aren't supposed to be sex objects. We're supposed to be valued for our words, our stories, and the impact that we leave on a reader's heart. Then again, Marka's books don't quite have that effect, their target focused more on arousal and less on emotional resonations. I rip off the head of a banana and chew, my fingers a bit slimy as I fire back a response.

> Ms. Vantly,
>
> I'm not going to take criticism from someone whose last book was titled *The Fireman's Hose.* Please return to your trashy smut and let the real authors work in peace.
>
> Helena Ross

Ha. Short and deadly. I send the email and smile, returning to my inbox, my mouse quick as I scroll past the other emails. A collection of uselessness. I unsubscribe to several solicitors, then chide myself for wasting my time. Three months left, and I'm cleaning up my inbox now? *Stupid.*

I take a final bite of the banana and toss the peel in the direction of the trash, watching as it settles into the white plastic bag. My headache, one that began this morning, is getting increasingly worse, a vise grip tightening on my temples. I let the email fester for a moment and stand, heading for the Vicodin upstairs in my desk, the banana enough food to keep it from hitting an empty stomach. I climb the stairs, and when I reach the top, the landing spins. I grip the banister for a moment and wait for everything to refocus. Maybe I should sit.

Lightheadedness, as of late, has become common. As has vertigo and blurred vision, the combination a bitch to my productivity levels. Another wave of lightheadedness hits and my hand loosens, not listening to my brain. I try to re-grip the banister, stumble hurriedly up the final steps, but everything becomes a kaleidoscope of gray and white and slick polished stairs.

My knees buckle.

Kate

Kate opens the door to her Manhattan condo, pulling off her flats as she enters, the dark room filling her with a moment of fear before her hand hits the switch and the space flickers to light. Two years since her divorce, and she still hasn't gotten used to the eeriness of living alone, the feeling that someone is there, hiding and waiting.

She opens a can of soup, dumping the thick mixture into a small pot and turning the burner on, her mind filled with thoughts of Helena. She put off calling the publishers, hoping that Helena will call her back, her sanity restored.

Of course she hasn't. Helena isn't the type to waffle over a decision or change her mind. The minute she gave Kate the order to pull out of *Broken*, it was done. Game over. Dead book walking.

It hasn't always been this hard. With Helena's first novel, she'd been almost pleasant to work with. Of course, she'd been younger then. A nineteen-year-old baby, one with big eyes and a solemn face, one who had driven from Connecticut for the sole purpose of terrorizing the Big Apple with her words. As a favor to a friend, Kate had met her at a coffee shop in Brooklyn. She'd watched the mousey brunette pick at a muffin as she'd described her novel… a second-chance romance that sounded exactly like half of Kate's slush pile. Kate had grown distracted, eavesdropping on a fight brewing at the next table, when she realized that the girl had grown quiet. Kate had flipped over the top page of the manuscript, her eyes sneaking down to her watch.

Then she'd read the first line.
The first paragraph.
The first chapter.

She, like all of America eventually would, *devoured* the words. From that plain, pale creature, one with ears and eyes a bit too big… came magic. She had forced herself to stop on the fourth page, her gaze darting up to Helena's. "You wrote this?"

Helena had nodded, then asked if she liked it.

"Yes." The answer had been too weak, and she had run her hand, almost reverently, across the page, trying to contain her excitement. "I need to read the rest of it. Tonight."

The girl had produced a CD-ROM from her messenger bag, pushing it across the table at Kate. "I've given this to five other agents." She'd said the words as if they were a gift, relieving the pressure off Kate, no need for her to pretend to like the material. But they'd had the opposite effect, the innocent information a threat, each minute that passed a possible opportunity for her phone to ring, the opportunity snatched from Kate.

"Okay." Kate had smiled weakly, her fingers lingering on the pages as she passed them back to the girl, the loss one she could *feel* in her chest. In contrast, the receipt of the CD had felt hollow, the case too light for the words which had already stamped themselves on her heart.

Kate had known, even before she opened the file, that she wanted it. She read the manuscript at her kitchen counter, peering at the screen over leftover Chinese and hot tea, her mouse constantly scrolling, the file re-saved and sent to her boss by ten PM. At ten-fifteen, she'd called Helena and left a voicemail. The voicemail she followed up with an email, one that promised a ten percent commission rate, a five percent discount that would risk her job but was worth it. She'd also guaranteed that the novel would go to auction in the six figures, another lofty promise that she couldn't back up, a figure she had never managed before. But she'd never represented a book like it before. This book could *make* her. This book could fix *everything*—their struggle to pay rent, her looming unemployment, the weak shelf her marriage balanced on.

In their dreary apartment, sending off that ridiculous beg for business… she hadn't known how high-maintenance Helena would turn out to be. She had grabbed ahold of the shiny novel, and hadn't even considered the headaches that might accompany its creator.

And the headaches have been plentiful. It isn't that Helena sets out to be high-maintenance, she is just very particular about what she wants, her quirks growing stronger over the last few years, and transitioning from requests to demands. The pleasant girl from that coffee shop has all but disappeared, withdrawing from Kate, the publishers, from any interaction with anyone. In her place, there has emerged a new Helena, one with which interactions are mine fields and keeping her happy? A balancing act.

On rare days, Kate regrets ever meeting the woman. But on most days, she just wonders about her. They say all geniuses are a little mad. Maybe Helena's madness just took longer to come out.

Kate opens a drawer and grabs a long wooden spoon, leaning against the edge of the counter and stirring the soup. Tomorrow, she decides. Tomorrow, she will call—or maybe email—the publisher and inform them of Helena's decision. An email will suffice, right? Something short and professional. If only she had more information, an excuse of some sort. She can't tell them the truth—that Helena is abandoning *Broken* for a new novel, one she wants to send to one of their competitors. Talk about burning a bridge. Word of this will spread through the publishing community like lice at a summer camp, every head infected with negative thoughts of Helena before the end of the week. She'll never be able to sell another one of her novels. Not that it really matters, since the woman is retiring.

She coughs out a laugh at the thought, and opens the refrigerator, pulling out a bottle of Moscato and setting it on the corner. Vodka would be more appropriate, something to toast the end of her career with. But she threw out all of the vodka when Rod left. The vodka, the bourbon, the small bottles she'd found tucked in every corner of their apartment. Turns out her husband had been quite the alcoholic, a trait she hadn't discovered until he'd left. Funny what you find out about people when they leave you. Or when your mind stops making excuses for all of their clues. The counselor had called those clues—his womanizing, his sloppy drinking, his lies—a call for help. "He was standing there, *screaming* at you with his actions," she'd explained.

"He was *begging* you for help."

It was bullshit. He was begging Captain Morgan for help. Not her. That woman, with all those fancy initials after her name, with her knowing smile and condescending tone, didn't know shit about real people, real problems, and real relationships.

She thinks of Helena, and of her stiff tone, her prickly demeanor that had poked at Kate through the phone line. Did Helena drink her problems away, or have any problems to begin with? Probably not. How many problems could someone like her have? She lounged around with all the talent and the money in the world. The damn woman is planning retirement at thirty-two, will spend the rest of her life sunning in the Caribbean, making early morning love to her husband, and growing fat with babies.

She turns off the burner, and taps the spoon against the edge of the pot. She tries to imagine Helena, screaming in the middle of the room, asking someone for help.

It will never happen. The woman would die first.

"Tell me about your books." His arm brushes against my shoulder when we walk, and I tuck my hands into my pockets, nervous at the thought of him reaching out, the uncomfortable join of sweaty palms.

I glance over at him, the wind rustling through the soft flop of his hair, the light from the bar's neon sign painting his face a rosy glow. "They're romance novels. You know. Boy meets girl."

He chuckles, and I like the curve of his lips, the way that his eyes light up when they look at me. "That simple, huh?"

I shrug, my own mouth lifting a little. "Love is pretty simple, Simon."

A dumb statement. But back then, I only dreamed about, yearned for, and wrote about love. I didn't realize what a brutal beast it could become.

There's a mouse in my house. I lie on my belly and hold out the piece of cheese, pushing it further underneath the couch, holding my breath as I hear the skitter of tiny paws across the floor.

I wish Bethany was here. If only... If only Mom could strap her into the car seat and bring her here, could walk in the door without knocking, just like she used to. Bethany could worm onto her stomach next to me, her tiny elbows against the wood floor, her eyes big. She would cover her mouth and giggle. Lower her chin to the floor and peer under the heavy leather couch. I could tell her that mice tails can grow as long as their bodies and that they eat 15 to 20 times per day.

I push the cheese with the tip of my nail and pull back my hand, waiting to see if the tiny creature will appear. Maybe he has a family, a tiny nest somewhere with five or six tiny pink bodies tucked in a cluster of scrap paper and misplaced threads, their miniscule mouths gaping open and begging for food. This piece of cheese can be their dinner, can pair nicely with the chunk of bread I left yesterday.

Maybe I should have let Charlotte WhatsHerFace in. The girl who showed up yesterday, armed with her questions, intent on ruining my day. Maybe her visit was just routine, a cop following up on Simon's death, a four-year check-in, and not an intensive investigation into the circumstances. Or maybe the Simon reference was an excuse, and she is actually my long lost sister. Our conversation might have unveiled a story of fire station abandonment, her youth spent in foster homes before she was finally adopted—probably by a wealthy sheik, one who crowned her a princess and is now marrying her off. She might need my help, wanting to run away to a happier life, one of freedom and sisterhood.

Ha. A terrible plot, full of holes, the first being that my mother would never abandon a child. She would have embraced a second child, especially one with Charlotte's delicate features and blonde hair. I bet she was a pretty baby. I bet she didn't refuse pacifiers or request more nutritious meals at preschool.

I turn my head, resting my ear against the wood floor, and watch the white chunk, waiting for the tremor of whiskers, a tiny nose peeking out, hesitant steps taken toward the food. I've never had a pet. Mother always crushed that possibility, appalled at the idea of drool, pet dander, urine and feces.

I shift on the floor, and close my eyes, a headache pinching hard, the pain almost blinding in its stab.

I push back from the laptop, my fingers trembling when I fumble with the edge of the drawer, pulling it open. I twist the cap off of the medicine bottle, shaking out two pain pills and popping them into my mouth. Another headache, my vision spotty from it. This morning there was a doctor's appointment, one where I laid out my symptoms and the doctor assured me they will only get worse. He gave me a sales pitch on chemo, along with a fresh script for pain meds. The chemo I passed on, but the meds I accepted.

I eye the bottom of my computer screen. Seventeen hundred words. Barely a chapter, and my fingers are stalling, my sentences grinding to a halt, my mind tripping over simple words it knows by heart. I've written fifteen books and never had such a complete whitening of thought, like a blizzard against your windshield, no options available but to pull over and stop. I push away from the desk, settling back in the chair and swinging my feet up, resting my socked heels against the wooden surface.

Three months left. That's what the doctor said. Three months, and a book that will easily run three hundred pages. I close my eyes and do the math, giving myself forty days to write, forty to rewrite, and ten days leeway for sickness. I'll need to write 8 pages, two thousand words each day. My stress rises. Ten days off in three months is a crazy schedule. And two thousand words a day is daunting, especially for me, who takes a year to produce a normal manuscript.

This will not be a normal manuscript. This is a heroine who will be closer to me than any other. A heroine whose shoes I filled, whose steps I took, decisions I made, sins I committed. Once I write her story, she will be real, she will be exposed, dead to edits but open to everyone's eyes. On their tablets, in their hands, grubby fingers and manicured nails skimming the pages faster-faster-faster until they reach The End and move on to the next. Done with that heroine. Done with that story.

I'm terrified at the thought. Thousands of words of truth and life, published and out for them to digest, creating the chance, the very small chance, that no one will buy her. Or that they will read her words and pick at them, reviewers typing away, their lips chit-chattering, musing about her motivations and her weaknesses and her actions and whether she is deserving of her fate.

I don't know what is worse, if they hate her or if they don't read her at all. She could end up in a clearance bin, a flashy 99¢ sticker plastered to her front.

I can't do that to her. I can't do that to *me*.

Maybe that's why I've waited until now, the moment when I won't be around to see the carnage, to deal with the police, the consequences, the judgement.

Two thousand words a day. Three months that are already whittling down. My stomach heaves, and I open my mouth, inhale deeply, a panic attack rising, my body suddenly hot, this office stuffy, the glow of the computer's screen too bright.

I can't do it. There is no way, not enough time, not enough hours to dedicate to what is the most important novel of my entire life.

I almost reach for the phone, dial Kate's number, and ask for help.

Instead, I lean forward, dropping to the floor, hand yanking at the plastic trash can beneath my desk, and vomit.

The summer I met Simon, I lost Jennifer. It was as if a hole opened in my heart, and he stepped right in, his hand where hers had once been, his smile replacing hers. Granted, they were different. She was eleven, he was twenty-two. She ran away...

I delete the last line, and then the entire paragraph. *Lies.* I am forgetting that this is not an ordinary novel, that I can't take fictional liberties, can't provide clues, or lead the readers down a path I didn't travel.

There is no Jennifer. Maybe if there had been, then I would be in a different place now. Maybe if I had had a friend, even an eleven-year-old one, then Simon wouldn't have been my everything.

I try to picture a friend of the twenty-year-old me, a girl whose interests had been singularly focused on reading and writing, her days spent at a notebook or computer, her mind preoccupied in thoughts of fictional characters and strange cities. Girls in my high school had seemed like foreign creatures, the boys leering villains. Another writer would have been my best bet. Or possibly a librarian, though none had ever given me the time of day.

I think of Marka Vantley, of our seven-year war, and make a face. Maybe another writer wouldn't have been my best bet. Then again, most writers aren't buxom supermodels who write trashy smut.

My gaze drifts over the stack of books beside my desk, all but one of my novels present. Missing is *Blue Heart.* The worst book I ever wrote. It was about a girl who gets a heart transplant as a child and—either due to the medical procedure or her God-given personality—is unable to love. Critics loved it and readers rushed out to purchase it, a million copies sold in the first year. Marka Vantly sent me a scathing email that spoke the truth. It said the book was terrible—flat and insipid, my attempts at matchmaking weak.

She had been right.

I hadn't responded well, reading the email and then pushing the laptop off the counter's edge. Simon had come home to find bits of the screen dotting our kitchen floor, punk music blaring through the house—an unsuccessful attempt to drown out her words.

I never responded to her email. I hadn't known what to say, my footing weak and unfamiliar. I'd solved the problem with a big sleeping pill, topped off with Chardonnay and hostility toward my husband. That email had been the spark that had started Marka's and my rivalry. The kindling had been our constant competition on the bestseller ranks, every week a new scorecard, our print runs and sales figures a giant tally that anyone with a Publishers Weekly subscription could access. That email had been the first of many, each release bringing another, my competitive nature unable to resist similar pettiness, barbs exchanged with increasing hostility.

I'd always told myself that it didn't matter what Marka Vantly thought. I'd convinced myself that she wrote trash, and couldn't tell intelligent talent from the smutty garbage she vomited out. But honestly, her prose isn't trash. If anything, behind all of the ass slapping and handcuffing and screaming orgasms… it's fairly good. What I hate—and what I can never confess in my emails to her—is that she is wasting such writing on smut. I write sex. I write, in the majority of my novels, a fair amount of sex. She can write sex and *still* write a great novel. And that's what infuriates me about the woman, even more than her perfectly pouty lips and incessant publicity. She's wasting her talent. She could be giving us more.

Then again, she might not have anything more to give. Maybe all she was blessed with is the talent to *tell* stories, and not the talent to *create* them. There's a very real distinction between the two. Maybe she writes drivel because *she doesn't have a better story to tell.* I feel a momentary burst of empathy for the woman, the sort of emotion I instantly recognize as condescending. But still, it's there, a crumbling of the hatred I've fostered for so long, a peace at the understanding of my adversary. Maybe that's why she sends such vile emails, the poor woman coming from a place of insecurity, jealousy, and frustration.

It's a good possibility, and I hold onto it, envisioning the positive scenario as an actual tree, giving it roots that dig into the earth and branches that reach into the sky. It is an exercise I haven't done in a decade, the concept taught to me by my psychiatrist mother, back when I was a bookworm without friends, a condition worthy of concern. I had a dozen painful appointments on her micro-suede couch before my mother gave up. In those appointments, I learned how to compartmentalize worries into an imaginary box in an attempt to relax. I also learned this stupid tree exercise, and how to bore clients while pretending to know a lot of stuff. Mom learned she was stuck with me and my 'oddities', which I'm fairly certain she blamed on my father's genes. If he loved learning, the dogged pursuit of a perfect SAT score, and setting the bell curve out of pure competitive spite? Then yes, we're practically twins. But I wouldn't know any of that. He took off two weeks after Mom told him she was pregnant. He left his wedding ring on the kitchen counter, along with divorce papers and a note. *I don't love you enough.* I'm a pretty cold, emotionally distant individual, but even my black heart can tell you that's just wrong.

I shove my Marka tree of happiness into a wood chipper and give up, pushing to my feet and abandoning the manuscript, moving downstairs in search of food and a distraction.

Seventeen hundred words down. Seventy-seven thousand to go.

Impossible.

chapter 8

Running. Wet grass tickles my legs, and I gasp out his name, pulling on his hand. He looks back and laughs, slowing to a walk. He tightens his grip, his fingers on mine, and tugs me closer, my shoulder bumping against his chest, the smell of his cologne mixing with the scent of moonlight and wildflowers. A foreign collision, my senses going wild, my chin tilting up, his mouth lowering to mine. The taste of peppermint and salt, his tongue so firm and confident, his hand sliding up my stomach and under my shirt.

"Simon..." I stop as his fingers work their way under my sports bra, my heart thudding at the contact of his palm against my breast. His kiss deepens, then breaks, and my shirt is pulled over my head, and he presses my hand to the buckle of his jeans.

"Touch me," he pants.

I sigh, leaning back, needing space from the scene, from the memories. My chest pounds, my breaths tight and painful, and I don't know if it's due to the cancer or the pain of the past.

There is nothing like young love. It comes at a time before the heart knows to protect itself, when everything important is raw and exposed—the perfect environment for a soul-sucking, heart-crushing burst. It burns brightest, hits hardest, and touches deepest. It's why Facebook flames erupt two decades later between high school sweethearts. Between two naive and innocent souls, anything can happen. Soulmates or Tragedy. And sometimes, both.

I had been completely exposed when Simon hit, his presence a glowing meteor through my life, one I had followed as blindly as a firefly to an electric light.

I stand, my knees cracking, back crying in protest, and it takes a few steps toward the door before I work out my kinks. I open the office door and step into the empty hallway. One lap through the house, one pill, one nap, and then back to work. It's an equation I've used for years, even before the cancer—only the pills back then were for depression, not pain.

I walk down the hall, my steps slower than they used to be, my breath harder. Bethany used to sprint down this hall, racing from our bedroom to hers. The media room to her bedroom. The guest room to the top of the stairs. The only room she never ran to and from - my office. That space had been "off limits", my rules unwavering, any violation met with swift punishment. I fix my eyes on the floorboards and try to push the image of her out of my head.

My lap of the house used to include the entire second floor. I would carry a damp cloth in hand, a Clorox bottle in the other, and clean baseboards, door knobs, and light switch panels as I went. On weekends, the Clorox was replaced with Windex, and the windows were taken care of. Each room got a once over, and when writers block would hit, the entire house gleamed. My lap changed four years ago. It now avoids the media room and our master bedroom. I don't carry cleaning supplies, and avoid the windows altogether.

My house, like the rest of me, is falling apart.

I head downstairs slowly, taking cautious steps, my hand tight on the wooden rail, no room in my timeline for missteps or injuries. I reach the last riser and lower myself to the step, taking a deep breath, my energy gone.

From this spot, I can see both front rooms, the sort of grand places that rich people like to put uncomfortable furniture in, back before formal living and dining rooms went extinct. When Simon and Bethany lived here, the left room was a den of sorts—filled with her toys, a comfortable chair I would read in, and an old firetruck from

Simon's youth. The right room had held a dining room set that Simon had found online—one that cost a fortune to ship in, but that had once belonged to Clint Eastwood, and should have been in a Colorado hunting lodge and not our McMansion.

Now, both rooms are empty, the front curtains pulled shut, the rooms somehow smaller without anything in them. My eyes drift over the bare foyer and to the great room, where a lonely sofa sits in front of a TV. The sofa I bought off a Craigslist ad, the TV off an internet special. Both purchases were made a few weeks after I sold everything, once I realized that my crazy had more room to grow, and its feed was boredom.

Sometimes novels aren't enough. Sometimes I need the mindless drone of a television, the brief escape of superficial housewives and train wreck relationships, something to assure me that Simon and I weren't alone, and everybody has problems.

If only our problems had been simple, the sort fixed by a marriage boot camp, or a romantic getaway, product endorsements and scripted discussions.

I close my eyes and try to summon the energy to stand, to make it the thirty or forty feet to the kitchen. Maybe food will help. Food and a pain pill. Then maybe I can churn out some more words.

KATE

Kate steps back from the imposing front door, one that most certainly belongs to Helena Ross, given the tiny angry sign above the doorbell, one that proclaims DO NOT RING! in angry handwritten font. If the tiny note wasn't enough of a tell, there is also the laminated list, taped to the center of the door. It is a list of rules, designed for anyone who dares to step on this property. Through Kate's worry, she is amused to note that this list is just as long and ridiculous as the one Helena once gave to Kate.

To read the list, you'd think a monster lives in the house, one who feasts on small children and gives stern looks when afforded a joke. You'd never dream that the same skinny fingers who typed these lines also created Eva and Mike, the couple who flies through the air when not falling madly in love. There is a sense of humor and wonder inside Helena, it just chooses to come out in her novels and not in her human interactions. Kate has spent many nights sipping wine and envisioning Helena's life, wondering whether her rules are in place everywhere or just in her interactions with Kate. She has pictured Helena with a big home, bookworm babies, and her adorable husband, one who tickles her while she writes, then pulls her into the bedroom to make love. Surely *that* is the type of world that creates the stories that Helena Ross writes. And why wouldn't she have those things? She isn't an unattractive person, almost cute in a sort of owlish way. And she *is* funny, with a bone-dry, off-beat sense of humor. You can't read a novel of hers without recognizing that. She manages to slip humor into the darkest of situations, adding just enough life to keep a reader's heart from stopping.

Her knock unanswered, she steps off the porch and looks at the house. The large home stretches into the overcast sky, two stories squatting on the top of a hill and peering down on the surrounding homes. It dominates the end of the cul-de-sac, the neighboring lots vacant and overgrown, their tall grass snug against the neat and perfect property line that is 112 Hilltop Way. Dark grass, stiff and short, blankets the front yard, its edge sharp and precise when it meets the bleached driveway. The stones that lead to the front step are also painfully white, set carefully in black mulch that matches the dark grey brick of the home. There is no color anywhere, everything varying shades of somber grey, and set off by the white blooms in the window boxes. The curtains are drawn at each window, no chance of peeking in, their edges stick straight and pinned in some fashion. It must be pitch black inside, with none of the warm sunlight that is starting to play across Kate's arms. This house isn't the world of Kate's wine-fueled musings. This house is a much starker, sadder reality, one that matches the darker, harder side of Helena. The side that creates rules and snaps at agents, the side that she fears. She peers up at the security cameras that point down at her from the porch eves. Lifting a hesitant hand, she waves.

Maybe Helena's husband is home. Simon, that was his name. He'd be a good one to talk to, could give her some insight into Helena's retirement. She'd met him once, a decade ago, at Helena's first and only attempt at a book signing. He'd been a great guy, super helpful, and seemingly immune to Helena's quirks. She waved again, then gave up.

This is silly. Helena isn't the sort to be okay with a pop-in. She should leave, get back into her rented Camry and drive the three hours back to the city, pretend this terrible idea never happened. Yet… she pauses. There are times in an agent's life when she needs to be there for her authors. And Helena's proclamation of early retirement *certainly* qualifies as one of those times.

She moves down the steps, stopping beside her car, and risks a final glance at the two-story Victorian.

Sad, that house. She can almost hear it crying, its yearn for a life not its own.

She opens the car door and stops short, catching sight of death itself.

The woman is almost skeletal, her sharp bones tied together with skin, her dark eyes sunken, her lips chapped and pale. She walks carefully, struggling up the inclined drive, her hair stringy and damp, her mouth pinched in a grimace of anger. No—not anger. Pain. Kate recognizes it in the hunch of her shoulders, the furrow of her brow, the halting stop. Behind her, a large bush hides a mailbox, the envelopes in Helena's hands a hint as to her origin.

"What are *you* doing here?" From the haughty tone, Helena's words clear and enunciated, you'd have never guessed at the condition of her body. In those words, she recognizes the author, even if her appearance has changed so drastically.

Seven years since they've last seen each other. Other clients would have hugged her. Or smiled. Yet, for Helena, the greeting is almost warm.

"I wanted to speak to you," Kate says, forcing her shoulders back, her posture into place. "About your retirement."

"Has seeing me answered that question?" Helena asks dryly.

It hadn't, until that question, that terribly simple clue that clicks all of the puzzle pieces into place. In the brief moment it takes Kate's heart to seize, she understands.

Helena Ross isn't retiring. She's dying.

chapter 10

It's interesting to see the reaction when it hits, the pale flush that covers Kate's generous cheeks, the widening of eyes, the stiffening of her chin, as if she's expecting a blow. I watch the action as an observer, the author part of my brain carefully cataloging the indicators for some future book that I'll never write. It's an automatic action and I stop myself before the pain of reality hits. It comes anyway. *I will never write another book again.*

Kate swallows, and she's aged in the last seven years. There are more sags in the skin of her face, more wrinkles on the edges of her red-stained lips. She's gained a little weight, her black pants suit a little tight in the thighs, her neck fleshier than I remember. She mentioned once, in an email several years ago, that she was getting divorced. Maybe her relationship was like mine—a careful chess match of secrets and power plays. Maybe her ex is responsible for that deep line in her forehead, for the extra pouches of skin under her eyes.

He probably isn't responsible for the wet dew of those eyes, the open inhale of that mouth, the spill of tears that suddenly leak out. My agent—the woman who is supposed to spearhead my career, fight for my novels, and stand toe-to-toe with New York's nastiest publishers, is *crying*. My opinion of her deflates, and I watch her wet her lips, and take a cautious step toward me.

"What's happened to you, Helena?"

What's happened to me? I have a story that I don't have time to tell. I have an empty house that reeks of death. I have no friends, no family, and no one to ask for help. I'm dying, and it's the best thing that has happened to me in a long time.

I shrug. "I've got a tumor. It's spread just about everywhere. The doctors gave me three months."

She sways, and I hope she doesn't faint, because I can barely make my own way into the house, much less cart her also. I sigh. "Would you like to come inside?"

She nods, and brushes a quick finger along her bottom line of lashes. "Yes. I'd like that very much."

I sit at the round kitchen table, one of the rare items that stayed in the house after that day. I don't have the energy to offer Kate a drink, and she doesn't ask for one, perching on the other chair, her gigantic purse on her knees, her eyes moving everywhere but to me.

"When did you move in?" she asks, her fingers tightening on the edges of the bright green leather.

"About ten years ago." I smile. "I'm not a big fan of furniture." It's the easiest explanation for my empty house, one that was once crammed with expensive items and life, noises and smells. Now, I prefer the echoing, empty feel of the downstairs, the bare walls, the lone items that look forgotten in the giant spaces. The only rooms left with life in them are my office and Bethany's room. The media room is also the same, as is my master bedroom, though I haven't stepped into either in years. This house occupies five thousand square feet of prime New London real estate, and you could fit all of its belongings inside this kitchen—this stark, utilitarian space, one currently crowded with two strangers and this uncomfortable conversation.

"Where's Simon?" She shifts in her chair and glances over her shoulder, as if my dead husband might suddenly appear.

"Gone." She knows better than to ask questions, and I'm thankful she never met Bethany, never knew of my pregnancy. I can handle many things, but the mention of her name is a knife in the heart. An attempt to explain her absence would yank it through my gut.

"Oh." She frowns, the fingers of her left hand pulling at the top of her thigh, at a loose bit of bunched fabric. "Who takes you to your chemo and stuff?"

I'm not doing chemo. Or radiation. Or any other "stuff". But I don't feel like a ten minute lecture on my responsibilities to myself, so I ignore that tidbit. "I drive myself. Or take a taxi."

Her eyes widen at the statement. She probably has a score of friends, all jumping at the opportunity to pick her up, fight city traffic, walk her inside, and sit patiently—through all the forms, the questions, the blood draws and sorrowful conversations. Not that I mind doing it all myself. I've had a book to entertain me—Marka Vantly's latest—an unfortunate choice, but I couldn't resist the competitive desire to know what my rival is up to.

"I can stay here," she offers. "Drive you places. Or," she glances around. "You know. Help you around the house."

"No." I can't think of anything worse. The conversation alone would kill me, her incessant chatter and offers and pitying looks… it'd be hell. A worse hell than the one I currently occupy, one where I have to struggle through basic tasks and am ignored by my mouse.

"When did you find out?"

"About ten days ago. I've been losing weight for a while, and my energy…" I don't even feel up to finishing the sentence. It hadn't just been my energy, though that had been the most annoying. There had also been the headaches, the nose bleeds, the equilibrium shifts and fainting spells. I think I've had mood swings, though it's hard to tell when I have so little interaction with others. "The doctor said the tumor is about a year old."

"Oh Helena." She reaches out, across the table, and I move my hands, underneath the table, squeezing them in between my thighs. I regret the action, her face pinching in hurt, her eyes dropping to her hand, and there is a painful moment of embarrassment before she recovers. Her back straightens and she opens her purse, pulling out a folder and pen. "I brought you the paperwork for terminating the *Broken* contract. You'll have to return the initial payment, of course."

I must have given something away on the phone, raised some internal alarm that caused her to print out this contract, drive three hours to New London, and hand-deliver it here. If I had the energy, I'd feel violated. Instead, I just want to sleep.

A notebook is also withdrawn, and I perk up at the sight of a pen, some sort of action eminent. "I understand you don't want my help," she begins. "But let's talk about what you do need." She raises an overgrown eyebrow in my direction. "Housekeeper? Cook? Oh!" She bends her head down and starts to write. I watch the word DRIVER appear in neat, block-like letters.

A year ago, I would have asked her what the hell she's doing, barging in and trying to take over my life. A year ago, she wouldn't even be sitting at this table. I would have ordered her off my lawn, told her to go back to the city, and then sent her a tersely worded email where I listed all of her errors while subtly threatening to fire her.

A year ago, I didn't need anyone's help. Now, I'm not in the position to turn away assistance, despite the snarl of my pride, which I swallow.

"So," she says brightly, as if this is a class project and she's been appointed our captain. "We can find someone to take you to the doctor, and pick up your medications and such. And a housekeeper and cook—are you okay with that?"

I pull at my bottom lip, considering the idea. Simon always wanted a "house manager"—someone to pick up after us, to handle the landscaping guy, and replace light bulbs, and tend to his every need. I had shot that idea down at every turn, panicked at the idea of a stranger opening my drawers, rearranging my things, and jumping into the middle of our lives.

"We can set private zones," Simon argued, his jaw stubbornly jutting out, his arms crossing over that broad chest. "She won't set foot in your office, or the media room, or..." he glanced around as if the kitchen might be up for discussion. "Or wherever else you don't want her."

Her. It had always been a her. And maybe that's why I hated the idea. I didn't need a woman in my house, laying claim to my processes, analyzing my marriage, or parenting, or personal quirks.

"I don't want someone here." I release my lip and look up at Kate, my muscles tensing for a fight.

"Fine," she smiles, and I am reminded of how annoying it is to be around overwhelmingly cheerful people. "I can look into daily meal deliveries, someone to just drop off the food." She eyes the floor and I wait for her to mention cleaning, to notice the dust bunnies that have begun to accumulate as my health has deteriorated. I watch her pen move, her attention returning to the page, and she writes DAILY MEAL DELIVERIES down, then looks back to me. "Do you need a nurse?"

"No." I'm suddenly hungry. It must be this talk of food, my stomach pinching at the thought of something fresh and home-made, my last few months spent sampling every TV dinner out there. But I can't mention food *now*. It'd only encourage Kate's pesky invasion, justify her meddlesome activity and give credibility to this stupid list she is intent on creating. I wonder if these daily meal deliveries can include desserts. I would kill for some strawberry shortcake. Or French toast. Or—

"Anything else?" She peers at me, and I can see in her barely hidden smile that she is enjoying *this*. Not my pain or sickness, I don't think she's a Munchausen Syndrome by Proxy candidate. But the action pleases her, the ability to assist me, to *do* something—that she enjoys. And maybe it's that understanding that causes me to open my mouth, to confess the need, the fear, that I hadn't fully yet faced myself.

"I need you to find me a ghostwriter."

KATE

A ghostwriter. Kate presses her tongue against her teeth in an attempt to not open her mouth, to ask for clarification on a concept that she never thought Helena Ross would ever, ever, consider. Forget swallowing the pride of having someone fix her meals. This was a job a thousand times more personal, more invasive—not to mention impossible. There is no *way* that Helena Ross will ever be okay with another set of hands touching her manuscript, reading her words, much less *writing* on her behalf. Kate carefully sets down her pen, sliding her hands into her lap and schooling her features into a pleasant mask of acceptance.

"You want to hire a ghostwriter," she repeats. "For the new book you're writing?" The book that she had driven here to talk Helena out of, hoping that a face-to-face with the woman might go further than a phone call.

"Yes. I'm worried I won't have time to finish it. A ghostwriter might work more quickly." Helena's eyes are on the table, on a long crack in the wood, one that runs down its center, then branches off to the left.

"The book that you want me to sell to Tricia Pridgen?"

"Yes."

Well, Helena could forget that possibility. As difficult as it would have been to sell that manuscript before—at least a Helena Ross novel had some value. A ghostwritten novel, under the Helena Ross name… that was poison, especially to someone like Pridgen. Kate pushes the value of a posthumous book out of her head, the concept still too raw to actually consider.

A dozen questions compete on the top of her tongue. Why is this book so important? Why write a book at all? Why not spend her last four months doing something fun and exciting, crossing bucket items off with a wave of her filthy-rich finger? Why not just make this book a short story? What compensation structure is she thinking about for the ghostwriter?

She chooses the most urgent one. "Do you have someone in mind?"

HELENA

For the first time since retaining Kate Rodant, I draw a blank. Bringing up the concept of a ghostwriter had seemed like such a huge step in itself. Thinking of who that ghostwriter might be… my mind seizes.

It reminds me of when I researched surrogacy. Not for myself, but for one of my characters. I spent twenty minutes on the phone with a Boston woman who had carried three babies for other women, and spoke about the experience with the detached air of a psychopath. Back then, I couldn't decide if I'd prefer a woman like that over one that would truly care about the fetus, and might develop an emotional attachment to something that was, in fact, mine and not hers.

I abandoned the storyline for the same reason I now want to abandon this conversation: it was exhausting to think about, the stakes just as high, the choices just as terrible.

I need someone with skill, someone who knows my writing style, someone with talent. Someone who doesn't need to tell their own story but can adopt mine. Someone who won't get emotionally attached to the story, someone without feelings at all.

It takes me longer than necessary to see the answer, one which pecks at the edge of my brain before pushing in.

I know who I need.

And I'd rather die than ask her.

KATE

"Marka Vantly."

Kate studies Helena's face, which holds no trace of humor, though the words must, surely, be a joke. Kate may not have known about her illness, or her strange empty house, but she knows one thing about her client: Helena *hates* Marka Vantly. Another agent in Kate's firm once represented Marka on a minor sub-rights deal and Helena had threatened to *fire* Kate for it, vehement that there be no association between their brands. It's why Helena has stuck with Hachette, though Random House has offered her far higher advances. Marka is with Random House, and any house who would sign a self-published author… Helena had shredded their seven-figure contract and mailed it back to Kate with an eloquent card that all but told them to go to hell, exclamation point, exclamation point, exclamation point.

Kate picks up her pen. "Why Marka Vantly?" She glances down at the page, carefully writing the woman's name down, and fighting to keep her features bland. Marka won't do it. The woman is a publisher's dream, her release calendar booked past next year. Plus, there is no secret of their rivalry. You might as well ask Darth Vader to water Luke Skywalker's plants.

Helena looks up, her eyes considering Kate as if deciding whether she is fit to receive the answer. "I don't know," she finally says, her words slow and methodical.

Even Kate, limited in her Helena knowledge, can hear the lie, the casual indifference seeped in a hundred secrets. "Are you sure?"

She watches Helena's hands clench, her head turning away, her gaze toward the window. There is nothing there to see, the blinds drawn despite Kate's repeated offers to open them.

"Yes." Helena's lips tighten around the word. "Call her agent and set it up."

HELENA

Kate doesn't understand. I can see it in the way she holds her cell phone, her shoulders stiff, eyes continually darting my way as if wanting me to stop her. She's asked three times if I'm sure, and I've made it clear she doesn't need to ask again.

Simon loved to question me. He was never satisfied with hearing something once, he felt the continual need to reassure himself of a response. When we bought the house, he asked me *seven* times if I was sure. *Was it the right neighborhood? The right price? Did we need a bigger one? Or was this* too *big?* I told him I liked it, reassured him it would be fine, but still, he worried. Fretted. *Pestered* me.

I remember walking into our kitchen on closing day, and thinking it was done. I remember inhaling the scent of fresh lilies, convinced that in this new town, away from his friends, from the noises and sounds of the city, that he would finally calm down, that we would get settled and be happy and that all of the questions would finally *stop*.

A woman should be able to celebrate her first home, but I only remember wanting some silence.

"I'm going to call her agent." Kate speaks from her place at the kitchen counter, her phone out, thumb poised, and I swear to God, if she stalls any longer I will chop off her finger and use it to push the buttons myself.

"Then do it already." I think a new set of rules may be in order. Kate seems to be stubbornly stuck to my side, and as bitchy as my rules may be, this is a shining example of their worth. Rule #1 could be something along the lines of When You Say You Are Going to Do Something, Shut the Hell Up and Do It.

Kate clears her throat and I glare at her fingers, the tension in my chest releasing as she begins to dial.

KATE

No one answers. Kate pulls her cell away from her mouth, her fingers tapping on the granite countertop, and turns to Helena. "Voicemail."

"Leave a message." Helena hunches forward over a ceramic mug of tea, the directive muttered in Kate's direction. Her moods seem to change with no clear stimulus, set off by triggers that Kate has yet to figure out. It reminds her of her own aunt, a schizophrenic woman who baked cookies in one moment, then snatched them from your hand and shoved them into the trash, muttering about poison and government conspiracies. Helena is a far milder case, her shifts more minute in nature, her highs and lows ranging from mildly entertained to irritable and depressed. This complete focus on a new book, on Marka Vantly—seems to come from nowhere. For her to walk from *Broken*, just weeks from the delivery, and spend her final months on a brand new book, one ghostwritten by Marka Vantly? It makes no sense. Helena Ross might need a shrink, or a stronger prescription, or a vacation in Tahiti, but she doesn't need a ghostwriter.

The voicemail ends, a tone sounding, her cue to speak. She leaves a message, a rambling speech introducing herself—and asking the agent to call her back. Ron Pilar has represented Marka for over a decade, her star one of a dozen in his stable. He is the agent she always dreamed of becoming, a dream that died years ago, around the time that gray hairs started appearing in her red curls. Ron won't know who she is; he probably won't even call her back. She ends the call and looks up to find Helena's eyes fixed on hers.

"Terrible message," the woman says mildly. "First time leaving one?"

Kate lets out a controlled breath. "To him, yes."

"Does he intimidate you?"

She smiles despite herself, the curiosity in Helena's voice so… fact-finding. At another time, Kate could have been a future character, an insecure woman in a yet-to-be-written novel. "Yes," she admits. "He's a very big name in our industry."

"And you aren't?" Again, such genuine innocence in her question. As if she doesn't realize how pathetic it is for an agent to have only one successful client.

Her lips tighten, the only crack she fails to contain. "No."

The answer doesn't faze Helena, her focus returning to herself, as it always has. "How long will it take for him to call you back?"

"I have no idea."

Helena checks her watch, a Beauty & The Beast timepiece with a chunky pink strap, fastened on the farthest hole. "I took a sleeping pill just before you came. If you don't mind, I'm going to lay down for a couple of hours."

"I have work to do," Kate offers. "If you don't mind, I'll bring in my laptop and work in here."

Helena's eyes move to the kitchen table, and then back to her face, as if she is considering the alternative scenario—sending Kate away, out to her car or worse, back to the city. "That's fine," she says slowly. "I'll be on the couch."

When she rises from the table, it is with sluggish effort, and Kate fights the urge to offer assistance, staying in place as Helena slowly trudges through the kitchen and into the great room, all but falling onto the couch and pulling a blanket over her body. "Wake me up in two hours," she mumbles. "Please."

Please? Had Helena ever used that word before? It's so strange to see this version of her, one so different than the woman she's experienced through emails and weekly phone calls. Seven years ago, the last time they'd met—a half-hour in Kate's office—her body had been comfortably fleshed out, her dry humor sharp, her directions given with an edge of superiority. She's always been private, never sharing details of her life, Kate's imagination left to its own devices, painting a life of color and wealth, family and dogs, evenings spent reading by a crackling fire, a chubby baby crawling before her on a plush rug. She'd always attributed Helena's irritability and strict communications to Kate's own ineptitude. Surely she wasn't like that with everyone, surely she…

Now, Helena silent on the couch, her gaunt figure swallowed by the blanket, the house eerily quiet, she realized the bitter truth of the matter. Maybe she doesn't have anyone else to be irritable with. Maybe, she doesn't have anyone at all.

A hunt for a phone charger brings Kate to the second floor of Helena Ross's home. She hits a switch, light flooding an empty bedroom and revealing stark white walls, pine floors and a slow moving ceiling fan. She flips off the light and steps farther down the hall, the sound of her steps ominous in the deserted house, the perfect prologue to any horror film.

The next room, another bedroom, also white, also empty. She moves on, the next door locked. It is eerie, all of the empty bedrooms. Why would Helena buy this huge house if she doesn't use the space? It doesn't make sense to waste all of these rooms, not when she has the money to fill each one with beautiful art and furniture, thick rugs and crystal chandeliers. Kate puts her ear against the locked door, wondering if it's bedroom or closet.

Downstairs had been a vacant showroom, the living room outfitted with just a couch and TV, the kitchen with only a table and two chairs. Every other room—the dining room, formal living room, foyer, and bedroom—all empty. Upstairs, the master bedroom had been the only room so far with any furniture. The king bed had been carefully made, and she'd resisted an urge to fluff the pillows or pull back the covers, her pause at the window long, the curtains left untouched. Maybe she could pick up some flowers at a local florist, something to put on her bedside table and give the room some color.

Or not. Helena's patience with Kate has to be wearing thin. Given different circumstances, she'd have already been asked to leave. Helena, most likely out of pure convenience, hasn't taken that path yet.

The door at the end of the hall is closed, and she stops before it, a piece of paper taped to its surface, one of Helena Ross's famous lists.

Only this list is different. Handwritten in colored pencil, the letters are big and loopy. This list closes a fist around her heart and squeezes.

The Rules of Bethany's Room

1. No boys.
2. Take off shoes.
3. If Music plays, you dance.
4. No touching my art.
5. No spankings.
6. Bring cookies.
7. Don't turn out the lights.

Sometimes, it only takes an instant to understand a person.

The feel of loss in the air… it isn't imagined. The life her mind had painted… at some point, it had been real. At some point, it had created this list-making child, one who hated spankings and loved cookies. Kate looks at the list and knows, without reaching for the handle, there is no one in the room. She gives herself a long moment to prepare, then twists the knob and pushes open the door.

Pale green walls, the shade of Eva's in *Forced Love.* A bed hangs from the ceiling by gold and pink ropes, the coverlet an organized mountain of pillows and stuffed animals. By a window sits a desk, the surface covered with drawings, pencils carefully lined up and organized by color. The right side of the room is a half-completed mural, supplies nearby, a forgotten doll on the floor.

The most heartbreaking piece is in the middle of the floor, a sleeping bag unrolled on the rug, the fabric rumpled and open, the pillow indented. So different from the stiff, unused bed in the master bedroom. This one reeks of frequent use, of sleepless nights and tears. Kate's throat becomes thick and she blinks, turning to leave the room before she loses all composure.

She doesn't look through any more of the home.

After that, she can't.

chapter 14

My house smells of bleach, the downstairs gone over by Kate, clad in surgical gloves and armed with a spray bottle and paper towels. She probably would have been a good roommate, one who understood my need for refrigerator conformity and organizational rules. Simon had always scoffed at my concerns, just as he did over my immunization research and the alarming air quality index in Brooklyn. My research, the fat envelope wrapped with three rubber bands, bulging with terrifying statistics, was why we moved to New London, three hours up the coast, a small town with an acceptable crime rate and clean air. I had grown up here, and embraced the idea of returning, my memories of the sleepy town filled with library visits and quiet afternoons reading in the backyard hammock. My mother had also jumped on board, buying a home a couple of miles away, her offers to babysit met with delight by Simon, and trepidation by me.

I watch Kate as she cleans the front of my laptop, paying careful attention to the keyboard, a bleach wipe coating the surface of the letters. When she finishes, she carefully turns it toward me, almost reverently, moving it to the exact middle of the kitchen table. A timer on her watch chimes and she smoothly turns, reaching for the cabinet and pulling out a bottle of pills, twisting off the lid and shaking out one. She holds it out to me.

"Ever thought of being a nurse?" I say wryly, reaching gingerly forward and taking the medicine, half-irritated, half-grateful. Maybe taking my meds as prescribed, on time and with food, would help my symptoms. I already feel better, revived after my nap, my headache down to a barely-noticeable ache.

"Don't laugh," Kate says, "but I did."

"Really?" I reach forward and press the laptop's power button, turning it on.

"Yep." Her snappy response makes me smile. Earlier, while she left Marka's agent another voicemail, I flipped through television channels and asked what she liked to watch, a question that was met with a recitation of Rule 4, in which—one grouchy day years ago—I stated that she must never share personal details of her life with me. It had seemed a reasonable request at the time, one designed to enhance my productivity. Now, it just seems bitchy. Recently, all my rules seem bitchy. And *super* controlling, which sucks, since that was Simon's most popular complaint, one I'd always dismissed without consideration.

My computer finishes its startup , and I open my email. There is one from Charlotte Blanton, and it takes my mind a moment to place the name. Charlotte. My doorbell-ringing, husband-inquiring, intruder. I click on her email with the heavy finger of the doomed. Any fantasies of long-lost sisterhood fly out the window as soon as it opens. It is short and cuts to the point, which I appreciate. Everything else about it, I hate.

> Helena,
>
> I am a journalist for the New York Post, and am writing an article on your husband. I have some questions to ask you, and some information to share. Please call me.
>
> Charlotte Blanton
> Investigative Journalist, New York Post

I've waited four years for something like this. For someone to pull a loose thread, a gentle tug that turns into more, everything unraveling until our secrets are bare to the world. This could turn into a media shitstorm. This could be the biggest story of the year, amplified by my pending death. I can see the headlines now. I can see the papers flying off the shelves, my cul-de-sac filled with news vans and microphones.

I can't let her do this. I can't let Charlotte Blanton ruin everything when I am finally ready to tell the story for myself.

I carefully drag her email into the SPAM folder, then block her as a contact. There. Done. Kate's phone rings, and she picks it up, her eyes connecting with mine.

"It's Ron Pilar."

"No." I press my fingers against my forehead, feeling nauseous, the condition either caused by the recent pill or the words that just tumbled out of Kate's dark red lips. "No way." It's one thing for me to reach out to Marka Vantly with a business proposition. It's another for us to *meet*, face-to-face, which is what she wants.

"We aren't exactly negotiating from a place of power," Kate says carefully, perched on the office couch. We moved upstairs after the call, me wanting to get to my calendar, my files, and out of that damn kitchen. She's wearing the same blouse, and it's a reminder that it's the same day as when I walked to the mailbox and watched her car pull in. It feels like a week has passed, her presence already turned from stranger to… not friend, but something in between the two. Thirty minutes ago, she walked straight to the bathroom without asking where it was. During my nap, she must have wandered around the house, discovering the empty rooms, the occasional bits of habitation. Did she try to open the door to the media room? Probably. No doubt she found Bethany's room, my bed there. From the change in her eyes, the softening in her speech, the fragile way she's handling me—she thinks she knows. Maybe, before she woke me, she did an Internet search on my married name. Maybe she knows about everything, or thinks she does.

She follows my eyes, looking down at her blouse, and smooths it self-consciously. "They said Marka will come here. You won't have to travel."

"No," I snap, my irritation rising, as much over her invasion as Marka's. "I'll outline everything, and we can communicate through email." Anything to prevent Marka Freakin' Vantly's sky-high stilettos clipping across my floor, her eyes on my empty house, on my sweatpants and greasy hair, a stupid smirk playing across her face as she taps those perfect fingernails against her sexy lips. Screw *that.*

"She hasn't agreed to anything; she just wants to talk."

Marka doesn't want to talk. She wants to ask questions, to peel back the layers of my soul and understand why, after a decade of insults, I chose her to write this story. She'll want to know about the ridiculously short timeline and my motivations. She'll want to know about the story and why it is so important—my next inhale is a struggle, panic tightening its grip around my heart. "No." I manage. "I can't."

"Are you intimidated by her?" Oh, the bitter irony, my earlier question so easily thrown back in my face. It is manipulative, same as it had been with me, my backbone straightening despite my knowledge of her motives.

"Of course not," I snap. "She's just not worth my time." I spin slowly in my chair, my eyes moving over the corkboard, focusing on the worn piece of paper, the blurb, stuck prominently in the center of the board. If Kate looked hard enough, she'd see it. If she thought hard enough, she'd figure things out.

"We could get a different author," Kate offers. "Maybe Vera Wilson or Kennedy—"

"No." I say, my eyes stuck on the opening line of the blurb. *If you lie enough times, no one believes your truth.*

"It doesn't *have* to be Marka," Kate persists. "I could try—"

"No," I repeat, my words stronger. Vera Wilson or Kennedy Blake or Christina Hendlake… they are all the same. Words on pages. Well-written, their craft holds no room for criticism. But it also holds no life. This story… my last story… it needs life. It needs a soul. It needs to be powerful enough, and I don't know if even *I* can do it justice. I need the next best thing, and with guidance, maybe Marka can be trained. Maybe, with a heavy hand of direction, she can pull it off in time. She writes quickly, I know that much. I'll do the outline, she can write her ass off, and I can heavily edit it. Steer her onto better ground when she goes astray. It *can* be done. It *has* to be done.

"Helena?" Kate has been talking, her last few sentences lost in the tangle of my thoughts, and I turn to her, raising an eyebrow. "Do you want me to call it off with Marka's people?"

"No," I grumble. "Let me email her first."

If you lie enough times, no one believes your truth. It is a good intro. I only wish it wasn't so true.

My beautifully worded email to Marka, one where I refrain from any insults or profanity, goes unanswered, a status that infuriates me. I hold firm for a full day, and then crack, giving Kate permission to call her agent and agree to the meeting. I've spent almost a decade battling the author. Now, with the pressure of my deadline, I give up.

I don't know why she's insistent on coming here. To make things worse, I can feel Kate's certainty that Marka won't agree to the terms. It's a legitimate possibility, one that I am afraid to consider. Hell, if Marka had reached out six months ago with a similar request, I'd have laughed at her. I would have taken perverse pleasure in turning her down, my email maliciously worded with the full intent to stab her when she was down. I would have been the biggest bitch on the planet about it.

And that's the main reason I'd initially refused her request for a face-to-face. The most likely scenario is that she is flying here for no reason other to embarrass me to my face. She will curl up that pouty mouth and laugh at my book proposition, at my timeline, and at my life. She will judge my uneven features and stringy hair. She will be just like the popular girls from seventh grade, only this time I *will* care, it *will* matter.

I need her.

But I'm also terrified of her.

With less than twenty-four hours until our meeting, I feel a wave of nausea and stumble for a chair.

chapter 15

When he meets my mother, it's like butter on hot toast, a melding of souls—an effortless union that I am merely a spectator to. I feel betrayed, seeing her laugh at his jokes, seeing him hold the door open for her, and his compliment on her work.

I prepared him for her stiff disapproval, for her judgmental stares, for her psychoanalysis. I didn't prepare myself for them to get along, for my mother to beam at me, for the two of them to unite.

Later, it will be war—but on that cool Sunday afternoon, it is just irritating. I—

The doorbell rings, and my fingers pause above the keyboard, the paragraph half-finished on the screen before me. My eyes move to the clock, worried for a moment that I have lost track of time, and that Marka is already here. But it is a quarter 'til four, fifteen minutes before our appointment. I can't picture Marka as an early arrival. If anything, I expect her to be fashionably late.

The doorbell rings a second time and I stand from the desk, saving my work and moving to the door, taking the steps as quickly as I can manage, suddenly filled with an urgent need to get to the door before a third chime of the bell.

I make it to the door and jerk it open, caught off guard by the man who stands there. I immediately toss the idea that he is Ron Pilar,

Marka's agent. This man, his face ruddy, hair wild, clothes crumpled—is not an agent, and is *certainly* not from New York. There isn't a polished bone inside his loose khaki shirt, one with an unnecessary number of pockets, a fish stitched onto the front breast. No salesmanship in his comfortable stance, one hand tucked in a pocket, the other lifting from the doorbell in greeting. I watch his hand move, noting the calluses on the palm, the cracks in the skin, the gold band on his left ring finger. If I look closely, there'll probably be dirt under his nails. I hope he isn't the driver that Kate found, showing up a day early. There's no way I'm letting a man like this take me anywhere.

"Helena?" The drawl of my name is deep and masculine, and I've described voices like it a hundred times, the rough kind that makes weak females swoon against fence posts. I will not be swooning. I will be kicking him off this porch, *immediately*, before Marka Vantly and her brigade pull in. I eye his vehicle, a white Ford truck that squats in the middle of my driveway.

"I have a sign." I tap it. "No ringing the doorbell. No parking on the driveway. And no soliciting."

"Ah." He smiles. "And I thought those rules were put up just for me."

I stare at him blankly, the response making no sense. Even worse, he is still *here*, his boots on my Go Away mat, precious minutes clicking by. I should be clearing my mind and composing myself. This distraction… I don't have time for this. "You need to leave."

"I'm a little early." His smile is still in place, and it is an amused one, his personal joke too freaking fascinating to share. "Would you like me to wait in the truck 'til four?"

I am a little early. Would you like me to wait 'til four? The words slowly click into place, and I blink, processing the possibilities, my next question a desperate attempt to buy time. "The truck in my driveway?"

He chuckles, and I'm glad this is so much fun for him. "Yes."

"Are you Ron Pilar?" He can't be, not unless Ron Pilar negotiates book contracts on fence rails before wrangling cattle.

"That prick?" He coughs out a laugh. "No." His mouth twitches as if he is holding something in.

So he knows Ron Pilar. Or he's crazy and bent on driving me to a similar mental state. Either way, this guessing game has gotten old. "I don't have time for this," I say sharply, my social graces drained. "Tell me who you are, or get the hell off my porch."

"I'm sorry," the man says, and he doesn't sound the slightest bit sincere. He extends a hand into my personal space, his stubble-framed smile splitting wide across that rough face. "I'm Mark Fortune. Better known as Marka Vantly."

Marka Vantly.
I'm Mark Fortune. Better known as Marka Vantly.

In the air, there is the hint of dusk, a softening of heat, the faint scent of honeysuckle on the breeze. In his eyes, there is amusement, a knowing gleam that scrapes a sharp knife along my heart.

"You're not Marka Vantly." The words stab out confidently, and I ignore his hand, crossing my arms over my chest in an attempt to fortify my stance. He's crazy. He's hacked into Marka's email, burst into this appointment early, and is trying to worm his way into my life. He's picked a terrible story to tell, Marka's image recognizable even to someone not in publishing, her perfect blonde specimen plastered on every square bit of ad copy that exists. This farmer… he couldn't be less plausible.

Unless.

Unless…

Unless I am wrong. There is intelligent arrogance in his grin, and I recognize that—the knowledge that you hold a card secret to others. I feel it when I write scenes designed to deceive, when I stack character traits and hidden messages against readers, setting them up for failure. He's amused by this. What does he know that I don't? Probably everything.

I suddenly feel small. Stupid. Angry.

I take the only path available, stepping backward, his eyes following, bushy eyebrows raising—and shut the door.

It may have been more of a slam. The wood sometimes swells,

requiring any action to be done in a rather forceful way, one that causes glass to tremble in panes and walls to shudder. It wasn't because I am temperamental. It was simply to ensure a good quality seal, one that won't allow for questions, or the stop of a hand, or whispered words through cracked openings. I shut the door, flip the deadbolt, and leave the delusional stranger outside. I'll let Marka deal with him. If, and when—I glance at my watch—she shows up.

Heading to the kitchen, I attempt to compose myself, the silent house comforting. There's a reason I hate the doorbell. After the funeral, it constantly rang, neighbors and do-gooders bringing over food and flowers, the house a repulsive scent of floral casserole, each ding-dong of the bell a fresh wave of intrusion. I ripped it off once, a pair of scissors seized, my frenzied hacking observed by a startled FedEx employee. Two days later, I had it fixed. I couldn't sleep at night, knowing that the loose wires were hanging out, a piece of the house incomplete, a visible reminder that I don't have a husband to fix it, or the self-control to listen to a tone of greeting. So instead, I left the repaired doorbell in place and posted the sign. It started out just one item, one rule.

DO NOT RING THE DOORBELL.

The one rule grew into two, then four, then eight. They serve as more than requests to preserve my sanity. They are also a measure of intelligence, testing both reading aptitude and the ability to follow simple and polite requests.

The idiot on the porch has already parked in the driveway. Strike one. He rang the bell. *Twice*. Strike two.
Lying about identity has never been a rule, but it could easily earn a spot on the list.

I get as far as the fridge when he rings the bell. It's not the polite tap of earlier. This time it is loud and insistent, one press after another, my psyche not able to handle the assault, my feet dashing, hand jerking open the door before my head comes completely off.

Before, the man was annoying. Now? I will kill him.

MARK

If fury is a person, it is Helena Ross. And if she owns a weapon, his next step is death. The woman violently swings open the door, her nostrils flaring, her eyes burning, one small fist reaching out and pounding on his wrist, stalling his next press of the doorbell. "Stop that. Stop, stop, stop, STOP." The words are a chant, her breaths coming harder, a painfully thin chest heaving under the cotton long-sleeve tee she wears.

So much anger in such a tiny body. He'd expected an older woman, one his age, with gray hair and delicate glasses, her regal shoulders pinned back, her panties the stuffy sort never seen. But this anorexic-thin stick of elbows and ears… she couldn't be much older than thirty. To think such a tiny thing has been the one who's told him off for the better part of a decade… it makes him want to throw back his head and laugh.

Laughing, it seems, would be unwise. She doesn't seem to have much of a sense of humor, her eyes sharpening every time he so much as cracks a smile. "I *am* Marka Vantly," he speaks quickly, before she shuts the door, his tone serious. "Call Ron Pilar and ask him." He holds out the worn business card, the only proof he has readily available. Who knows if the number on it is accurate, the card one he'd been given eight years ago, back when Ron was a stranger and he was just another poor writer with a stack of declined manuscripts. There had been no auction on that novel, no *Publishers Weekly* write up and six-figure advance. There'd just been a desperate flail for attention from the industry's top agent, the first contact a moment of celebration, the resulting business card a coveted item.

She straightens, one hand still protecting the bell, her gaze moving down to the card, which hangs in the space between them. Her large eyes dart back to his face, narrowing, squints of skin that breathe fire in the form of pupils. A perfect glare, one that belongs to the claws that pecked out all of those vicious emails filled with jealousy and spite.

Her hand snatches, and his bit of nostalgia is suddenly gone, a victim of her grasp, her gaze darting suspiciously between the card and his face. "Wait here." She steps back and grabs the door jamb, pausing for a moment as she eyes him, then her doorbell, then him again.

He raises his hands in innocence and steps back, away from her and the tiny button that seems to annoy her so. God, to think of all of the emails he had mused over, carefully selecting the right words to drive her mad, and all it took was the ding-dong of this bell.

She snorts, and shuts the door, leaving him alone on the porch, for the second time in five minutes. What an interesting woman.

He turns, stepping away from the house and to the rail of the porch, his eyes moving over the perfect lines of the yard, a stark contrast from the wild acreage of his Memphis plantation. He tries to imagine the conversation occurring inside, Helena's interrogation of Ron Pilar. Ron will behave, swallowing his snark under a blanket of kiss-ass. Helena… who knows how Helena would handle it. So far, his plan to play nice has gone slightly astray.

There is the click of a lock and he turns, pushing off the porch rail. Helena stands in the open doorway, a house phone gripped between her hands. There is a long moment of quiet as her eyes drift over him, examining him with renewed distrust. He says nothing, the waiting game stretching out slowly.

"You should have told me you're a man," she finally says, and damn if there isn't a bit of sadness in her voice, as if he is a cheating spouse, or an unfaithful friend.

"It's a secret very few people know." He tucks his hands into his front pockets and wishes, for the first time in his life, he wasn't so big, so tall, so widely built. One of her hands move to grip the doorframe, and it's as if she needs it to stand, her frailty so out of place amid the fire that burns from her eyes.

She considers that, then nods. "I can respect that. But I can't respect you playing with me." Her face hardens, and he pities her future children. This expression, the steel in her voice—it is a force, one scary to stand up to. "Don't screw with me."

"I won't." It is a promise he will have to keep, the hurt that permeates the edge of her stance… a familiar pain. In it, he sees his daughter's first tears over a boy, her withdrawal when Stanford rejected her, the crack in her voice—just last week—when she was snubbed by a friend. This hurt, he had caused, all in an immature need to humiliate Helena Ross for pure entertainment. "Can we start over?"

There are small cracks in her facade, a relax of her narrow shoulders, the general untightening of fingers around the phone, her lips parting, a sigh of breath escaping from them. She meets his eyes and nods. "Okay." She turns, opening the door and waiting for him to enter.

Taking a deep breath, he moves across the threshold and into the house. He had come here to meet Helena Ross, and turn her down. Already, he can feel himself waffling.

My mind can't move off the fact that Marka, the blonde siren of romance, is this crumpled old pile of masculinity. The fingers that drum the table before me, scarred and cracked, with short nails and knuckle hair, are the ones that wrote *The Virgin's Pleasure.* His eyes, watery blue knives that peer at me as if they can read my soul—they reviewed proof copies of *Teacher's Pet.* Underneath this thick head of silver and black is the mind that wrote some of the best and worst pieces I have ever read. *A man.* Had I known, I would never have called him here. A man can't help me tell this story. A man can't, won't, ever understand.

We are in the kitchen and I take the second chair, the place I used back when Simon sat across from me, his shoulders hunched over his coffee, Bethany streaking past us, full of morning energy, a toy or two in hand. I remember sitting in this seat and marveling at how beautiful my life was. I remember sitting in this chair, the morning after it all happened, and planning my suicide.

"Helena?" His voice is impossibly gentle, one that can't belong to the woman—person—I hate. The person who wastes their talent on filth and sends me such nasty emails. I look up at him and blink, the view blurry. *Hell. Am I crying?* I wipe at both eyes and focus. He wants to know why he is here. That, at least, I can manage.

I clear my throat and begin my script, one that I've practiced three times now, each delivery less wooden, more believable, each delivery practiced for a goddess and not this chunk of AARP that sits before me. "I have a story I want to publish, but I don't have the time to write it. I work at a much slower pace than you do… normally I take a year per book. Given that this one is a little more complicated than my others, it would take me even longer. I'm looking to hire someone who can write the bulk of it, and I will handle the rewrites. Each chapter will be provided in outline format—the ghostwriter—you, will only have to fill in the copy." I look up from the table's worn oak surface. He watches me intently, the lines of his forehead furrowed, one giant hand now running across his mouth.

"What's the length?"

I shrug. "I'm not sure. Probably eighty thousand words."

"Longer than my normal works."

"It's not your normal works. It's not erotica."

I know the next question before he asks it. I had dreaded it from Marka's mouth, had pictured one perfect brow lifting, her lips bright and red as they pouted out the words. From him, it is different, gruff as gravel, his fingers dropping from his mouth as he speaks. "Then why me?"

"As much as I hate to admit it..." I swallow, my hands fisting underneath the table. "We have similar writing styles. I wouldn't have to do extensive rewrites. Your work has, even with your ridiculous plots, heart. You know how to write motivations and difficult scenarios. I think, given the right direction, you are trainable. Improvable."

One short laugh sputters out of him, his body leaning forward as he levels me with his gaze. "No."

I squared my shoulders and waited, the bones of my bottom digging into the wooden seat.

"I'm not looking for a mentor. Especially not one as young as my daughter. I'm perfectly happy writing my trashy little stories." He pushes off the table, his body lifting to its feet and this can't be it; he can't leave *now*.

"Wait." I reach out and grab his wrist, the motion an unplanned lunge, one that causes a sharp pain in my chest, my breath to wheeze, my face twisting in pain for a moment before I regain control. "Sit down." His eyes drop to my hand around his wrist and I release it. "Please." I add, and don't like the way he peers at me, his gaze skating across my face, my body. In preparation for battle, I had covered up, worn layers. Put makeup on, and brushed my hair. I fear, in his new and more critical appraisal, that I haven't done enough.

"You sick?" He stays in place, his palms flat on the table, stiff arms that support strong shoulders, the hunch of him intimidating. Still I return to my seat, needing the distance from him even if it puts me in a weaker position.

"Yes." I shouldn't have to say more. A polite individual would let that sit.

"What kind of sick?"

"I have three months. Maybe less." I hadn't planned on telling Marka. I don't plan—with Kate already aware—on telling anyone else. Yet, with this man, for some reason, I do. I think part of it is desperation, his refusal still fresh off his lips, my heart still panicking in my chest. Part of it is because, in his eyes, there is something there. An edge of grief that I recognize, a pain that I understand. I don't know anything about him, but I know—suddenly—that I need him. Even if he is a man. Maybe he *will* understand.

He finally sits, a heavy lumber into his chair, the back of it creaking as he settles into place. He is a much bigger man than Simon, the largest the chair has ever held. His eyes stare off, in the direction of the fridge, and there is a long moment of silence before they return to me. "People outlive those prognoses all the time."

I make a face. "I'm not that type." I know those types. The kind with families and children, the kind who *must* live longer because there is simply no other option. They do acupuncture and juice, they try meditation and have thousands pray for their healing. They abandon stress and devote everything, *everything,* to beating the odds. Everyone's journey to death is different. The contrasts between them and me are numerous.

"Is this a publisher contract thing? You accepted the advance and can't pay it back?" He looks around the deserted kitchen, and if I thought he missed my empty foyer and dining room, I was wrong. "Hell, you been selling furniture to pay your medical bills? Because I can—"

"No." I snap. "This isn't for a publisher."

"So, it's just a book." He delivers the sentence slowly, as if trying to understand the concept.

"My books aren't like yours." I shift in my seat and try to think of the nicest way to put it. "They aren't *just* books. The characters are special to me, and their lives are living, breathing stories. This story in particular—it's one I need to write before I go. It's important to me."

"You can't pull out the dying card and just expect me to jump on board."

"I'll pay you." I name a sum, one that catches his attention, his brows rising. I don't know what kind of advances Random House is paying him, but I know what Kate gets me, and I've matched that figure.

"And you want me to ghostwrite? Not co-author?" It is an important distinction. As a ghostwriter, readers will never know about his involvement, only my name listed on the cover.

"Correct." When I prepped for this discussion, it was with Marka Vantly in mind, a woman I was convinced loved the spotlight. I had been concerned over this part of the negotiation, certain that she would want her name in gold print along the spine. I have no idea how this man will respond. He's published for all this time in secret, hiding behind some blonde Barbie, his real name and identity a secret. Is ghostwriting any different?

He runs a hand through his hair, scratching at his scalp, the resulting effect wild, a man with little thought for appearances. I want to slice through that hair and open up his skull. Feast on his thoughts and taste his motivations. Why does a man like this write smut? Why has he agreed to this meeting? Why did he ever email me to begin with? And what, right now, is he thinking?

His hand falls from his hair and he turns his head, fixing me with a stare. "Tell me about this story you have to tell."

"You'll do it?" The words rush out too eager, and I try to collect myself, to calm my features.

"Maybe. I need to know the story."

I'm not ready to tell him that. I can't even manage a decent outline, my pen still stalling over the white page, my mind unable to yield despite the urgency of my timeline. How can I pitch him on a story I can't even work through in my mind?

"It's about a family." I pause, and I need a shot, a plug off the bottle above the fridge, the one that I hide from myself, the one that makes me think of her and him and ending it all. I don't move to my feet, I don't grab the shot glass, the one that sits in the bottom drawer, all by itself. I should. *I shouldn't.* He is watching me, and I am past due for a sentence. I clasp my hands tightly together, knotting them in my lap. "Well, it starts earlier than that. A love story. Guy meets girl, they fall in love."

"And then?"

I twist my hands, my knuckles bending, and maybe I could break them. That would distract from this painful conversation, could buy me hours of time and possibly a few more sympathy points. "They marry and have a child." I take a breath and the next words rush out in one long line of vowels. "It's a tragedy. In the end, the wife loses them both."

He blinks. "Loses? Define that."

No, thank you. "I haven't pinned down every detail yet."

His pupils don't move, their fix on me almost disturbing in its focus. "What—"

"Those are the bones of the story. I'll fill in the holes for you later. I'm still working them out." The response snaps out of me, and I clutch to the sharp tones of the words. *Yes.* This I can do. Abrupt. Snarky. This will keep my fingers from breaking and my eyes clear from tears.

"It sounds..." His eyes finally move, a slow sweep away as if in search for a word. The one that finally comes out would disappoint thesauruses everywhere. "Sad."

"Duh." I straighten in my seat, and can feel the end of this conversation approaching, the drone of its finality growing louder. "I know it's sad."

"Something's missing." He leans back, his arms crossing over his chest. "What else?" I watch his eyes narrow, as if suspecting me of something.

"That's it." I haven't lied so much since that night.

"It's not going to be successful."

"I don't care." There is a freedom in that. This will be the first book that I won't fret over. The first book where I don't wait by the phone, nauseous over where my latest release comes in on bestseller lists. I'll never know if this book sells five copies, or five million. I'll never know if readers, or even the editor, loves or hates it.

He is struggling with something. I can see it when he leans forward, one hand closing over the other, his eyes down on the table before he lifts them to mine. When he speaks, his question is the last thing I expect to hear. "You really want to spend your last months writing?"

"Yes." He's asking a druggie if she wants another hit, an overweight child if they'd like more cake. There is nothing in my final days I want more than to create worlds. There is also nothing I dread more than to dive further into *this* particular book.

But it has to be done. I can't die with this book unwritten, with these truths buried among my bones. It needs to come out. Someone has to know the truth.

"You can't be serious." His hands part, flex, then find each other again, his fingers closing over a wedding ring, which he rolls around his finger. Simon never wore his ring. I should have asked him about it, during one of the hundred times that I noticed it. I should have taken it out of his bedside table and waited to see how long it took him to notice. After he died, I gave mine to a homeless woman, her eyes unmoving as I dropped it into her cup. Sometimes I wonder what she thought when she dumped out her change and saw the diamond. I wonder, when she pawned it, if questions were asked, if the police were called. Mark's hands move. "You should travel. Do everything you always dreamed of. Sit on a beach and sip umbrella drinks. Get massages every day and read. Hire some Italian to rub lotion on your feet and screw you into next Sunday."

I have to smile at that. "You have an unnatural fascination with Italian men, you know that right?"

"Don't change the subject."

"I'm serious. *The Italian Stallion*… then that slutty little novella set in Venice, the one where both guys—"

"The only thing you're proving is how much you obsess over my books," he interrupts.

I snort, and the change of topic feels good, the corners of his mouth turning up, a bit of levity in the air. "Do we have a deal, Mr. Fortune?"

"A million dollars?" He raises his eyebrows and glances away. "I need to think on it overnight."

"What is there to think about?" I can't lose him. Not now. Not when I've wasted an hour on this meeting, and several more setting it up. Plus, a part of me likes him, his rough edges and quiet manner. Even if he did ignore my rules and seems uninterested in my novel. It is surprising, given that I don't like many people. In fact, I don't really like *anyone.* I push forward the contract, the one Kate prepared, nineteen pages long, with nine of the pages devoted to my "requests." That's what Kate is calling my rules, though *requests* is a terrible substitute, one that poses the items as negotiable, even though they are absolutely not. "Here's the contract. You'll get a million dollars for something you can knock out in a couple of months. Write quickly, and you could be out of my hair even earlier than that." I smile, and he doesn't return the gesture, pulling the contract closer, our levity of earlier already gone.

"I'll think on it." He pushes to his feet, and I watch the contract follow him, the paper folded in half and tucked into a back pocket, a terrible vehicle for such an important item. He isn't going to think on it. He probably won't even read the contract. I've lost him, and I don't know why.

"One million five." I'm pathetic, and desperate, and I never realized that until now. I follow him, my hand tucking a bit of hair behind my ear, and he turns, his eyes meeting mine. His shoulders sag a little, and, if I thought my weak negotiation would empower him, I was wrong. He reaches out and lays a hand on my shoulder, the weight of it heavy, the squeeze of it doing nothing to reassure me, a dump of fuel on my fire of internal panic.

"It's not about the money, Helena." He releases my shoulder and smiles, a grin that doesn't meet his eyes, his steps toward the front door slow.

"Then what is it about?" I call after him, clutching the chair rail.

He stops, but doesn't turn. "I haven't said no yet."

"That doesn't answer my question."

He turns, and the afternoon light hits his face, the weathered skin almost pink in its light. "I have a daughter," he says slowly. "Her name is Maggie. She's nineteen."

"Good for you." My daughter's name is Bethany. Three weeks ago, I should have lit ten candles on her cake. I straighten, and when I lift my hand from the chair rail, I am still standing. "What does that have to do with my book?"

"I wouldn't want her to spend her last months, stuck in an empty house, working on a book with someone like me."

"That's not for you to decide." I step forward, and suddenly I *don't* like this man. "It's not really any of your damn business."

"My name's on this contract, it's my business." He lifts the pages, and I suddenly wish I'd added another short and simple *request* to it. *Don't be an asshole.*

I open my mouth to tell him off, and instead, the truth falls out. "The book is about my husband and my daughter. They're gone. I'm dying. I'm sorry that you don't like it, or my agenda for the next three months, but *this* is what is important to me. Their story… it's all that matters to me." I turn my head, looking back at the table where we sat, my jaw clenching with the effort it takes to keep my tears at bay. If I look at him, I will fall apart. If I say another word, it will be a sob.

He steps toward me and kindness isn't what I want. I can't…

I can't.

MARK

She's breaking. He can see it in the rigid grip of her stance, the clench of jaw, the tremble of her entire frame. He can feel it in the air, the rough pain that emits, and this is so much deeper, so much stronger, than her own mortality. In that news, there had been no emotion. In this, she is a raw current. He doesn't know when it happened, or how, but grief is a song he is well versed in.

There are few ways to comfort a person like this. He was her, gripping his mouth so hard he left bruises, when they told him about Ellen. He was her, in the middle of a hospital hall, when the orderly touched his shoulder, asking to get by. He was her, when he smashed the man against the wall, when he sobbed into his chest, then tried to punch him, again and again, for no reason at all.

He steps closer, and she flinches. She blinks, and tears fall. He wants to hug her, he wants to cry for her, but he doesn't *know* her, and that is the problem.

"Stop." She lifts a hand, and he does, watching as she closes her eyes, steeling herself, swallowing everything. It can't be healthy, that inhalation of emotion. Then again, maybe if he had inhaled more and drank less, he'd be in a different position, with a lot less regrets. "I'm fine."

It's a lie if he's ever heard one, but she is stronger when she turns her head, her gaze meeting his, her chin raising. "I'm fine," she repeats, almost as if to convince herself.

Silence grows between them, the hallway suddenly warm, and he reaches back, touching the contract in his pocket, the terms unimportant now, everything rooted in her confession.

"Will you help me?" The words are dead, spoken by a woman who has given up hope.

"I don't know." He needs to think, needs fresh air and sunshine and to be out of this miserable house. He needs to drink, to fight, to climb onto a stallion and gallop so hard he loses his breath. He needs to live, and to forget, to abandon this girl and her death wish, her depressingly realistic book. Then, he thinks of his daughter. If she is ever in this situation, if she ever needs help… will he be there? And if not, who will? Who will spend those final months with her? Who will help her with the most important tasks she has left?

In that light, he really has no choice.

HELENA

"Okay." He pulls something out of his back pocket and it's the contract, his steps slow as he walks forward and flattens it against the wall. I watch, and feel the tears start to clog my throat. I'm terrible today. I haven't cried in years, yet I'm now welling up like a fountain. He flips to the last page and holds the paper there, the other hand pulling at a pocket on his shirt.

"You'll do it?" My heart skips when he pulls out a pen. He crosses out Marka Vantly and writes in his true name, his handwriting tight and messy, the scrawl of his signature even worse. "There is a lot in those pages," I say. "You might want to read it—"

"I don't care." He caps the pen with his mouth and returns it to his pocket, holding out the paper to me. "I'd like half of the funds up front."

"Okay." I glance down at the agreement, and feel the first crack of relief. "The amount is wrong; it still says—"

"It was kind of you to increase the amount, but I'm not taking advantage of your situation." He steps toward the door. "A million is more than fair." He is swinging open the door when I get there, and I reach out to stop him. Something needs to be said, something other than contract logistics.

"Thank you." I don't know when I last spoke those words. I know that right now, they seem inadequate, two syllables that say nothing, yet mean everything to me.

He looks down at me, and there is vacancy in his eyes, a lack of connection that I don't understand. "It's fine. I've got to go… some things to do."

I've got to go… some things to do. It's the last thing he says, his boots heavy on my porch, his trot down my stairs hurried. A minute later, I watch his car jerk into drive and down the street.

And to think, people consider *me* odd.

I was once told that marriage is a facade. I ignored the wisdom of the words, mainly because they came from a fifty-two-year-old swinger, one who believed that monogamy was a self-destructive concept, and a good orgy is the answer to everything.

But that slimy stick of sex appeal was right. Not about the orgy, though I never tested that concept out. Marriage is a facade. Simon and I... our facade started early and grew, deep and dark, a pit of secrets and lies.

I loved my husband. But I also grew to hate him.

Prologue: Helena Ross

I never write out of order, yet the prologue comes to me as Marka's—Mark's—contract scans in. I hand-write it quickly, before I lose the thought, my pen scratching over the notepad as the machine hums. When all of the pages are done, I staple the contract together, using a fresh pin to stick it to my board, a wave of relief pushing through me at the sight of his messy scrawl. *Mark Fortune.* He hasn't written a single word, yet I already feel relief, a lift of the pressure that's weighed me down since my diagnosis.

I look down at the prologue, reading over the content. Good stuff. It will intrigue the reader, while also confusing them. I tap the final line and step to the side, my fingers softly dragging across the laptop keys, the screen coming to life from the pressure. I look over at the prologue and feel a familiar stirring. I click on the book file, the feeling growing.

I should be eating something. And take some meds. But first, I'll just write a paragraph. Maybe two.

When I finish the scene, it is almost five the next morning, fourteen hours after Mark's departure. I turn off the music and save my work, stretching in the doorway before dropping on the office's couch. I hug a pillow to my stomach.

I'd written four thousand words, my last for a while. I finished the initial courtship of Simon and set a hopeful tone for the book, one that Mark will spend the next few months strengthening, then decimating.

A part of me fears the passing of the torch, exposing my secrets, telling him everything.

A part of me fears how, in the final novel, I will come across.

A part of me is terrified. The rest feels almost giddy with liberation.

Soon… my final story will come out, and everyone will know the truth.

The knock comes five hours later, at a time too early for visitors. I practically crawl down the stairs and open my door, squinting up into Mark Fortune's face.

At least he knocked, proof positive that men *can* be trained. I lean forward, far enough to see the driveway. *And* he parked on the street. Two points in his favor. Both of which are moot because the contract, of which I emailed him an executed copy, *clearly* states that he is supposed to be at home. Far away from me. I work alone, he writes alone, and everyone is happy. I look down, at the leather duffel bag in his hand, and raise one eyebrow.

"Good morning." He's back to the charmer I first met, his smile dipped in a casual familiarity that instantly irritates me.

"What are you doing here?" I emailed him the manuscript before I went to sleep. He should be at his desk, reviewing that content, and gently poking me, via email, for an outline.

"You forgot the attachment." I stare at him blankly. "In your email," he explains. "There wasn't an attachment."

"Oh." It's a distinct possibility, my all-night writing session leaving me a little loopy, my forgetfulness with attachments a common occurrence. A missing attachment doesn't explain his presence on my front porch, at ten on a Saturday morning. "I'll resend it."

"I thought I'd just read it in person." He smiles, and I stall, my mind torn between a desire for feedback and a visitor-free morning.

The feedback wins, and I step back, opening the door wider, and beckoning him in.

It's not that hard to write a book. The words are easy. What's difficult is the ability to breathe life into them. I chose Marka because her words jump. They have life, they have feeling. I chose Marka because I can see myself in her characters, I can *feel* their emotions.

The same man who wrote those words, those characters, just *scratched himself.* He's reading my first chapter, in the midst of my freaking *love* story, and reached down, his hand gripping the front of his pants, the action one without thought, a disgusting habit that he probably does ten times a day. *This* is why I avoid men. This is why I avoid people in general. We are a disgusting, foul race, only a few centuries past smearing our faces with feces and dancing for rain.

"What's wrong?" He's looking at me, his eyebrows raised, plastic-rimmed glasses perched on his nose.

I bite my lip in an attempt to stop the curl. "Nothing."

He returns to the page, his thumb licked before he flips to the next.

The thought of him reading my work is unnerving. There is a reason that I don't allow anyone to see works-in-progress before completion. I once walked in to see Simon hunched over my computer, the mouse moving, my manuscript scrolling by. I'd snapped. It'd been our first big fight, one where I screamed and he'd scorned and we'd finally agreed, four hours and a hundred tears later, to never ever, *ever* touch each other's stuff. I wouldn't mess with his World of Warcraft laptop, and he wouldn't so much as enter my office without prior permission.

He lifts the pages, and I tense, watching his face closely. "This is good."

It isn't a gush, but I still feel a knot between my shoulders relax.

"You wrote enough for me to get the tone of it. And I feel like I have a good handle on the characters." He stands, one hand supporting his lower back, and I wonder exactly how old he is. Fifty? Old enough that I feel confident that he will never attempt a pass at me. Not that that's been a common problem during my life. Most men dislike me, a condition that Mark will eventually reach, assuming he hasn't already hit that precipice.

"Why do you love me?" I whispered the question against Simon's back, my hand running along the skin, from freckle to freckle, connecting the dots.

"I love everything about you." His voice was barely audible over the television, and I wanted to mute the sound, and ask the question a hundred more times.

"Even my quirks?" I was hesitant to pose the question, a small part of me worried that, somehow, in our year together, he hadn't noticed them. Maybe, once he did, he'd run.

At that, he turned, his big frame shifting in the bed, his profile illuminated for a brief moment by the television's glare before he was facing me. "I love your quirks most of all. You're the most unique woman I've ever met, Helena. It's what first attracted me to you."

"I thought it was my supermodel looks."

"That too." He leaned forward and I felt his arm slide around my waist, the sheet between us, almost a cocoon of embrace as he pulled me closer and pressed his lips to mine.

"I'm starving." Mark speaks, and it snaps me back to present, the memory of Simon replaced by an old guy who could use a good round with some ear clippers. "May I take you to lunch?"

May I. How pleasant on the ears, a simple rule that Bethany never could master. With her, it was always 'can'. *Can I…* I'd corrected her a hundred times, but she still learned by example. And Simon was a terrible example.

"Helena?" Mark is standing now, looking at me with an expectant air. Now that he's here, we should knock out some work. There is still an outline to do, rewrites to complete, plus the awkward act of depositing him into his truck and nudging him in the general direction of the New London airport.

My stomach picks that unfortunate moment to growl. I look down at it and weigh the idea in my head. "Okay," I concede. "But just a quick lunch."

He's barely had this truck, yet it already smells of male. It's been so long since I've been so close to a man, so long since I spent this much time with anyone, other than Kate. And Kate knows my limits, she doesn't press my buttons, and she understands her place. This man is different. He will be a bulldozer, one who slowly grinds over my carcass and then backs up to complete the job.

"What do you feel like eating?" Mark shifts the truck into drive, the lurch of the cab causing me to grab at the door, the other hand tightening on my seatbelt. He doesn't look over, his eyes on the road, his voice calm.

"Thai." It's an easy answer, a food I have been craving for years. In the Life After, I eat at home, an easy way to avoid an Approach: the sympathetic and slow shuffle of a stranger, their hands reaching forward for a handshake or hug, an overwhelming need to say *something* to the widow of Simon Parks. You'd think that, four years later, locals would have forgotten, but they haven't. That's the problem with a small town and a beloved teacher. Anything tragic sticks in their history books. I need an action and reach forward, opening the glove box, finding and pulling out a vehicle rental contract.

"Mark Fortune." I read, settling back in the bench seat, and tucking one foot under my thigh. "Sounds like a porn star."

"Helena Ross sounds like a librarian."

"Ehh…" my voice drifts off, my life comprised of little more than books and regret. "That shoe kinda fits." I read further. "So, Mr. Fortune, you're from Memphis." I eye the top of the contract, one dated yesterday. *He stayed the night.* In this little town just off the Sound, where no one but soldiers and college students live, the wee bit of locals a hodgepodge of whaling descendants and nosy families.

"Yep. Born and bred." He stops at the exit of my neighborhood. "Right or left?"

"Left. What's Memphis like?"

"It's nice. I have a ranch on the outskirts. My daughter goes to Ole Miss, so it's close."

His daughter. I shift in the seat, remembering that painful fact. "She's a freshman?"

"Yep." He turns to me, the corner of his mouth lifting ruefully. "The house is a little empty with her gone."

My bad luck continues. A year earlier, and his callused life would have been busy with teenager drama and prom fittings. He certainly wouldn't be sticking around, sucking up my days with dining and conversation and other time-wasting events. He reaches forward and flips on the radio, a country song softly rolling out from the speakers. I return to the contract.

"This thing is eighty bucks a day?" A bump in the road jostles the contract and I look up. "Turn left. You should have gotten insurance."

"Insurance is a rip-off." He seems unworried, steering the wheel with only one hand, his eye contact with me unnecessary given our high rate of speed.

I distract myself with the page, my stomach twisting when I get to the extension of the rental. "This contract is for a month." I shove the pages in his direction.

"I figured I'd stick around." There is a spot of traffic ahead and he lifts his foot off the gas, his calmness growing more frustrating by the second.

"I don't *want* you to stick around." I mean it, but the words come out flat, as if I'm having second thoughts. I'm not. I want my empty house back. I want my rules and full control over every aspect of my environment. I want something that, two weeks ago, my prognosis stole from me. Once Mark starts writing, I'll be at the mercy of his pen. Can I tell him my story? Can I give him my heart and trust him with it?

We come to a red light and he turns his eyes from the road to mine. "I won't get in your way. Just give me a little bit of time each day, and we can knock this out. Two hours a day, whenever you want. In a month, this could be on its way to the publisher."

An entire book, written in just a month. He could do that? It sounds like heaven, to have everything off my chest in that length of time. It also sounds like hell, to go through all of that pain, that quickly, with a stranger.

I look away from his eyes and pull on the top of the seatbelt, my chest suddenly tight. "I don't really work well with others. Literally and figuratively speaking. Plus…" I hesitate, unsure whether to mention the elephant sitting between us. "You and I don't have a history of getting along."

"You're referring to the emails." He tosses out our history as if it's minor, a cutesy squabble between friends.

"Yes."

"I thought we got over that."

Did he? He thought that all of these years, all of these hateful words… had they not meant anything to him? Maybe the issue is that he knew. He *knew*, for all these years, that he wasn't Marka Vantly, that it wasn't a gorgeously annoying supermodel who was showing me up on bestseller lists, and outselling my print runs. He knew, and probably guffawed his way to the bank, and found me and all of my snide remarks amusing. My face flares with embarrassment, and I've never felt so stupid. "Stop the truck."

"What?" He glances over, his foot not moving from the gas pedal, the truck still humming along at a pace that will surely kill me. "What are you talking about?"

"I don't want to ride with you." And I don't want to write with him either. How could I? Everything I knew about him is false. "You're a liar."

"A liar?" He finally slows, pulling the truck to the side of the road, the vehicle bumping over a curb and coming to a stop on the shoulder, so close to the guardrail it almost kisses it. I reach down, fumble for the handle, and crack the door open, the guardrail in the way, preventing it from opening. I feel claustrophobia swell and think of the safe room, the locked steel, being trapped. "Helena."

I turn to him. "I'm stuck. Pull up and give me more room."

"We're on the side of a highway. I'm not letting you walk down it in this traffic."

I close my eyes, slow my breathing, and try to think of a giant meadow, of wind, of open space. "Then pull forward. Start driving. NOW."

I don't open my eyes but I feel the truck lurch forward, the ease of the seatbelt as it loosens, and I relax, reaching forward and hitting the window control, welcoming the burst of fresh air.

"How am I a liar?"

He's either an idiot or obtuse, and I'd place a bet on either. "You're a man."

"Yes." He turns his head, one hand loose atop the steering wheel, and I glance nervously down the road. "And that bothers you?"

I shift in my seat, trying to formulate an explanation that I haven't yet worked through myself. In some ways, I'm happy—overwhelmingly so—that he looks the way he does. I'd been intimidated by Marka's perfection, her pouty lips and sex appeal. When you combined that with her writing, her sales, her following… it had been unfair, had pissed me off, put our relationship on uneven footing that had always left me the loser. Now, that intimidation factor was gone, the competition diluted, my vision of her gone.

Still, I knew how to battle with *her*. With a man, with HIM, everything is different. He smiles when I would have expected her to jab. He chuckles when she would have sneered. His eyes soften, are dipped in compassion and understanding—qualities I hadn't expected her to possess.

In this fight, I don't even know where to stand. I swallow. "You should have told me the truth."

"I'm sorry about that," he sighs, and he actually sounds sincere. It must be a cowboy thing, the ability to drag words along the ground and kick up emotional dust. "I'm not in the habit of telling anyone. My daughter and my agent. That's all who know." He leans forward, turning down the air conditioner. "Well, and now you."

"And Kate." I add quietly, and cracks form along the ridge of my anger. I, more than anyone, understand secrets. I understand how one person, one whisper of truth, can crumble empires, destroy lives, reveal monsters.

There was a day that I was a monster. And this man… he will soon have to carry that truth, hold that secret, guard that pit.

Maybe it isn't a bad thing he's kept this façade for so long. The man can keep his mouth shut. It's a tool that will, in the next few months, come in handy.

I look out the window, and feel some of my hate fade.

"It won't be that bad." He puts on his turn signal and merges into a space between two cars that an elephant would find tight. "I talk less when I write. It can only be an improvement to *this*." He gestures in the open space of the cab, and I smile despite myself. This: (a noun) the awkward exchange of words between two opposites.

He turns right, and I watch a jogger stop, bouncing up and down in place, her eyes meeting mine through the window. "I can't even picture you writing," I admit. The thought of this man hunched over a laptop is amusing. He probably pecks at the keys with his pointer fingers. He probably double spaces the start of each sentence and forgets to save his work.

"It's a very masculine endeavor. A lot of grunting and flexing."

I laugh, the sound barking out of me, and I lift my hand to my mouth to cover the slip. "You're not going to take this seriously."

"It sounds like a dark book, Helena. You're going to need some comic relief at some point."

I turn to look at him, and his eyes are soft, the kindness in them clear. It's cute that he thinks he can handle this, that he can take in my sad story and create a novel from it. But all he knows is that I lost my family. He doesn't understand how.

And it's the how that is the most twisted piece of it all.

We end up at a Taco Bell drive-through, the Thai restaurant closed, a sudden yearn for chalupas rearing its head. There is a storm coming, the air electric with anticipation, the sky dark enough to be dusk. We head back to my house, racing the rain, his foot heavier on the gas, my eyes watching the clouds. He holds his hand out toward the takeout bag.

"Pass me a taco."

I tighten my grip on the bag. "Not in the car." If I had a rule book handy, I'd outlaw drinking, eating, and talking in the car. I'd insist that only eighties music be played, nix any air fresheners, and require absolute control over the car's climate.

"I'm a grown man. If I want a taco *I* just paid for, in *my* truck, I can have one." He shakes his hand and I scrunch up my face, digging in the bag and unwrapping one of the six tacos he'd ordered. Six. Who needs *six* tacos?

"Here." I shove it into his hand and look away, closing my eyes briefly at the crunch made when his jaws close around the hard shell. There will be bits of cheese everywhere, strings of lettuce falling into the floorboard, his hand one dirty mop that will touch the steering wheel, gearshift, and door. In my purse are hand wipes, and if he thinks he's stepping into my house without a thorough wipe-down, he's crazy.

He puts on his turn signal and makes the turn without me telling him, his sense of direction better than mine. I used to constantly get lost. I once drove to a meeting in New York and ended up in Princeton. It was a lack of focus issue, my mind wandering through the pieces of my latest work-in-progress, miles and important turns slipping by unnoticed. Now, there are probably apps that keep you on the road, constant reminders of upcoming actions, a way to easily see where you are in your journey. But back Before, all I had were maps, ones with directions scribbled in the margins, my chances slim of getting anywhere on time. Simon always drove, his hand occasionally leaving the steering wheel to reach over and touch my knee, the weight of his palm comforting, his smile at me shy, as if I might push his hand away.

"Are you married?" The question is a hollow attempt to push away the memories, Simon's eyes, and the curl of his fingers around my bare knee.

"No."

I recognize it immediately, the clip of words, the tightening of his shoulders. I don't want to think about the past, he doesn't want to talk about his present. It's too bad for him, because he isn't allowed to cut my head open and then protect his own. "Why not?"

"I was married. She passed away."

I suddenly understand the look I'd seen in his eyes, the haunt of grief that hugged the edges of his smile. No wonder I feel a kinship with him. We've both lost someone, his pain still as raw as my own. I look away. "How'd she die?"

"Cancer."

Go figure. I sigh. "That's encouraging."

"Sorry. It's a popular disease."

"You could have been more creative with it." I risk a glance at him. "Told me that she got trampled by elephants while on safari."

"Fine. It was a band of cannibals. They broke in and feasted on her. I barely escaped with my life."

"Oh my God…" I try and swallow a smile. "Please tell me that she passed ages ago, so that this isn't terribly painful and rude."

"Three years ago. But conversation with you seems to lean toward painful and rude anyway." He finishes his taco and I watch as he crumples the wrapper into a ball and tosses it into the floorboard. I wouldn't have thought that littering in a vehicle needs a rule, but it obviously does.

"I'm sorry about your wife."

"Thank you."

There is silence, and against the windshield, the first drop of rain hits. I watch it, then a second, then there are a hundred blurry dots across the smooth surface, his hand reaching up to start the wipers.

"Have you outlined anything yet?" He has to speak up over the rain, and I turn to him.

"No. I will this afternoon."

"I won't need a lot, just an idea of what is next."

"Have you worked off an outline before?"

"No." He grins at me sheepishly, like it's any confession whatsoever. I could have told you that five chapters into any of his books. His writing lacks the organized structure that comes from an outline. It wanders in places where he should be concise. He has plot threads that sometimes dangle, as if he'd planned to go one route, then unexpectedly switched courses.

I've told him this, of course. I have criticized his sloppy execution in plenty of emails—dozens of them. They haven't made any difference in his work, my criticisms ignored, his own path consistently and stubbornly retread, book after book, like a broken record played by a deaf DJ.

"You'll have to learn to work off an outline." He may push every rule I set, but this is non-negotiable. If he can't stick to the path I give him, it won't work.

"I'll be fine." We are on my road now, passing homes of people I used to know, of children Bethany once played with. He turns into the driveway and parks.

I didn't realize I was lonely until I met him, until he fused himself into my life so completely that there wasn't Helena and Simon, but only US.

And once I got used to US, I didn't want to be alone any more.

The rain fills our silence, hammering against the kitchen's window. It took twenty minutes to eat. Ten more to organize ourselves and devise a system. Now, two hours later, and neither the rain, nor our hands, pause for breath. I outline a chapter, write the first paragraph, and pass the page over. He picks it up, reads it over a few times, and begins to write. I was correct. He *is* fast. Not just his writing, but the execution of it. I had envisioned a hen-peck-typist—but he surprises me, his prowess that of the 100 wpm variety. I listen to him go and my fingers ache from just the sound of it.

We are still in romantic country, and he jumps in where my first four chapters left off, finishing the story of my first year with Simon—the giggling, happy girl that I became in his presence—the way my virtue crumbled with something as simple as flowers. I was so young back then, so inexperienced in love and courtship. Simon took me to the movies, and I bought my own popcorn. He interrupted my sentences and I ate up his words. When his hand snaked up my shirt, I let it. When he pushed my palm to his zipper, I obeyed.

I fell in love impossibly early, just months into our relationship. I thought it was cute how Simon would drink too much and hang all over me. I felt sexy when he pushed me against a tree in the darkness of the park. I told him about my books, and he listened. I cooked dinner for him, and beamed when he ate it.

He wasn't all bad, and I wasn't all naive. In between the idiocy, there were a few moments of sweet young love. In between the lies and the secrets—especially in the beginning—we did love each other. At least, I loved him. Fiercely. Blindly. Stupidly.

"You think he didn't love you?" Mark speaks and I look over at him. I've almost forgotten that he is here, my mind and my mouth running away with me, spurred on by the wine, the bottle now half empty before me. I haven't had alcohol in years. I forgot how weak it makes my throat. How much it opens my heart. I stopped drinking because it made me feel too much. I stopped drinking because I was worried, after pouring a glass, what I might say, what might slip out. A stupid fear for a woman with no friends, no drinking buddies, no social media accounts to corrupt.

"You think he didn't love you?" I hadn't said that exactly, but I understand where Mark gets it. Half of the time, I convince myself that Simon didn't love me—that he was married to our big house and the lonely girl that worshipped his words and overlooked his faults. But I think he did. Early on, I think he fell just as hard for me as I fell for him. I tell Mark and he nods, as if unsurprised, as if there is anything likable in my emaciated frame and bitter words.

"I need a scene," he says, lifting the bottle and filling my glass. "A good one between the two of you. A happy memory. One to add before this. One pre-engagement."

I sit back in my chair and bring my knees to my chest, cupping the wine glass with both hands, its contents the color of pale sunshine. I close my eyes and try to find one scene—one happy moment when we were in love, reckless and passionate, our minds void of all sense.

I don't come up with one. I think of a hundred.

Midnight. The glow above us, his hands tight on the rungs of the ladder, a skinny one that snaked up one leg of the water tower. A spray can stuffed into the waist of his pants; he lifted one foot and hesitated, looking down at me, the terror on his face illuminated from above. He made it fifteen feet and stopped, our initials quickly sketched on the leg of the tower in bright orange paint, a shaky heart around them. When he made it back down he was panting, his armpits soaked in sweat, his face disappointed when he saw the short distance that he'd traveled. I told him that it was beautiful. He kissed me and his lips trembled.

I finish off the glass and blink, my eyes wet.

Our first time. His sheets smelled like hamburgers and sweat. We turned on the fan and the hum almost drowned out his roommate's tv. I was nervous and we were both drunk, our night spent at a bar, celebrating my print deal, my head spinning from too many appletinis. He didn't have a condom and we discussed it, our slurred conversation filled with immature logic and groping, the act begun and finished before any conclusion was reached. He pulled me onto his chest and told me he loved me. I closed my eyes and calculated my ovulation window, given the date of my last period.

Mark pushes a napkin across the table at me, and I pick it up, looking down at the pattern, pink apples stamped into the thin paper, their cheery repetitions occasionally interrupted by a green leaf. Kate must have bought these.

"Let me get you to bed."

He's standing now, his hands helping me up, the kitchen dim, the afternoon light gone. What time is it? I look at the oven but the numbers on it blur, either from tears or intoxication.

"I can make it." I step away from him, then think better of it. "Never mind." I reach out and he takes my arm. He's thicker where Simon was thin, his arm hair coarse where Simon's was fine, and he's taller, by at least four inches. "My room's at the top of the stairs." I'll have to lay down in our old bedroom, that stiff four-poster bed where Bethany was created, the one I haven't slept in since That Day. I'll move, once he leaves. I'll only have to lay there for a few minutes, for the sake of appearances.

I say goodbye to him at the entrance to my room, and walk into the space I rarely enter. I drag back the covers, and half-crawl, half-fall, into bed. The sheets still smell like Simon's cologne. I can still feel his lips on my collarbone when I pull them up to my chin. It isn't just this bed. The memories of him, as much as I fight them, exist. In the shower, I sometimes think of his kiss. In the car, I remember how he would reach over, his hand cupping mine, his thumb caressing the back of my hand, and tighten imperceptibly at quiet moments—a hug of sorts. I remember how much we laughed. Our inside jokes. How he would beam at me when I said something witty. When I hit my first bestseller list, we opened cheap wine and sat on the floor of that apartment and made a ramen noodle bonfire. That night, in bed, a laptop open, his arm around me, we'd looked at houses. "The sky is the limit," he'd said, and we'd gone crazy, flipping through homes we never thought we'd be able to afford, envisioning lives beyond belief. We'd known. We'd known that this was our new life, and that there would be more bestsellers. We'd thought that everything, from that point forward, would be perfect.

I close my eyes and, despite every intention not to—feel the pull toward sleep. I hate Simon with my entire soul, and I love him with every other inch of my body, and neither really matters because he is dead, and I killed him.

My new worst friend somehow tags along to my doctor's appointment.

"Helena Ross? Are you *the* Helena Ross?" The nurse looks up from my bracelet, her pierced brow pinching upward as if concerned by the concept. She can't possibly read my books. She has a rainbow magnet stuck over a photo of her and a "friend", one with more body hair than me, and we all know *that's* saying something. If this girl reads my straight-laced romances, complete with the obligatory male/female pairing, then she needs to expand her library immediately.

"No, I'm not. But I get asked that a lot." I try to pull back my hand, but she holds it firmly, two fingers pressed against the underside of my wrist.

"Wait, sweetheart. I need to get your pulse."

My pulse is probably perfect, calmed by the lie. I've always been a liar. Maybe that's why writing came so naturally. A thousand lies, disguised in a character's voice, bits of my life sprinkled through the pages, the perfect camouflage for whatever it is I feel the urge to say.

"I got a great parking spot." Mark comes from somewhere, a grin on his face like he has accomplished something other than irritating me. I'm still not sure why he's here. We wrote all of Saturday and most of Sunday, finishing off the weekend with some well-needed alone time. Then, this morning, he was there—on my porch—all but insisting that he bring me to this appointment, even though a taxi was on call and available.

"Yippee." I watch as the woman drops my wrist and reaches for the blood pressure cuff.

"This place is nice. The chemo area has little cubbies. Much nicer than where Ellen was."

Ellen. His voice softens when he says it. I feel a pang of jealousy and poke out. "Please don't make this entire thing a tribute."

His nostrils flare a bit and I watch with interest. He has more minute reactions than Simon ever did. Like flared nostrils. I always thought that was a book thing, one of those literary reactions that never actually happens in real life, like swooning heroines or angrily shook fists. I expect an apology but he says nothing and I like him a little more for it.

"Looking good!" The woman says brightly, and I don't know how *that* could be possible, but I can't bitch at a woman wearing purple kitten scrubs. "Let's get you in to see the doc."

The doc is different than the one who handed over my death sentence. He's an oncologist, and will handle my crumbling body for the remainder of my life. I stare at the Harvard diploma on his wall as he explains, without introduction or cushioning, the next few months, and how my body may react to it. He is an enthusiastic prescription writer, and fills out five different scripts, passing me the stack that will allow me enough drugs to weather a gunshot wound. I tell him that I've done just fine on my current meds, but he doesn't seem to care. He's pure doom, wrapped in pale skin and too much ear hair, his voice clinical and dull, the kind that has me ready to nod off within minutes. He doesn't meet my eyes, he doesn't smile, and if there was an empathy class at Harvard, he flunked it.

We'll get along just fine.

Two hours later, I walk through my front door and pass a stranger. She is a short squatty woman with an apron, one who avoids eye contact and shuffles past—the cook that Kate found. I bite my tongue, listen to Mark drill her senseless, and make it to the sunroom, settling into the recliner and leaning it back. I turn as Mark enters, his guard dog duties complete, and watch him set his giant leather duffel down. "You don't need to be here." This is the third time I've said it. *I don't* want *you here.* The revised statement lies on the end of my tongue, pushing, easing its way out. He moves to the kitchen, and hunger stops my statement. I watch with interest as he opens the fridge and pulls out a container of food.

"Debbie—that's the chef—said she put the food in here."

I look past him, at the open door of the fridge, my perfect alignment of water bottles and Cherry Cokes now crowded to the side and replaced with enough Tupperware containers to get Octomom and her brood through three Thanksgiving dinners. I eye the container in Mark's hand, watching as he opens the microwave and sets it inside. "What's that?"

"Lasagna." He presses a button, and the electronic hum of radiation fills the air. "I'm thinking you need an official poison taster. Just in case Debbie read one of your novels and wants revenge. I volunteer as tribute."

"Ha." I say flatly, but smile despite myself. "Chivalrous of you."

"It's a cowboy thing." He sniffs the air, and I'm almost angry at how good it smells. Maybe I should have hired a chef before. If this tastes good… if I've been missing out on four years of edible enjoyment… I'm going to be pissed at Kate for alerting me to this mistake.

Mark glances at me. "You hungry?"

I tilt my head, distracted by a knock on the front door. This is what happens when you start talking to people. I go from a life of solitude to Grand Central Station. Mark moves forward, his back straight, and my mouth twitches at the protective stomp of his stride. I hear the crack of the door, murmured voices, a female apology, and the sound of clunky feet tripping toward me. A heard of giraffes would be quieter, and I know, even before I see the bright pink clogs and polka-dotted socks, who will be there. I groan.

"Helena!" Kate sounds surprised, as if we are bumping into each other at the grocery store, and not inside my house, three hours away from Manhattan. "Hey!"

"You *really* didn't need to come back." I told her this. In every single email, and the phone call this morning, I *told* her not to come. "You *shouldn't* have come."

She steps further into the sunroom, and completely ignores me. "I know. You didn't want me to come and I'm *not* here to stay, I promise." She turns to Mark with a smile. "I'm Kate. Helena's agent."

"Nice to meet you, ma'am. Mark Fortune." I watch Kate's face redden as he extends a hand. Perfect. I'm so glad we're eHarmonying up my house. If the cancer doesn't make me nauseous, all of this togetherness will. I clear my throat and they both turn to me. "If you aren't here to stay, why *are* you here?"

"Well… When I left the city this morning, before you called me… I didn't realize that Mr. Fortune would be here—" She flashes him a quick smile. "And I'd thought you might want some company."

Oh, yes. That's me. A companionship addict. I say nothing and the silence grows.

"Well." Kate wheezes out the word, and awkwardness hangs in the air. The microwave dings, and she brightens. "That sounds like food. Let me get it."

Mark follows her into the kitchen, and I relax my head against the recliner, the only item in this room. The big overstuffed chair was a Lazyboy special, one I often write in, and—just as often—fall asleep in. There is something soothing about the act of writing, a drug that lures you into another world, but then forgets to stop, and sometimes carries you all of the way into sleepdom. I kick my feet free of the blankets and look at the backyard. The windows in this room have gotten filthy—the outside caked with years of pollen and grime, the bottom screens littered with dead bugs and the occasional leaf. I used to wash them every summer. I would get a giant bucket of soapy water and a sponge, put on a bathing suit and a 70's playlist, and give them a thorough once-over. Bethany would try to help, her tiny hands gripping the big sponge, her reach only accessing the bottom panes, her attention gone at the first sighting of a lizard, or spider, or Simon's call.

I remember the smell of hamburgers, the baseball cap Simon wore, the taste of his kiss as he would pull me against him and brush fallen pieces of hair from my eyes. We once danced, out on that patio, the grill sizzling behind us, Bethany singing beside us, his eyes tender as he looked down on me.

In that moment, during that Rod Stewart song—there hadn't been the arguments, the competition. There hadn't been my mother, or any rules. There had only been a love song, and the sway of hips, and the scent of charcoal in the air.

In that moment, I would have sworn we were going to be okay.

Three months later, he was dead.

MARK

Helena moves to the sofa, where she falls asleep, a half-eaten tub of ice cream on the floor beside her, the television on, housewives arguing in seaside mansions. He turns the volume down and pulls the blanket over her, her face relaxed. She looks so young, not more than a few years older than Maggie, though she must be at least a decade older. He pauses at the ice cream, then leaves it in place, his earlier attempt to remove it met with violent opposition.

He walks into the kitchen, passing an empty glass to Kate, who dips it into the soapy water. "Is she sleeping?" she asks.

"Yeah. The anti-nausea medicine they gave her is pretty potent. I wouldn't be surprised if she's out the rest of the night." He steps next to her and pulls open an empty drawer, then another. "You know where hand towels are?"

"Here." She hands him one. "She seems to have only one of everything. Most of these drawers are empty."

"That seems to be a recurring theme in this house." He glances around, at the stark kitchen. "Book sales struggling?" It's a joke, and he's pleased when she smiles.

"Ha." She passes him a plate to dry. "I think she's just the opposite of a hoarder."

She thinks. The intrigue surrounding Helena Ross grows. "So you don't know her well." A sad realization, the only two people who care enough to be here—both strangers.

"No. She likes her space." She pulls the drain on the sink and shoots him a wry look. "Which is why I'm a little surprised to see you here."

"I sort of elbowed my way in. She seemed like she needed some help."

"Huh." A single syllable seeped in suspicion. She turns to him and folds her arms across an ample chest. "She's not the easiest thing to work with."

"I know. I'm trying my best with the content." And he has, truly, tried. He's put more effort into their chapters then he's ever put in anything before. Part of it is because he understands how seriously she is taking the project. The second motivation is an insecure desire to please a legend. A legend now snoring, one arm hanging limply off the couch. A legend who has read everything he's written so far, and yet hasn't given a line of feedback. He must be performing well, must be nailing the feel. Otherwise, she would lash out, and give him some of that famous Helena Ross hell.

"She'll rip your heart out, but she doesn't mean it." She pauses, and he can feel the assessment in her stare. "I think she needs you. More than just your words. She needs *someone* to help her through this."

"My wife." He stops and collects himself. "I've been through this before, I can—"

"No." Kate shakes her head. "That's not what I meant. This *book*, that's what she needs help with, that's where her focus is. Her death?" She meets his eyes. "She treating it like a side effect."

chapter 25

As a child, I only loved myself, and even that was a love dipped in confusion and self-criticism. As an adult, I learned to love in a stilted fashion, my relationship with Simon similar to that of my first ski lesson. Slow at first, my hand gripping the safety rope, my breath in my throat, waiting for the eventual fall, the eventual tumble. After I began to trust him, that's when the danger really started. That's when the hills became taller, more like mountains. And my risk went from that of a skinned knee to something much more deadly.

I wake up on the couch, the words echoing in my head. I grab a stack of Mark's latest content and write the paragraph in the margins, the room dark except for the television. There. The beginning of the next chapter, done. I set the pages aside, my entire body aching when I stand and stumble into the kitchen. There, the light is on above the microwave, pill bottles in a perfect line along the counter, a note in front of them.

Wake me up.

I don't recognize the handwriting, but it can't be Kate's. It's messy and male, and missing a *please.* I am turning to the stairs when I see his feet. They are bare, jutting off the end of my recliner, and there is the low sound of a snore. I plod into the sunroom and peer at him, his mouth hanging open, features slack. Men are so ugly when they sleep, and Mark is typical, the second snore coming louder than the first, his face twitching as it struggles through the inhale.

He didn't need to stay here. I'm perfectly capable of sleeping on my own. Chances are, given Kate's prior visit, any dishes are done, the trash taken out and toilets cleaned. He should be sleeping in his hotel, that duffel bag somewhere other than my floor.

Speaking of which… I consider the bag, which slouches next to his chair. Settling onto the cool tile, I pull it toward me, my eyes lifting to him for a moment before I pull the zipper open.

The contents of the bag are fairly unexciting, a grab bag of old man underwear and clean shirts. There are no pants, and I eye the leg of his jeans, which hang off the edge of the recliner. I relax a little when I find his dopp kit, his toothbrush and razor inside, his invasion of my home not creeping into a bathroom. I find myself mildly disappointed that there is no porn magazine, or flask, or pill stash—no well-creased photograph or love letter hidden inside a book or passport. I do find a wallet, my hands careful as I pull out the overstuffed leather billfold. Lots of cash, over a thousand dollars. A driver's license in the name of Mark Fortune, his birthdate putting him in his early fifties, his height a generous six foot, weight of 205. He is an organ donor, one point in his favor, and has a motorcycle license. I thumb through the other cards, my hands plucking them out as I go. An automobile association card. A—

"What are you doing?"

I glance up, from my spot on the floor, watching as he slowly hefts the recliner upright. "Going through your wallet." I hold up a black American Express card. "I thought you had to spend a million dollars a year or something to get one of these."

"Worried about my finances?"

"You still have a *Blockbuster* card?" I don't wait for a response. "God, you're old." I pull out the AARP card. "Is this teensy discount worth destroying your sex appeal?"

"That's the determining factor in my inability to get laid? An AARP card?" He eases his way out of the chair and I hear the actual creak of limbs as he stands.

"It can't help." I flip to the other side of the wallet, moving past a Discover card (who still uses those?), a concealed weapons permit (good to know) and a player's card for a New Orleans casino. "Speaking of which, do you have a girlfriend?"

"No." He shuffles to the kitchen, and I watch him pass, wondering if the bottom of his feet are clean. "You want anything to eat?"

I drop the wallet and consider the question, my hunger warring with my fear of sickness, my head a bit loopy from the drugs. "Maybe some toast." He moves farther into the kitchen, and I hear a cabinet open. "Thank you," I call out, turning to look over my shoulder, his movements slow and careful, those of someone still half asleep.

"You're welcome." He finds the toaster and I turn back to his wallet, examining an insurance card before moving onto the last item, a laminated photo of a girl, thirteen or fourteen in age.

"This your daughter?" I ask, turning over the photo in my hand. On the back, there is writing, neat and pink and cursive.

I love you. Maggie

Original girl. Bet she thought about that inscription for ages.

"Yep. That's her. It's an old photo. You like jam?"

"No."

"Good." He shuts the fridge. "You don't have any."

"You get along with her?" I slide the photo back into the leather sleeve and close it, dropping the wallet into the bag and standing. The room tilts, and I grab the recliner and wait for a moment as my vision returns to normal.

"I do." He scrapes butter over crisp toast, and glances up at me. "Sit down. I'll get you some water. You should drink as much as you can, it helps to flush out your system and the meds."

"And she's at Ole Miss." I say, remembering our earlier conversation. I try to picture the daughter of this man, what she looks like, acts like. "Sounds like the name of a cow."

He shakes his head, a smile tugging at the corner of his mouth. His shirt is stretched out, there's two days' worth of stubble on his face, but I can still see where he was, decades ago, attractive. "It's a nickname, for the University of Mississippi." He turns away, walking to the fridge, and I watch as he fills a glass with ice water. "What's with the lack of furniture?"

I shrug, taking the glass. "I'm a minimalist."

"I'd say."

The sarcasm pokes at me and I can't stop the bristle that moves along my spine. "I got rid of most of the furniture once I was alone." I rip off a bite of toast and chew.

"You could have sold the house. Moved into somewhere smaller."

"Yep." I take a sip of water and feel my first hard stab of nausea. Selling the house used to be a common suggestion. Right after the funeral, I got flyers and market reports from realtors, all boasting about the stats of the home, none mentioning the stigma that might follow it. I looked it up once, the effect on value of a home that has hosted death. It's not a fact that has to be disclosed. These walls could hide blood splatters and a home-made dungeon, the oven used to cook organs, and we'd never have to tell a soul. But in this small town, everyone knows. Everyone knows about the strange widow in the big empty house, and the day it all fell apart.

Mark doesn't seem to know. The newspaper articles and obituary both used my married name, Helena Parks. I've Googled my maiden name and Bethany's, my maiden name and Simon's, my maiden name and death, and nothing comes up. I am protected, though I can't say the same for him. Last night I Googled Mark Fortune, and a treasure trove of tragedy emerged. He told me about his deceased wife. The rest, the DUI, the bankruptcy, the rehab… he hasn't mentioned. It's fine. I have my secrets, and he has his. The book is what matters.

"Did you buy this house with your husband?"

I feel the action a split second before it comes and I lunge for the sink, my chin barely clearing it before I vomit, the toast rough and painful on its exit, the taste hitting my gag reflex and I retch again, spraying the spotless surface of my sink.

Mark slides a water bottle toward me, and I grab for it, rinsing and spitting into the sink, my hand clutching at the faucet handle and pulling it, needing to wash out the sink. I run the disposal, the counter vibrating under my forearms, and I don't have the strength to look when Mark gently touches my arm. "I'll clean that. Let's get you into bed."

I can't take a second night in my old bed. Eventually, I'll show him Bethany's room, the tattered remains of my heart. For now, I push away from the sink. "I'll sleep on the couch. You should go to your hotel."

"I'm fine in the recliner. I'm too tired to drive, assuming you don't mind me staying."

I do mind. I want to be alone. I don't need his ice water, his concerned looks, his constant mothering. I want my house and my privacy back. I want my happy place, which is in Bethany's room, in my sleeping bag, surrounded by her things. "Whatever," I mutter, slowly moving past him and toward the living room.

The couch flickers with color, still lit by the television, and I pull back the blanket and crawl onto my belly, pulling the pillow against my cheek, my eyes closing. The last thing I remember, before falling asleep, is him feeding me more pills.

The phone wakes me. It is a siren, loud and incessant, and I roll over on the couch, pulling the pillow over my head and waiting for it to stop. Then, I remember Mark, hear the click of a door as he moves through the house, his weight creaking the floor boards, his steps echoing through the empty house. I throw off the pillow and lift my head. "Don't answer that!" I fall off the couch, my fingertips scraping along the floor, and then I'm standing, my steps drugged and confused, the room tilting as I move through the dim room and toward the kitchen. "Don't answer—" I run into his chest, my fingers curling against the flannel of his shirt, and I look up into his face, surprised.

"I'm not answering it." He supports me, and looks around for a chair, nothing around, and I feel his hands tighten on my forearms. "Let's get you back to the couch."

"No." I straighten, my bearings found, and stand, pushing against his chest. "I'm fine." The phone stops, and we both fall quiet as the machine beeps from its place in the hall, one room away. I let out a sigh of relief when a telemarketer's automated voice comes on. I've dreamed of Charlotte Blanton, her visit, her email… a call must be next.

"Are you hungry?" Mark's voice is mild, as if my drunken sprint to the phone was normal.

"I think so." I make it over to the stove and eye the scrambled eggs in the skillet. "You cooked these?"

"Yes. They're edible."

The eggs look more than edible. They look delicious. I grab a paper plate from the cabinet and spoon some onto it.

"You can take more. I've already eaten."

"This is enough." I consider the toast, which sits beside the stove. I move on.

"Coffee?"

"Yes please." I sit down and see a stack of papers, crisp and double-spaced. "Is that new content?" I was so hesitant, at the beginning, to read his work. I watched him type, I answered his questions, and I waited. My hesitation was a mix of fear and worry. I was afraid he wouldn't do it justice. I was worried his words would be flat.

My fears had been unfounded. I'd known, when I started the first paragraph, one that had smoothly continued what I had begun… that he would do fine. He easily captured my voice, followed my outline well, and kept the tone I wanted.

"Yep. I swung by my hotel and printed it." He sets down a cup of coffee. "How do you like your coffee?"

"Black is fine." I eye the pages, the eggs forgotten.

"I wrote some more this morning, but haven't had access to a printer."

I nod, pulling the pages closer. "Can you grab me a pen? There's some in the drawer to the left of the fridge."

I sit back, kicking a foot up on the opposite chair, my fork stabbing absently at eggs as I read on. I finish the plate and barely notice when he replaces it, cut strawberries appearing, everything gone by the time I finish the content, my stomach full, my fingers tapping against the edge of the final page, itching to write some words of my own.

"Can you email me the rest? I can print it here."

"Already done." He shakes a medicine bottle. "Want some medicine?"

"The anti-nausea please. Whatever's been knocking me out…"

"That's the anti-nausea."

I make a face, but still hold out my hand for the pill. "I'm not very entertaining."

"I disagree." Our eyes meet as I take the pill.

I roll my eyes and turn, glancing at the clock. 10:14 am. In the last twenty-four hours, I've slept over sixteen hours. I should be wide awake, but all I want is to lay down, my fatigue even worse than yesterday. "Let's move to my office."

"You're the boss." He picks up the pages, glancing down at my notes, before he straightens. He doesn't move, and I realize that he doesn't know where my office is. I've lived in a world of my own creation for too long, one where the sole character is a neurotic, nosy individual who can't receive a stranger's mail without opening it. If you had put me alone in his house, I'd know his social security number and the condition of his air filters by now. This man has seriously wasted his time, fixing me food and typing away. Now, with my legs in working condition, my mind somewhat clear, he's lost his chance at invading my privacy.

The steps have gotten higher in the last two days and I literally wheeze at the top, taking a moment to catch my breath, Mark patient as he leans against the banister.

"It's a steep flight," he remarks, as if my struggle is normal, and I glare back at him.

"Bite me." He should be better at this. He should know not to coddle or be kind. He should know that, within this pathetic body, I am strong and independent.

I point down the hall and at my office door. "In there."

The last guest in my office was Simon. Some days, during the winter, when the heat rattles on and there has been no fresh air for days, I can smell his scent. It invades this space, my hand clawing at my neck, the fan useless against it. On those days, I open the window and let in the freezing burst of fresh air. I huddle in a blanket, my space heater on, and work. The cold is worth the erase of him, and when summer comes, it's like he never existed at all.

Mark takes the couch and I sit down at my desk, powering on my laptop, his email one of several. My first attempt to print is unsuccessful, and I groan as I lean over the printer, unplugging the back and then resetting it. There should be a rule in the universe, one that states that mortal problems will fade with a terminal diagnosis. I'm dying. I shouldn't have to deal with petty shit on my way out.

Once the pages print out, I take a seat next to him on the couch. We both read, him going through my notes and me marking up his new content. His writing is only getting stronger—falling into the rhythm of the story, staying vulnerable while visually stimulating—and it's a giant level above his normal novels. When I look up, he's settled against the cushion, his eyes closed. "Can I ask you something?"

"This should be interesting," he replies, without opening his eyes.

"If you can write like this…" I lift the pages, "why don't you? Why write the… *stuff* that you publish?"

One eye opens and he manages a glare. "God, you're offensive even when handing out compliments." He exhales, sitting up and rolling his neck. "And the *stuff* you refer to is the only thing that I can manage to sell. I've written other stuff, good stuff." He nods to the pages in my hand. "Better than that. Self-published it. But no one bought it."

"So you reduced your quality for *sales*?" It is a stupid concept, even to my drug-muddled brain.

"Without sales, *this* is all a hobby." He gestures to my office. "When I was first published, I couldn't afford a hobby. Romance was flying off the shelves, and no one cared about contemporary fiction with heart." There is a sharp edge to his words, and I glance at him, trying to understand the irritation in the vowels. Does he hate smut? I can't imagine hating the novels I write, spending months in a story that I don't respect.

"So you sold your soul and invaded my world," I muse, looking back down at the paper.

"Readers seem to like my stuff."

I twist my mouth, swallowing the things that I want to say. Marka captured a lot of the lower end market—their tastes not exactly literary nor picky.

"Your notes…" he lifts the papers in his hands. "They're kind." He sounds so surprised that I smile. "I've been expecting a lot more red."

"So was I." I shift in the seat and feel the first wave of sleepiness, the nausea pill working its magic. "But your characters are good, and the tone is right."

"It's not hard to imagine a happier version of you."

I smile, but it is forced, my cheeks tight when I stretch them apart. I barely remember my happier days. Sometimes I think that my memory is inventing them, filling in blank slots of time with Hallmark-movie clips. "I'm not certain that version of me ever existed." I sit at my desk, grabbing at a pen, desperate for a task. "Let's do a few more scenes."

chapter 27

I had never been a girl to think about marriage. The institution of it all had bored me and the romance had intimidated me, the fate reserved for prettier girls, ones who kissed more and slouched less. When Simon first brings up the notion, I laugh. When I watch the strong flex of his hands as he carefully opens the ring box, when I see the intense mix of vulnerability and hope as he asks the question... I almost cry.

In the beginning, it was wonderful. Simon seemed oblivious to the flaws that society loved to point out in me. He didn't care about my lack of friends, or curves, or sex skills. He gave me space, yet chased me down. He brought me flowers, and impressed my mother. And his proposal, ten months after we met, hadn't seemed too quick, but just right.

"How?"

I look over at Mark, irritated by the interruption. "What?"

"Tell me the story. The proposal." He shuffles through the pages. "You're skimming over it here."

"Oh." I lean back in the chair and cross my arms over my head, stretching. "It was at a restaurant. You know. Wine. Candles. One knee." The ring had been tiny, but that hadn't been the problem.

"You said no?" He is guessing, and my flat tone must have given something away.

"I wasn't ready. I wasn't prepared." I made a list that night, though I never gave it to Simon. Five Rules for a Proper Proposal. Don't put the woman on the spot. Don't have an audience. Don't eat garlic before the act. Don't check out the waitress's ass mid-proposal. Don't ask unless you are certain that the answer is yes.

I drop my hands and sit up. "I went home and thought about it. I wrote down some pros and cons." I still have that list. If I reach right and open up the bottom drawer, it'll be there, filed under his name, the tab marked HISTORY. My pro and con list on Simon Parks.

Pros: He has nice teeth.

Cons: Sometimes, I don't trust him.

That first con, I should have listened to. There were seven more, underneath it, but that one right there... it was the only thing I needed. And I ignored it, like the stupid lovesick girl I had been.

I swallow. "He had several good qualities, which I listed. Those, coupled with the probability of anyone else ever wanting to pair with me... followed by an analysis of whether I wanted to be single or married..." I shrug. "I decided to go for it."

"That's the most unromantic story I have ever heard." He looks dismayed, so much so that I laugh.

"Disappointed in the Queen of Romance?" I tease. *The Queen of Romance.* Such a joke, the title handed down by my publisher, a New York powerhouse that doesn't have the foggiest idea of my innermost thoughts.

"Heartbroken." He sighs, and leans forward over the page. "Do you want to tell the proposal like that? It's a little awkward."

"I suppose you did it better."

He rubs a thick finger over his forehead, and I'll be damned if the man isn't blushing. "I did okay."

"Tell me." I scratch an itchy spot on my nose.

"It wasn't anything major. We were at her parents' house—a tiny crackerbox of a place in Mississippi. I asked her father, then asked her to go on a walk. Did it there." He blinks, and I can see the vacant stare of a memory in his eyes, one edge of his mouth lifting up.

"It was getting dark, and the mosquitos were so bad, you could barely pause without waving one off. She hadn't wanted to go for a walk—and was complaining up a storm… about the heat, about the bugs. I finally stopped her under this big old tree and told her to shut her mouth long enough for me to propose."

He looks at me, and his mouth fully breaks into a grin. "She missed the proposal entirely. She just kept smacking at bugs and looking up into the tree like she might scale it. I had to hold her arms still and get her to look in my eyes. Then, I asked her again." He shrugs. "And she said yes."

"That's sweet." And it is, in a redneck sort of way. "What kind of girl was she?"

He surprises me, laughing. "Reckless. You ever met a Cajun woman?"

"No."

"They're hell. I thought women from Texas had backbone. Half our relationship, I was terrified of her. The other half I spent trying my best to protect her from herself."

"Meaning what?"

"She was wild. Not afraid of anything. She'd climb on our wildest stallion and try to break him. She'd walk into the worst bar in Memphis and make friends." He looks down at the page, his smile drooping into something more melancholy.

I'd envisioned his wife as a chubby ball of Southern hospitality, one with an apron on and Christian music softly playing. Instead, she sounds fascinating, the type of woman I want to get on paper, right away, before her vision fades, before he says another word and ruins her. "Is your daughter like her?"

"Not really. I think God looked at the two of us and picked out the better parts. Maggie is quieter. She thinks through things before she acts. And she doesn't drink or smoke—has no interest in either." I glance at the soda before him, knowing the answer but still wanting to voice the question.

"Who was the drinker?"

"Both of us. She with wine, me with liquor. Luckily, we were both friendly drunks." He runs a hand over the knee of his jeans. "Ready to get back to work?"

It is an abrupt change, and I watch as he stands and stretches. "Sure." I pick up the pen and eye the clean page before me. Part of me wants to go back to work. The other part of me wants to abandon the novel altogether, to run away from Simon and his crooked smile and all of the ways he used to make me feel.

We all have a Happily Ever After, each story just needs to pick the right time to claim it. And at this stage in the Simon and Helena story, this is as good as it got: his proposal, my carefully considered acceptance. After this? After our wedding?

It started to go downhill.

As Mark writes, I steal out of the office and down the hall. I stop at Bethany's door, gulping at air, and I don't know if I'm breathless from the exertion of movement or what I'm about to do. When I finally reach forward, my hands tremble, carefully pulling at the edges of the tape, undoing the handwritten piece of paper—one of her first lists—from the door.

"My rules!" When she screamed, I could feel it in my bones, brittle parts of me breaking inside. "You said that I could request reasonable things and that my feelings would be respected!"

"We can't remember all of your rules, Bethany." I turned to Simon helplessly. This is why I hadn't wanted a child. I had fifteen hundred words left to write, and she was throwing a temper tantrum over me turning off her bedroom light.

"Why don't you write them down?" Simon suggested, crouching down before her, his hands gently holding hers. "Write down your requests, and we'll vote on them, as a family. If they are all reasonable, then you can keep them, and we will follow them."

"You promise?" It wasn't a request, but a threat, her eyes cutting to me, accusation in them. "You'll follow the rules, Mommy?"

"Yes," I said exasperated. "I'll follow the rules."

My rules had always been an unorganized set—lists I kept in my head, though I certainly vocalized them enough during my life. It wasn't until Bethany created her own, her practiced script posted on that empty door, that I realized how much simpler it was when the rules were properly stated and communicated. Less than a week after we voted on Bethany's rules, I began recording my own. Some, like Kate Rodant's, I shared with the applicable parties. Others, like my Ten Rules for Dealing With My Mother, or my Five Rules of Sex, I kept to myself, in a notebook, frequently editing them, depending on my moods. I didn't write a set for Simon. If I had, they would have drained my pens of ink. He was a walking pile of mess and disorganization, a man who enjoyed hangovers and dripping nachos, impromptu sex and a lack of retirement planning.

I may not have been a good mother. I may have been—as my attorney and mother believed—unfit, but I had followed Bethany's rules. When music played, I danced with her—our arms swinging through the air, our hips bouncing in time to the beat. I didn't touch her art. I brought cookies—Fudge Stripes, wrapped in a paper towel, and formally presented to her as if payment for passage.

I open her door and reverently carry the paper to her desk, softly setting it down, realizing the ridiculousness of my precautions as soon as it flops onto the surface. I am treating it as I would have before, back when I needed to preserve her things for the rest of my lifetime. Now, with that timeline chopped, I don't need to use such care. It only needs to last another two and a half months.

When I close the door and twist the key in the lock, I can see the faint outline of where the list sat, sticky residue still present along the corners. Before my prognosis, I would have immediately cleaned it, unable to move away from the door until it sparkled. Today, I can barely stuff the key in my pocket, my lungs tight, my heart in pain as I move away from her room and toward the stairs.

I have to lock it up. I'm not ready for him to see it or hear about her. Not yet.

chapter 28

I grip the sides of the white granite counter, my breathing short and shallow, my vision spotting. I close my eyes, focus on my inhalations, the exercise doing little to calm the gallop of my heart. I turn away, leaning against the counter, and press my fingers on my eyelids in an attempt to stop the tears from falling.

There is a soft knock, and I am not fast enough to reach for the knob, to flip the lock. The door creaks open and Simon is there, those handsome features tight with concern. His gaze darts to the counter, to the white stick there. The word PREGNANT is stark and final, and there is a break in his expression, a moment of clear and uncontained joy. He gathers me against his chest and I sob, his happiness causing a fresh injection of panic. He whispers my name, wraps his arms tighter, his kiss soft against my forehead, my tears. "It will be okay," he swears. "My beautiful, sweet, girl. I promise you, this will be the best thing that has ever happened to us."

He was right, of course. She was the best thing that ever happened to me. The best, but also the worst.

The new medicine is turning me into a zombie. On Thursday, I hear the mail when it comes, the squeak of the vehicle's brakes, and I lift my head off the recliner, considering the effort to get up, walk through the house, down the steps, and to the end of my drive. The doctor promises that next week will be better, that my body will adjust to the medicinal cocktail, and I'll feel almost normal. In the meantime, he stresses, I need to have as much activity as possible, and drink lots of fluids.

Activity is a joke, unless moving a pen across a page counts. Drinking fluids has been an easy directive, the floor littered with empty bottles, my energy level too poor to pick them up, and I can feel my pristine environment slipping away with each pill I take.

It used to be that the clean and empty house calmed me. It was why I got rid of all of the furniture, all of the memories. It was too painful to look at the furniture, photos, and bits of our old life. I didn't want to sit on the couch where Bethany lost her first tooth, or at the table Simon and I once made love on. I didn't want the Peter Lik that I bought with my second bestseller, or the crockpot we got as a wedding present. I wanted it all gone, each item attached to a memory, each day an assault of What Used To Be. I wanted a fresh start, and it worked. The blank slate felt like a different house, one without secrets and death, one where I hadn't been a fool, one where I had loved Bethany properly, and done everything right.

Now, with Mark and Chef Debbie's presence added to the house, it just feels odd. He suggested I use a heating pad that I don't own. He asked for a bucket when I was nauseous, needed a wrench to fix the sink, both things I threw out four years ago. Debbie has bumped around with the limited dishes I own, my kitchen too bare to make much of anything, and finally started cooking elsewhere and just bringing the food here. Kate has been buying enough items to bankrupt us both, her frustrating appearances coupled with shopping bags full of useful items, and I *hate* that she keeps popping up, and that their presence is helping me. I am useless, empty and lacking in every sense except for the creation of plot.

There is the hum of an engine, and the mailman drives off. I should go out there. It will give me some exercise. Plus, it's been a solid week since I checked the mail. The box is probably full, an engraved invitation to anyone plotting to rob my house. Two months ago, I'd have welcomed them in with a smirk, hoping to fight to the death. Now, with this book off and running, my life is too valuable, a joust not worth the risk.

I lower the footrest of the recliner and stand. I bend over and grab a few of the empty bottles, then straighten, making it to the trashcan, then across the kitchen and to the front door. There, I rest. Mark is gone, back to his hotel, plans to shower and change and hunt down some Thai food for dinner. He's written eight thousand words in two days, an impressive feat, one that he barely blinks at. During that same time frame, I've slept and complained enough for three toddlers. Occasionally, in between snoring and bitching, I've marked up some of his work.

It doesn't need a lot of changes. He has talent, more than I had expected. I'd planned to mold him, to water his talent and watch it grow, to rewrite his weak words and create something from their framework. But in them, there is already greatness. My tweaks are small, the majority of his work left alone, my lack of effort almost disappointing. Almost. These last two days have been hell. I twist the knob and pull, the door unsticking and swinging open, the afternoon breeze coming in. It's beautiful outside, one of those cheery days of fall, when a hint of heat is still in the air. It reminds me of summer days, spent on this porch. We had a tarp Simon would set up on the grass, a hose put at one end, the gradual hill of our lawn providing the perfect slide for Bethany. We added dish soap to make it slick, and she'd shriek with excitement as she slid down. It became an event, Simon adding balloons to our mailbox, and inviting the other kids on our street. Some weekends, we had as many as twenty kids streaking around that lawn, Bethany exhausted by the time the sun set and we cleaned it all up.

I take the front steps carefully, moving among the memories, each one both painful and sweet, like poisonous chocolate, the sticky taste lingering far after I swallowed the piece. At the mailbox, there is a thick stack of envelopes, and I flip through them slowly. A utility bill moves aside and exposes a thin white envelope, my eyes narrowing at the sender's name. Charlotte Blanton. I stop, one foot on the first step of the porch, and stare at it. What could it contain? What could this woman possibly need? Her behavior is stretching the limits of my patience. First her visit, then her email, and now *this*. I hold the envelope away from the stack, considering it.

I'm afraid of it. Scared in the way that I was right after the funeral, the grief/guilt/paranoia cocktail contributing to my short-term dependency on pills, then alcohol, then work. Writing is what pulled me out of it, my characters pulling me away from the Ambien and wine, an impending deadline being the final push I needed to forget *everything* but my word count.

Now, with just her name in the return address, I feel my throat close. "*May I ask you a few questions?*" Lying, my forgotten friend, would save me. If I had to, I could handle questions, just like I always have. "*Please. It's about your husband.*"

Inside the house, I feed the envelope into the garbage disposal, watching the white envelope spin to its death without any desire to see what lies inside.

I have only nine weeks to go. Dodging Charlotte Blanton, during that time, is certainly doable.

I lay back on the couch, my feet on a pillow, Simon's head on my swollen belly. He turns his head, pulling up my shirt and presses a kiss against the skin. "How about the name Jacklyn?" he asks.

I groan, running my hand through his hair and note, with affection, the way his hairline is changing. "No. How about Bella?"

"No." He shakes his head. "I knew a Bella once."

"You seem to have known a lot of girls," I pout, tugging at a tuft of hair. "Good thing I'm not a jealous woman."

He grins, and I love the soft huff of his breath against my skin, the warm weight of his body as he lowers it against me.

"You're the only woman for me." He kisses me, and I smile against his mouth, loving the gentle curve of his fingers over my belly.

Mark's cell rings, a muted tone from inside his shirt pocket. I look up from my spot on the floor, my back against the couch, pages of his work spread out before me. He doesn't react, his butt perched at the edge of my chair, his fingers busy against his laptop. It rings again, and I wonder if he can hear it. "Your phone—"

"Shh." He doesn't look at me, his eyes glued to the laptop screen as the clattering of keys reaches a crescendo. He hits a key with finality and sits back, one hand working open the pocket on the front of his shirt, his chin tucking into his neck as he peers at the screen. When he answers the phone, I set down my notebook, interested.

His voice is friendly, then changes, worry creeping into the tones, the one-sided dialogue confusing. By the time he ends the call, I'm lost.

"Is everything okay?" I watch him rise to his feet and I can see the distraction on his face, his cell phone twisting in his hand. I think of his daughter, and concern flashes through my mind.

"It's Mater. She—" he sees the look in my face and hurries to explain. "She's one of my cows. And she's birthing early."

Marka Vantly has cows. All the times I've envisioned my arch nemesis, it has been in an elegant penthouse, one that smells of perfume and fresh flowers, her days busy with waxing appointments and massages. *Marka Vantly has cows.* My imagination couldn't have been more wrong. "So…" I try to understand the worry on his face. I don't know anything about cows, but birthing seems to be a normal part of their life cycle.

"I need to go home. Just for a day or two." He pulls on his right ear, and glances toward his laptop, still open on my desk. "I'm sorry. She's one of my oldest. I need to be there." His hand falls and he looks up at me, a new light in his eye.

I recognize the glance—the *aha* moment of a dumb idea. Simon used to get it all the time. *You know what…* he'd start, a thoughtful look crossing his face. Then he'd propose a "project," like pushing out the guest room wall and turning it into a game room, one with pool tables, a bowling lane, and wet bar. Or the idea of throwing an Easter egg hunt for the entire neighborhood, complete with a bunny petting zoo and giant furry costumes for me and him. "All the kids can come," he'd said, as if that was a *good* thing, as if I wanted hundreds of tiny feet all over our yard. That idea, he'd actually implemented, using Bethany as his pawn, me helpless against the two of them and their ideas of *fun.* Such bullshit, all of it. All lies, all selfishness and I was so stupid to enable it all, to stand there and foot the bill for what he wanted.

"Why don't you come with me?" He nods, as if this idea makes sense. "I got my plane. We can be in Memphis in two hours. I've got plenty of room at the ranch, and we can keep working—not lose this momentum."

"No."

"It'd be better for me to be around, in case you need something, or don't feel well."

"You're not my nurse, Mark. I'm a big girl. I managed just fine before you."

"When's the last time you took a trip?" He steps back and leans against the desk, and I eye the legs of it, wondering at its strength. Bethany used to sit on that desk, her legs swinging, arms twirling, typically when I'd be trying to work. Her forty pounds couldn't compare to him, his big shoulders, his wide thighs relaxing against the edge of the desk. It's easy to imagine him around cows. Simon, in comparison, was small, like me. His t-shirts fit me well, and his chin came just over the top of my head. I remember buying him 32 inch jeans. I remember thinking, as I searched for that ridiculous size, that I was *above* this. I had more important things to do, words to write, deadlines to hit. I was Helena Fucking Ross, and there I was—pushing a shopping cart, a baby drooling in the carrier before me, a freakin' pacifier tied to my belt loop.

I rub at my forehead, anxiety growing as memories collide with the present. I glance at Mark and realize he is waiting. Oh yes. His question. When *was* the last time I took a trip?

It's both the easiest question and the hardest. Did my overnight sprint to Vermont—just four weeks ago—count? I decide it doesn't, and squirrel those two days away in the *Never Going To Talk About* bucket. That trip aside, my last trip was with both of them, Bethany strapped in the backseat, a cooler loaded into the back with juice boxes and yogurt sticks, our snacks covered until we hit the Canadian border. The seven-hour drive ended up taking ten, and we were all in a terrible mood by the time we hit the ski resort in Tremblant. It had been a rough start to a great weekend. I'd sprained my ankle within an hour of strapping on skis, and spent the next three days by a crackling fire, getting hours of uninterrupted writing time in while they explored the resort. We had gourmet dinners in the tiny village, one out of a fairy tale. Bethany had shrieked and splashed her way into the hot tub, her pink bathing suit sprinkled with snowflakes, the steam rising into the air, and I'd told her a story of a witch who cooked little children in her big cauldron, one that bubbled over a fire—and we'd turned the lights of the hot tub to red and I made evil faces and pretended to stir the cauldron, dunking her into the water every once in a while to make sure that she was evenly cooked. It was an incredible trip, even if Simon and I did fight on the ride home. Even if he did let her order chicken fingers and soda off the French restaurant's menu—robbing her of a rare opportunity for culture. Instead, she ate tan sticks of chicken that had been nuked in a microwave somewhere, with a side of fries. Not even poutine. Just plain old French fries, dipped in fat globs of ketchup.

"Helena?" Mark speaks gently and I blink, the room coming into focus.

"It hasn't been that long," I say. *Five years.*

"It'll be fun, I promise. And it will help clear your head. While you feel good, let's go."

It'll be fun. It will most definitely *not* be fun. I don't know what Mark Fortune's version of fun entails, but it probably involves sweating and bugs.

While you feel good, let's go. Do I feel good? I take a self-assessment. This week has certainly been leaps and bounds above last, my nauseous reactions to the meds gone, my dizziness reduced to rare bouts, my energy almost back. "Feeling good" isn't really the phrase to describe it, but I certainly feel more capable, less shaky, and a little bit like my old self. According to the doc, the short-term effect of the meds will help, but my energy will begin to wan, my headaches will worsen, my appetite lessen, and I'll be practically bedridden within another month. Mark's right. If I am ever going to travel, this week is the time. Where he's wrong is his assessment that I have any interest in the journey, although getting a peek into Marka Vantly's world *is* tempting.

"Thank you for the invite," I shake my head. "I'm going to pass."

"Ever seen a baby cow be born?"

"I've never seen a lot of things, that doesn't mean that I'm interested in any of them."

"Stop being stubborn." He smiles kindly, and I hate the comfort I find in the gesture. "It's September in Memphis. It's the most beautiful time of the year. And Mater's like you—old and crotchety. You'll get along well." He holds out his hand for me and I take it without thinking, his strong pull getting me easily to my feet.

In my thirty-two years of life, I've only been to a handful of places. New York. New London. Tremblant. Maine. Washington, DC. Vermont. They've all been the same. Cool, both in their people and their climate. I like Northerners. I've read stories based in the South, in cities like Memphis, and am appalled at the people described. The type who throw their arms around someone right when meeting them. The kind who trust too easily, ask too many questions, then gossip that information all over town. In New York, if you invite random strangers in for tea, you'll be raped and dead within a week. I think that's almost the way it should be; we should all have a healthy fear of each other.

I realize that Mark has packed up his things, the cord of his laptop stuffed into his leather duffel, the papers I had spread on the floor now stacked, a paperclip found and securing their corners. His laptop slips into the bag, and he eyes my pajama pants. "I'll go downstairs," he announces, "and grab some snacks. Don't worry about packing too much, you'll fit into Maggie's clothes if you need anything."

"I'm not going." The words stop him at the door and he pauses, a heartbeat of time passing before he turns.

"Helena."

It is not a simple name. In just the three syllables, he manages to pack in everything that he is doing for me, for this book. He is saving the final days of my life. He is allowing me my confession. He will, one day soon, keep my secrets until I die. And he wants me to go to Memphis. It seems, on this good day of health, like a small concession.

"Okay." I purse my lips. "But only a couple of days."

"I'll take you home the minute you ask."

I nod, a grating movement that almost creaks from unuse, and his face splits open in a smile. He is jogging by the time he moves down the stairs, the heavy vibration of boots against wood echoing through the house.

Oh, how quickly a life can change.

chapter 30

I haven't mentally prepared for the flight. The drive here was too short and dominated by Mark, his jaw not pausing since the time we climbed into his truck. I expected lines of security, an x-ray machine, some liquid restrictions—but none of the woes of travel, everything I've read about—occurs. We walk from his truck, through a small lobby, and are suddenly *at* the plane, everything in motion, us minutes from taking off.

Something in my belly flips, and I feel a wave of panic, one strong enough to cut through the anti-anxiety pill I took before we left. His plane looks small, too flimsy to lift off the ground and barrel across the sky. I examine the vessel, a two-door aircraft with one giant fan stuck on the nose. I don't know planes, but it seems that two propellers would be better than one, and that the larger the plane, the safer it will be. The wind whips around us and I clutch my jacket closed, the weight of my backpack reassuring, my laptop hard and flat against my spine. If we die, I'll have the manuscript with me. I'll die knowing I fit in as many words as I could, even if I don't get into the root of the mess.

"You look worried." He pushes something into the underside of the wing, and then holds a small bottle up to the sunlight, examining the liquid level in it.

"I haven't flown before." The confession darts from me, the words almost carried off by the wind.

"You haven't flown private? Or haven't flown at all?"

"At all." It's ridiculous, I know. I'm thirty-two, for God's sake. This should have been knocked out in my twenties, my chubby bank account taking me to Paris, or Alaska, or some other glamorous locale. Instead, I stayed stubbornly in the New England area, any trips outside done by car or train. It isn't so much that I have a fear of flying, it is more that I've always been a little too educated in its danger potential. I read *Alive*. If we crash on a mountain range, I'll be the first to succumb. I'll die, knowing that he will turn cannibal and eat my scrawny forearms. I swallow a gruesome smile at the thought and nod to the deathtrap. "It looks dangerous."

"It's the safest plane you'll ever step foot in," he says, moving forward and peering at the front wheel. "It's got a parachute on it. If something goes wrong—hell, if I keel over and die while flying—you can push a button and it'll get you to a safe altitude and open the chute, and you'll float down to the ground." He straightens and makes a swaying motion with his hand, like that of a feather falling. "The impact might sting a little, but nothing that a few visits to the chiropractor can't fix."

A parachute makes me feel enormously better, and I watch him circle the end of it, his hand sweeping over the metal in the way you might check a horse. "What are you doing?"

"Pre-flight check. Why don't you climb on up? This'll take me a few more minutes."

"I'm good." Truth be told, I have no idea how to *climb on up*. There are no stairs, or a ladder, and I can't see a door handle. I stuff my hands into my pockets and wait.

"Suit yourself." He looks over at me and pauses. "I'm a good pilot, Helena. I'll get you there safely."

The wind howls and I look up to the sky, not a cloud in sight. At least the weather is clear.

I stare at the screen, at the red and yellow bands that flicker across it, and feel a wave of panic. The plane dips, and I grab at the door, cursing Mark Fortune with every word in my dictionary. All I can picture, as rain peppers the windshield, is that damn parachute. It won't float gently down, not in this storm. Gusts of wind will grab ahold of its sail and whip us from side to side—like one of those carnival rides that only stupid teenagers enjoy. I close my eyes and breathe through my nose, my hands sweating against the seatbelt straps.

"Relax." The word drawls out of him, and I turn my head, my peripheral vision catching the loose fit of his hands on the stick. "We're going around the storm. We're in no danger."

As if to defy him, the plane rocks, and I whimper despite my best attempts to control my hysteria.

"Just turbulence." He turns to me. "I'm taking us higher. It'll calm down in a moment."

"How much longer before we arrive?" I wish I could reach my water. It's in the side pouch of my backpack, which I tossed in the back seat without thinking. My mouth feels dry, my face clammy, and as the plane shudders, I feel nauseous.

"Two more hours. That seat reclines, if you'd like to take a nap."

The man is crazy. *Anyone* who would sleep, at a time like this, is crazy.

By the time the small plane reaches Memphis, my heartbeats have slowed. He was right—the turbulence calms the higher we climb, and we skirt around the storm, the view almost magical from our place in the sky. By the time we descend, I am almost calm, Mark's competence proven, the small cockpit roomy and comfortable. Mark reaches over and taps at my belt. "You can take that off now." He cracks a window and cool air rushes in, the plane rolling forward, down a long runway and towards a set of buildings, WILSON AIR CENTER on a sign big enough to see from the sky. I unbuckle and stretch my legs, pushing my toes against the floor. Looking out of the window, a larger plane passes, the sun glinting off its back.

We pass a stretch of buildings, and end up in front of a hangar. I crawl out the door and hop off the wing, my backpack in hand. Mark motions me to the side and I drop my backpack on the ground and untwist the top of my bottle, chugging the lukewarm water. It is an interesting production, the gassing up of the plane, the roll of it into the hangar, and fifteen minutes pass before Mark stands before me, keys in hand.

"Ready?" he asks, and I nod, grabbing my backpack.

His vehicle—a vintage Bronco—is parked in the hangar, the top of it down, and I open the door carefully, admiring the polished wood accents and the pristine leather seats. They are two-toned, dark green and white, and I slide inside, admiring the showroom-ready finish. I think of him eating the taco, bits of lettuce fluttering to the floor of his rental truck. The floors of this truck are wood strips inlaid with rubber, and I can guarantee that he's never eaten here. "How old is this?" I ask.

"1976." He climbs into the truck and the frame of it shifts, his elbow bumping against me as he twists to get his belt. "I've had her six years now, did the restoration myself." His voice flexes with pride, in a way I haven't yet heard. "Do you like it?"

"It's beautiful." I recognize the loving way he brushes his hand over the dash before reaching for the ignition. Simon loved cars in the way a rich woman loves shoes. He loved the purchasing of the item, being the first to drive it, a brief affair with a shiny new toy that he always grew tired of. I had married a conservative man, one who stressed over the price of a fancy cup of coffee. But I became the widow of a spoiled man, one who spent almost every dollar I made, our house and garage quickly filled with the best of everything. It's another reason I threw it all away after he died. Every time I saw the jet skis in our garage, the line of expensive watches, or the framed sports memorabilia, I hated him a little more. I had enough things to hate Simon for. I didn't need the extra negativity of his consumerism.

Mark glances at his watch, his push of the pedal more aggressive as he reaches for his phone. I watch as we move through the airport gates, employee hands raised in parting, familiar smiles given as we pass through the parking lot. There is the faint sound of a voice, and Mark speaks into the phone. "I'm in the truck. I'll be there in twenty. How is she doing?"

I look out of the window, watching a large commercial plane take off, dust swirling behind it. From the one-sided conversation, I pick up that the cow is still in labor, and that there's cause to be concerned. Mark hangs up, and I look over at him. "Will she be okay?"

"I'm not sure." He puts on his signal, and the truck rocks a little as we pass a minivan, a smiley face drawn in the dust of the back window. I had a minivan. In the winter, Simon drove it, putting a reindeer nose on the front of it, his festive side a lot more enthusiastic than mine. "She's thirteen. It's a little old, for a cow. This will be her last baby."

"How many has she had?" I turn away from the window.

His mouth twists and he uses one hand to rub at the back of his head. "Oh… seven, I think. One died during birth, a few years back."

"What do you do with the babies?"

"I keep the heifers, sell off the males. I don't need more than one bull, he keeps us busy enough as it is."

"What's wrong with her now? Is the baby going to make it?"

"Nothing's wrong, necessarily. She's just uncomfortable. Taking a little longer than usual."

I hope his cow doesn't die on me. My life story is chock full of sadness already. I don't need to travel a thousand miles to get more of it. If I want grief, I can just open up a photo album, or visit the cemetery.

"I was thinking of having Maggie drive up, Friday night, for dinner."

Maggie? It takes me a minute to remember. His daughter. The freshman. I picture her sunny smile, beaming out from that crinkled photo. I don't say anything.

"She's curious… I think. Me staying in Connecticut—"

"I didn't ask you to stay." A ghastly thought occurs to me, and I turn to look at him. "She doesn't think we're—" I can't voice the words, and he grins in understanding.

"Nah. She's just been asking a lot of questions. She's a little protective of me, has been ever since her mom died." He clears his throat. "I didn't tell her you're sick. I'd prefer her not to know."

I make a face. "She's an adult. She can handle—"

"I don't think she can. And I don't want her thinking about it. I'd just rather, if you don't mind, her not know."

Simon constantly wanted to protect Bethany; it was our most frequent fight. But how can a person trust someone that lies to them? And how can a person know what they can handle if they aren't challenged by life? One day, probably soon, Maggie will find out about my diagnosis. She'll know she was lied to. And everything else Mark tells her will be received with a seed of doubt. I voice my opinion, and am met with a stretch of silence.

When Mark finally speaks, the words stab through the air. "Fine. I'll tell her not to come."

I shrug, looking out the window, watching trees pass, their leaves a bright canvas of yellow and orange, the ditch between us filled with water. We are on a two lane road, the truck shuddering when a semi passes, and a small house moves by, twin rocking chairs on its porch, a limp orange Tennessee flag hanging off a pole normally reserved for an American one. When we drove up to Tremblant, we passed through country like this, homes like these, everything covered in a thick mat of snow. I remember thinking how peaceful it must be to live in such a place, one free of nosy neighbors and architectural review boards, one where you could sit on your porch and not be disturbed for days. I'd been deep in the fantasy, a small smile crossing my face, when Simon had sighed. "I don't know how people live out here," he'd said, turning to glare at a man walking along the road. "I'd think you'd just *die* of boredom." It had been such a clear clashing of our mindsets that I had laughed. When I told him what I had been thinking, he'd looked over with a wry smile, and leaned over, kissing my cheek. "Crazy Helena," he'd whispered, his breath warm against my jaw.

Crazy Helena.

For once, he'd actually been right.

I don't know what to expect, but after seeing Mark's plane and his pristine Bronco—I built an image in my head of his Memphis home, one of spotless Southern grandeur. When we pull off the road and down a gravel drive, I lean against the seat belt, and wait for the entrance.

I am disappointed, the trees clearing and revealing an open field, tall grasses and wildflowers on either side, no animals in sight, though a fence does run off in the distance, behind the ranch home that sits on the top of a hill. It is long and flat with a large porch, a chimney coming off one end. It looks so… normal. I frown.

As we approach, I notice the small details. The rose bushes that grow wild before the front porch, their thorny stems swaying in the breeze. The pillows on the front rockers, faded blue ones that probably once matched the front shutters. The bike that leans against the side of the house is almost buried in overgrowth, its basket rusted, handlebar grips dotted in bird droppings. It looks like a house that time forgot, one lived in but neglected, as if one day—maybe three years ago—someone stopped caring.

We park before a detached garage and he opens his door. "You can leave your bag. We'll go in the house later."

I unbuckle and ignore the directive, quickly pulling on the backpack and stepping out. "If you're dealing with the cow, I can just wait on the porch for you. I've got my computer, I can work."

"You're coming with me." He steps to the garage and opens the side door, stepping into the dark interior, the door rumbling open a moment later. I follow him, my hands twisting on the straps of my backpack, my flats sticking to the concrete floor when I see what he is climbing onto.

"You want me to ride on *that*?" It's a four-wheeler, one with big muddy tires, the handlebars far apart, the headlights big—the entire thing menacing, as if it will buck underneath its rider and scale a rock front.

"I've got two. You can either hop on behind me or ride Maggie's." He nods to the one next to him, one with a bright pink helmet, in every other way identical to his.

"I'll just wait here." I step backward and my elbow collides with the edge of the door. I grab it and wince, the pain shooting through me.

"Helena." He reaches over and snags the helmet, holding it out toward me. "Just put this on. I'll drive slow. The barn is a mile away. It's too far to walk, and we're short on time."

I hesitate, and he shakes it at me. "Carpe Diem, Helena."

I never envision *seizing the day* aboard a filthy death machine. Still, the challenge spurs me on, and I take the helmet, carefully pulling it on, the pad of the strap fitting on my chin, no adjustment needed. I don't even consider the second vehicle, climbing on the back, no need to touch him if I lean away and grip the rear set of rails. I feel secure as we reverse out of the garage, my feet knocking against his calves—then he bumps the ATV into drive and presses the throttle, the leap of it causing me to rock forward. I give up on the rails and grab at his shirt, moving up on the seat until I hug him. "Sorry," I call over the roar of the engine.

"Hold on tight," he hollers back. "And hit my shoulder if you need me to stop." He pulls past the home and I turn my head to see a huge backyard surrounded by a chain-link fence, a big yellow dog inside it, his tail wagging, body bounding forward, alongside us. Mark lifts his hand in greeting, increasing our speed and I smile as the dog sprints faster, his tongue lolling from his mouth. I swear he's smiling at me, even as he skids to a stop, reaching the end of his yard, his tail constantly moving. "That's Midas," he yells. Then we go on, and I burrow my face in his back, my arms reaching around and gripping his stomach.

It's a different world out here. The air smells like sunflowers and dirt, and bees hum past as my hair whips in the wind, pieces coming free from my ponytail. It's a world that is free of Bethany memories, and I feel a small ease of the constant grip on my heart. We turn off the beaten path and climb through a ditch, my fear mounting as I grip him tightly, the tires digging into the hill and holding, our journey moving into thick woods, the crackle of dead leaves sounding as we rumble through the trees, falling leaves drifting through the crisp fall air.

There is a moment where I feel outside myself, where I examine the soft flannel of his shirt in my fists, the smile on my face, the quiet enjoyment in my chest. Is this happiness? I haven't felt it in so long I almost don't recognize it.

A path appears and Mark takes it, going a short way, then turning at a break in the fence, the vehicle rocking over a row of pipes, and Mark points down at them. "Cattle gate," he calls out, and I nod, as if he can see me, as if I understand. When I look out, I see them. Cows, their bodies dotting over the field, a chorus of brown and red, their huge heads lifting, jaws in motion as they watch us move. I've never thought I'd be scared of a cow, but in this open field, our path taking us within charging distance… I hold my breath, my hands tightening on Mark, and am suddenly grateful for the four-wheeler's impressive speed. "Will they attack?" I ask, and he turns his head.

"No. But don't mess with the bull." He points, and I follow his finger, seeing the huge animal under the shade of a tree, watching us, his horns scary, even across the hundred-acre field.

"Wasn't part of my plan," I call out. He guns the engine and we head for a low barn, another four-wheeler parked out front. We come to a stop next to it and he kills the engine, waiting for me to climb off before he follows. I step to the side and watch as he strides to the barn, sliding open the big doors, wheels squeaking as they part, and he moves sideways through the opening. I hesitate for a moment, then follow.

The barn has a wide center aisle that's open on the far end. The ceiling is high enough to accommodate the giant tractors parked to our right, the left side a row of open stalls. I glance in the empty stalls as we pass. My toes feel gritty in my flats and a pebble of some sort has worked its way under the leather, each step digging the annoying stone further along my sole. A man leans against a stall at the end, and he straightens as we approach. There is the masculine grip of a handshake, then they turn to me. "This is Helena, a friend of mine from Connecticut."

"I'm Royce." The man nods, and I push my hands into the front pocket of my jeans, before he has a chance to extend a hand.

I nod. "It's nice to meet you."

"Ever seen a cow give birth?" he asks, and I eye the dingy baseball cap on his head, the brim nearly black from dirt. Behind him, Mark opens the gate and steps into straw, his voice low as he says something.

"No." I step forward and grip the top of the stall wall, rising to my tiptoes and looking over. A cow is there, her belly huge, her red fur close enough for me to reach out and touch. She is standing, and I move back a bit as her body turns, her head coming around to Mark, who runs a hand down the side of her face. On the flight here, he told me about cows—how they have contractions before birth, just like a human does. They can deliver standing up, or lying down. He told me that the front hooves come out first, then the head. I move closer, shooing away a fly, my eyes drawn to a pile of manure against the back wall of the stall. When I had Bethany, the room smelled of bleach and sterility. Simon wore booties over his shoes, a gown, and a hairnet. He had a mask over his face, and the doctor's hand, when it touched my inner thigh, wore a latex glove.

No one here has gloves on. There isn't a medical kit in sight, nor a disinfecting station—not even a clean rag. The idea that—any moment—a baby cow could be produced… my head swims with the terrible possibilities. I feel unprepared, uneducated. At least with Bethany, I *knew*. I knew that five out of every ten-thousand births required cardiac surgery on the mother. I knew that complications during post-delivery stays had increased by 114% in the last decade. I knew what to eat, and drink, and how to exercise just enough, but not too much. I had known everything. And now, looking at the gigantic animal before me, I know nothing, have researched nothing, and I *hate* the feeling of stupidity, of not knowing the situation I have put myself into. The cow's front knees buckle and I grip the dirty plank, watching her pitch to the ground.

MARK

Mater sinks to the dirt, a heavy wheeze coming out of her, and Mark steps back, giving her room, his eyes picking up on all of the details. Her wide eyes, the white of them showing. Her nostrils flaring, the twitch of her legs as she lowers her head to the ground, her hooves swinging in the air for a moment. He remembers when she was born. She'd laid, just like this, covered in blood and mucus, for so long that he thought her dead. Ellen had cried, one hand whipping over her mouth, her long legs shifting back and forth as if she was both anxious and afraid to step forward. He had gathered her to his chest, pressing a kiss to the top of her head, and they had prayed together, asking that the calf would make it. When Mater had twitched, her head lifting, Ellen had cheered, her shoulder rocking against him, her smile big enough to light the whole barn.

"What's wrong?" Helena's words are tense and tight, her face lined in worry.

"Nothing." He relaxes against the wooden railing. "She's just trying to get comfortable. Her contractions are getting stronger. It won't be long now."

"Are *you* worried?" She hangs on the question, her eyes darting from him to Mater, as if her sanity depends on his response.

"I didn't fly here for nothing." He shifts, finding better footing in the dirt. "But it'll be okay. No matter what. Mater's had a good life."

"I need a statistical probability." Her nails are unpainted, and he watches them dig into the wood, the grip turning her knuckles white.

"What chance is there for complications?"

Behind him, Royce chuckles, and the sun casts his shadow as he steps out of the stall and gives them some privacy.

"What difference does it make?" he asks Helena, meeting her dark solemn eyes.

"I'd like to know. I don't want to be here if—" she gestures to Mater, who picks a terrible time to groan in discomfort.

"It's okay," he smiles. "She can't understand you. If she dies?" he supplies helpfully. "Or if the calf does?"

"Yes."

He rubs a hand over his chin, feeling the growth of stubble, a week's worth of missed shaves. "Fifteen percent." He uses his thumb to scratch the side of his check. "Fifteen percent chance of complications."

"You flew us here on a fifteen percent chance?" She is irritated and suspicious, stepping away from the railing and crossing her arms in front of her chest. "There's an eighty-five percent chance that she's going to birth this baby cow just fine and we came all the way here for *nothing*?"

He raises an eyebrow at her, trying to understand the source of her agitation. "So… you *want* there to be a complication?"

"I want the truth." She points an index finger toward Mater, who—as if on cue—bellows, her head swinging against the ground, her discomfort obvious. "Fifteen percent?!" She spits out the number as if it is ludicrous.

"It's my wife's cow." He steps closer to Helena and lowers his voice. "Ellen used to ride on her back. She fed her tomatoes every harvest. I'd be here if there were a one-percent chance of anything going wrong."

There is a long moment where Helena doesn't respond, her eyes studying his as if reading the truth in them. Finally, she nods. "Okay. I just .... me coming here isn't something I necessarily feel comfortable with. It was a big deal to me." She finishes the statement with a wary look, as if he has lied or misled her in some way. And he wonders, in the moment before she steps back to the railing, her forearms flattening on the wood, her chin resting against the top of her hands, what happened in her life to make her so suspicious. Maybe she was just born that way. Maggie was that sort of child, one who peppered him with questions, never satisfied with his first response. Helena, even now, with her weight relaxed against the railing, has coiled muscles, an alert air. If he startles her, if he screams BOO, she will take off running. She'll sprint through that barn and never look back.

I stretch out my legs and examine the toe of my flats, their paisley surface stained around the edges from dirt. I'll have to throw them away. These jeans too. I shift in the dirt, finding a new spot to sit in, and look toward Mark. Between us, Mater shifts for the gazillionth time. She's a very loud birther. Lots of wheezes and sighs, plenty of loud collapses onto the ground, then laborious struggles to her feet. The first four or five times, I was worried, my hands clenching into fists, body stiffening, as if I could will her into comfort. After a while, I followed Mark's lead and relaxed. Mater, which is the dumbest name I've ever heard of for a cow, seems to be taking her time. At the moment, she is standing, her head down, her eyes closed.

"What if we miss it? When her water breaks?"

"You're not gonna miss it." His elbows rest on his knees, his butt on an upside-down bucket that's already cracked along one edge. I watched when he sat on it, the plastic bowing a little under his weight, but the crack didn't grow.

The silence returns, and it's comfortable now, just the two of us here, Royce leaving fifteen minutes ago. Mater wheezes, and the sound joins the hum of crickets, the falling night interspersed with streaks of fireflies.

"You have a lot more fireflies here," I say, watching one fade into the shadows. "We don't have as many up north."

"We got a lot of flying critters," he drawls. "Stick around for summer and I'll introduce you to a million and a half mosquitoes."

"No thanks." I won't be alive in summer. I won't ever feel the warmth of sunshine on my shoulder, or hear the sound of the ocean, feel the scratch of sand against my soles.

"Maggie always loved fireflies." His head turns to the open door, and he waits, a chorus of them appearing, as if on stage.

"So did Bethany." I smile sadly, remembering summer nights on our front porch, her feet darting across the front lawn, hands outstretched, swinging a jar through the air in an attempt to catch one as her prize.

"I got one." She beamed at us, her tongue pushing the gap between her top and bottom teeth. "He was too slow, and I got him." She held out the glass and I carefully took it, Simon and I moving apart, her tiny rump settling down on the step between us. "What should we name him?"

"Hmmm." I wrinkled up my face, and soberly considered the small fly, which settled on the bottom of the glass. "What about Doug?" It's a terrible name, intentionally picked. Bethany took the naming of items very seriously, and awarded extra attention to anything that ended in "y".

"Dooooouuuuug?" She stretched out the name like it was ridiculous, her eyebrows pinching together in the creation of an alarmed look. "That's a terrible *name!"*

"Okay," I allowed. "Then you pick one."

"What about Lighty?" Simon interjected, and I tightened my hands on the glass, fighting the urge to reach over and smack him.

"Lighty!" Bethany cheered, and pulled the mason jar from my hands, raising it high in the air. "Great name, Daddy!"

It wasn't a great name. It's a terrible name, as bad as Doug, only not in an intentional, funny way. It was the most unimaginative name, supplied at a time when I was trying to grow Bethany's creativity, and give her her own, original voice. 'Lighty' didn't accomplish anything toward that goal. 'Lighty' was the personification of bland, average, uninspired normality.

I tried to smile, my lips pressed together in an attempt to fight a grimace from forming. "Do you know why the fireflies light up, Bethany?"

"Yep!" Her response had such confidence that I stalled, my eyes darting to Simon before returning to her. She didn't know, not unless Simon told her.

"Tell me." The request came out all wrong, hard and accusatory, as if Bethany was a defendant on the stand, and not a four-year-old with a Dora the Explorer Band-Aid on her elbow.

"It's their mini flashlights," she said solemnly. "It's how they see in the dark."

There is imagination, and then there was stupidity. I was a strong believer in the first, and a staunch disapprover of the second. It's a point of contention between Simon and I, and I could see the stiffening of his spine as I shook my head. "No, Bethany."

"Yes," she insisted, stamping one of her shoes on the step. "Daddy said!"

"Bugs can see in the dark. They don't need flashlights."

"Then why do they have them?" she asked plaintively, as if I was old and stupid and she was humoring me. I hated *that tone of her voice, the over-enunciated speech of an insolent child.*

"It's how they communicate. Mostly, it's how they attract mates." I pulled her onto my lap and lowered my voice, using the hushed whisper that she liked. "The males fly around, flashing their light and showing off. The females settle on branches or grasses and watch the males perform. If they see a male that they like, they'll flash their light." I pointed to the tree at the end of the drive, its branches silhouetted against the street light. "Watch the branches of that tree. See if you see any of the females flush their lights."

She didn't look. Instead, she examined her jar, her eye close to the glass. "So… Lighty is a boy*?" She said the word as if it was offensive. "I wanted a* girl *firefly."*

"What's wrong with boy fireflies?" Simon interrupted, scooting into the place that Bethany left, his leg brushing against mine in the most annoying way.

I tightened my grip on Bethany, and leaned forward, hugging her with my arms. "And did you know that some species of fireflies are cannibals?"

"What does that *mean?" She turned, and the soft skin of her cheek brushed my neck.*

"It means that they eat—"

"Ice cream!" Simon interrupted, in the jolly voice of a town idiot, his body springing off the porch step and landing gracefully on one of the stepping stones.

"Fireflies eat ice cream*?" Bethany asked with suspicion.*

"I'm not sure," he said grandly, as if being ignorant was fun and exciting, and fury exploded in me at the same time that Bethany pulled out of my arms. "But I do! And I think I'll get some right now!" He reached out and snagged her, the mason jar swinging through the air as he picked her up and spun, giving the poor

firefly a carnival ride from hell.

I closed my eyes, my skin prickling from the cool night air, and counted to five, each number releasing the tension from a different part of my core. He will ruin her. He will fill her head with fluffy and false information. He will rot her teeth on junk food and ruin her grammar. I opened my eyes and, from across the dark lawn, a firefly glowed at me from the thick of the tree.

I closed my eyes and counted again.

"Did you know that some species of fireflies are cannibals?" I speak quickly, before Mark changes the subject, before this final opportunity to share this information—probably the last of my life—passes by. "They are very sneaky about it. They replicate the female mating flashes of a different species of firefly and—when the males come closer to investigate, they swoop in for the kill."

"Very interesting." Mark drawls.

I hesitate, watching him, unsure if he is being sarcastic. He seems fairly genuine, and I soldier on. "Also, some species are aquatic—they have little gills, just like a fish. But most are like these." I wave my hand toward the streaks of light. "And when fireflies are attacked, they shed little drops of blood that are really bitter and poisonous to some animals." I relax my shoulders against the back of the post. "It's their defense mechanism. Because of it, most animals or opposing insects, learn to stay away from them. They have very few natural predators," I finish.

"You know a lot about fireflies," Mark says, the words carefully delivered, in the same way someone might politely broach a terrible subject, like bad breath or a rip in someone's pants.

"I read." I say flatly. "You should try it sometime." That summer, I had read an entire book about night insects, for the sole purpose of educating Bethany about the caterpillars we might encounter, or the fruit flies that always ended up inside, no matter how often I emptied the garbage disposal, or examined our fruit. I had had the perfect educational opportunity that night on the porch. Simon had ruined it, as he so often did, waving his arms about and distracting her with words like *ice cream.* I don't know how any kids in his class ever learned *anything,* as fanatical as he seemed to be about education disruption. Then again, he was probably just that way with us.

"Speaking of reading," Mark sighs, leaning back, the bucket creaking under the weight. "Did you ever read my novel *The Milk Maid*?" He chuckles before I can respond. "Never mind. You did. I think you referred to it as 'hick porn'."

I glare at him. "I hope you're not suggesting we spend this time—"

"I'm not." He cuts in, almost sternly, with a look that warns me away from finishing the thought. In the novel, a farmhand and a lost socialite get stuck in a barn during a snowstorm. They spend the next five hours in a variety of sexual positions, most of which had me setting down the book—the scenes uncomfortably graphic. "I was just going to say…" He gives me a look of mild contempt, like *I'm* the one with the dirty mind, and he's the picture of innocence. "I wrote that book right here in this barn. On a night like tonight. Waiting on a cow to birth."

"Shocker." I drawl, though the information does interest me. My ideas always come from the strangest places, the most random of situations. Bethany once cut her hand on the edge of her dollhouse, and I—while cleaning the cut—had the idea for a colony of blood-dwellers: minuscule people who live in our bloodstreams, their lives in continual upheaval, depending on tiny things that occur to our bodies—the flu for example, or a cut such as hers. The idea had been so strong, so visually *there*, that I stopped in the midst of the first aid, hurrying down the hall and to my office, a scene sketched out on paper—right then, before it slipped my mind. Simon had come home to find Bethany still standing on the stool by the sink, her sleeve soaked in blood, the water running, and had flipped out. He'd interrupted my scene, my entire thought process, with his yelling, face red and furious, as if she'd been *dying* or something. He always did that. Over-exaggerated the unimportant and under-focused on the things that had mattered. He'd told my mother about the instance, and a simple writing sprint had become another building block that was later used against me. So much drama, all over a book I had never ended up writing.

It's funny, how book ideas often seem *so* brilliant when they first appear. It takes weeks of work to really discover the potential of a story, if there is any at all. Looking around this big barn, the privacy of it, the dusty smells in the air… it's not a giant stretch to see what he had imagined. The door creaking open, a blonde head peeking in, worry across her face, her designer heels wobbly on the loose dirt. And then, around the corner comes a six foot tall, muscular man, his jeans dirty, t-shirt stretched tight across broad shoulders, a shy smile breaching that gorgeous face. Because, you know—all farmhands are undiscovered male models. And all super-hot blondes drive alone, cross-country, through snowstorms.

"So you wrote all of it?" I ask, glancing over at him. "The entire thing? While waiting on a cow to be born?"

"Not all of it. But the first six or seven chapters." He stretches his neck to one side and yawns, his Adam's apple bobbing amongst the stubble on his neck. "I keep some notebooks in the storage room. Just in case inspiration strikes. I can grab one now if you want to work a little."

I consider it. "No, I'm good." Right now, the thought of diving into the past and discussing it with him is exhausting. Maybe later tonight, if I don't get sleepy—we can work. Already today, I've thought too much about the past.

Mater's head suddenly lifts, and I watch her tail swing upward, a motion that has happened a dozen times in the last hour. My shoes jerk back when her hind legs flex, a volley of liquid spewing from her rear, and I scramble to my feet at the same time that Mark straightens. He smiles at me and raises his eyebrows. "Looks like the excitement is starting."

I pull down on the edge of my shirt and examine the fresh pool of liquid, one quickly absorbed by the dirt. I move along the stall wall, my butt bumping against the wood as I edge around to stand beside him, my eye nervously fixed on Mater, who was sniffing her discharged water as if surprised by it. "Is it coming?" I ask.

"Soon. She'll most likely lie back down to have it."

Another change in position. My heart goes out to the big girl, one who seems so laborious in her movements, her joints creaking whenever she struggles into place. I steal the bucket from him and sit. "Does it always take so long?"

"I suppose you were faster?" he asks, and I don't like the question. I wasn't faster. I was a terrible birther. I prepared for every possibility and still came up short, all of my perfectly timed huffs and puffs and pushes—all inadequate. It was as if my body agreed with my heart and put up a roadblock against the oncoming child. After all, I'd never wanted a child. It had been Simon who had pushed. Pleaded. Begged. Threatened. I had merely, after two years of arguing, given up. *One baby*, I had made him promise. Just one. And, after that day in the hospital, after that emergency surgery… that promise hadn't really mattered. One baby was the only possibility that remained.

"Helena?"

"I wasn't faster." The words nip off my lips, and anyone with any sense would leave it alone.

"Tell me the story."

"No."

"You're going to have to tell me at some point. Might as well be now."

He's right. A few days ago, he wrote the wedding scene—the small church packed with strangers, all Simon's guests, Simon's friends, Simon's family. My mother had been the lone face in the crowd that I had recognized, her face beaming, a handkerchief gripped in her hand as if there was a chance of tears. Two days ago, we wrapped up our first year of marriage, and covered much of the pregnancy. We are only a chapter or two away from Bethany's birth. I tug on the end of my ponytail and a few strands come free.

"Helena?"

Mater has stopped her sniffing of the water, and I watch her back stiffen, muscles flexing in effort. I sigh. "We were at home when my contractions started. I was writing—working on *Deeply Loved.* We started to time the contractions, with a plan to go to the hospital when they were four minutes apart."

He nods.

"It was on the way to the hospital that I realized something was wrong. I told Simon to stop, to pull over. I was cramping, and wanted to move to the backseat, where I could lie down. But he wouldn't listen." I swallow. "He was so intent on getting to the hospital. He screamed at me to shut up and breathe. That's what he said. 'Shut up Helena. For once, just *shut up*.'" And I had, one of the rare moments when I listened to him. "The pain—I remember closing my eyes and wondering if I would pass out from it." I hadn't. I'd been conscious when he'd slammed to a halt in front of the emergency room doors. My head had hit the window and I'd cursed at Simon. *The baby*, he had said. *Don't curse in front of the baby.* His voice, when he said those words—I can still hear it now. The excitement, the happiness that had been in those syllables. They had sparked something in me, a flood of anger. I was there, in such *agony*, and he was happy. Happy over this thing that he had done, that *he* had wanted, that he had caused. Yet, he wasn't the one whose back ached. He wasn't the one who had leaked pee all over his panties. He wasn't the one that wanted to die, the fat woman that had crammed her swollen feet into sneakers, the one being pulled out of the car by strangers. Even now, the memory of that voice infuriates me. It shouldn't, but it does.

Mater moans, and I wish I could do something to help her.

Two hooves come out first, pinned together so tightly I thought they were fused. They travel slowly, like thick honey from a bottle, and then stop, right at the knees, the hooves sticking straight out as the cow appears to give up, her head dropping, her contractions ceasing.

"What's happening?" I look to Mark, thinking about the baby calf, his tiny lungs struggling to breathe, squashed inside her body.

"Relax. Give her a moment."

Her moment stretches painfully long. I am lightheaded by the time her muscles clench, and there is another slow push that uncovers the nose, then the face, and I lean forward as it comes out.

Oh my god. It's amazing to see, the rest of the calf suddenly out, slick and sudden, and my heart grips as his body slumps onto the dirt. He is soaked in internal fluids, his eyes closed, pieces of the embryotic sac still around him. He doesn't move, hasn't done so much as twitch, and a sudden pain flares in my chest. I can't be here. I can't be watching this. What if he's dead? I suddenly regret it all—getting on that plane, the wind on my face as we'd ridden across that field—this isn't exciting and different, it's dangerous on my psyche, on my body. I could get a respiratory infection from breathing in this filthy air, I could get pneumonia if the chill drops further. I don't have an extra jacket, have exhausted the hand sanitizer in my bag, and have nothing to shield my heart from the possibility that this calf, this beautiful creature as big as Bethany, is dead.

Mater lumbers to her feet, her tail swiping across the calf in the process, and he doesn't flinch, doesn't react, doesn't MOVE. I stare at his side, and *will* it to expand. He should be breathing, I should be able to see the lift and drop of his ribcage, *I should see something.* I step back. Mater's body pivots as her head comes over to the still body, her nostrils flaring as she huffs along the length of him. Her tongue, dark and purple, comes out, and I blink back tears as she licks him, her movements firm and purposeful. She doesn't realize he's dead, and it's heartbreaking to watch her clean it. Her body swings closer, and my view of the calf is blocked as she rocks his body with her muzzle, dirt caking to his wet and bloody skin.

"Helena," Mark's voice is soft and he waves his hand. "Come here. Look." He points to the calf, and I move quickly to his side.

The baby's eyes are open, and as I watch, his head shakes in a quick, sudden shudder of movement. A gasp slips from me, and I lift my hand to my mouth, turning to Mark for a quick moment. "He's alive!" I whisper. I can't help the goofy smile that yanks apart my lips, and I curl my fingers against my mouth, grinning like an idiot as the baby lifts his head. It took so long for me to just have eye contact with Bethany, for her to be able to focus on my face and understand what she was seeing. In contrast, this calf seems to immediately grasp the situation, and he surveys his position on the ground, most of his wet fur caked in dirt, his mother already moving away, her head lifting as she settles into a more comfortable stance, her eyes dropping closed as if to say *There. My job is done.* Mark steps to the side, flipping over the bucket and turning on a spigot, filling it with water, her eyes flicking open, one ear tilting toward him. "Mark," I cry out, watching the calf get one of his back feet planted, then a second. He's doing it all wrong, his front knees still on the ground, and he's going to topple over at any moment.

"Give him time," Mark says, his hand on Mater's forehead, his voice dropping as he says something to her, the bucket bumping against his thigh as he holds it for her.

"Something's wrong." The calf is now hobbling around on his front knees, his journey taking him close to Mater, who could easily step left and crush him. "Something's wrong with his front legs." A cow can't live, not like this, his knees not sturdy enough for everyday life. He will be ostracized by the other cows. Maybe Mater will refuse to let him drink her milk. Maybe this is why, less than ten minutes after birth, she is ignoring him, her head dropping, eyes closing.

"He'll figure it out." Mark hangs the bucket on the wall and comes to stand beside me, his arms crossing over his chest, his elbow bumping gently into my shoulder. "Just watch."

There is nothing to watch but a crippled little baby cow, one who is crawling on his front knees, underneath his mother's belly, pitifully short without the full contribution of his front legs. Then…

I hold my breath as he gets one hoof up, his head lifting as he heaves his weight onto it, the movement almost triumphant as the second hoof joins the first, his initial stand one of the sprawled legs, uncoordinated variety.

I lean my head on Mark's shoulder without thinking about it, filled with a sudden burst of happiness, one that blooms brighter as the calf turns his head and looks back at us, as if to say *See what I did? All by myself?* "He's beautiful," I whisper.

"She." Mark reaches forward and points. "See? A girl."

He is right. With Bethany, I missed all of this. I was put under for surgery and woke with a screaming baby in ICU, one I was told was mine. I didn't get to see her like this, covered in blood and mucus, straight from my womb. I didn't get to see the moment she opened her eyes, or the miracle of her birth.

Maybe if I had, I would have felt differently about her.

Maybe if I had, I would have loved her more from the start.

I look into that baby cow's eyes and I swear—as stupid as it sounds—I see the twinkle of Bethany's spirit in those giant dark depths. I feel her spirit in the first triumphant step. And I feel her in the immediate love I have for this giant spindly bundle of bovine.

It makes no sense, yet still, the happiness is there.

"It's not a vacation. We're *working*. Mark had to come home, I came with him." I shift my weight, leaning against the kitchen's doorframe, my voice lowered as I speak into the cell phone. My explanation sounds wrong, like it *is* something different, like Mark and I are *friends* and not just business associates. "So we could *work*," I repeat.

"Are you having… fun?" Kate delivers the question doubtfully, and this conversation is already stretching too long.

Mark taps a spoon on the edge of the pot and I glance at him, then turn away. I ignore Kate's question. "Did you call for something?"

"I was just checking in. I do want to talk to you about your book… the one you are writing with Mark… whenever you have a chance."

"So talk." *Whenever I have a chance?* What a dumb thing to say.

"Oh. Well. I mean, we don't have to talk about it right *now*."

Irritation flares. "You just brought it up. So talk about it."

A long pause. "Oh-kay." She sighs, as if she is about to step into war. "I need more information so I can prepare a pitch."

"No." The word falls instinctively off my lips. At some point, someone will read these words. Millions will. But not now. Not with Kate.

"No?" The word squeaks out, and she clears her throat. "Then when?"

It's not a ridiculous question. By now, I should have sent over an outline. Kate would review it, send back some questions—and it would be packaged and sent off to Jackie—the editor of my last eight books, the editor who always loves everything, and always pays whatever we demand. But this book is different. Jackie will hate it. That's why I picked Tricia Pridgen, an editor who likes twisted books drenched in truth and void of a happy ending. But Pridgen won't buy a book she knows nothing about. I know this, yet I can't bring myself to do an outline, or even a summary. I can't deal with that emotion, and I can't yet share this story with Kate.

"Soon," I lie. "We need to get further on it first." I watch as Mark turns off the burner. "I've got to go."

"Okay. Be safe."

Be safe. The last words I said to Bethany. *Be safe.* Did I tell her I loved her? I've tried, for four years, to remember. I don't know that I did. I'm afraid I was too distracted to do more than kiss her goodbye.

"Helena?"

I squeeze my eyes tightly shut. "I'll talk to you later." I end the call and push the phone into my back pocket, struggling with the simple task, my hands thick and clumsy.

"Everything okay?"

"Fine." I step into the kitchen. His home is so different from my own. Rich brown leather, burlap curtains, wood-stained walls and clusters of family photos. In my house, I've removed every reminder of Bethany and Simon. Here, even in the kitchen, Mark is surrounded by images of his wife, her wide body pressed to his side, her arms slung around his neck, her astride a horse, by a waterfall, and next to a puppy. Maybe he fears forgetting her. Maybe he thinks that, if he has enough reminders of her, it's like she's still alive.

But it isn't. I've spent over a thousand nights surrounded by Bethany. I've wrapped myself in her sheets, smelled the clothes in her drawer, and flipped through photo albums until my fingers bled from paper cuts.

Nothing replaces having her in my life, her feet pounding down my hall, her shriek of laughter in the air. And nothing makes the loss easier. Distractions are the best we can hope for. Short windows of time when the sadness breaks.

I lean against the edge of the counter, watching as he turns on the faucet and washes his hands. "I don't have pictures of Bethany in the house." I have to speak loudly to be heard over the water. I should step closer, he'll hear me more clearly if I do, but I don't think I can support my own weight right now.

He stops the water, turning to me, his movements slow as he dries his hands.

"It's not because I don't love her." I say desperately. He needs to know this. He needs to show that in his writing, in the pages of this book.

"I know." He says softly, kindness in his face. But he doesn't know. He doesn't know anything yet. He knows I fell for a boy. He knows I had a baby. All he knows are the first lines of a song. He hasn't even heard the melody yet.

"You don't know." I say. "But you will."

My mother once told me that I was too selfish to love. I was thirteen at the time, our argument held across a sticky tablecloth in a Red Lobster. She had planned a trip to my grandmother's house, one that would correspond with her seventy-first birthday. The trip would have caused a complete disruption of my writing calendar, one I had reviewed with her and posted on the refrigerator door, five weeks earlier. This trip hadn't been mentioned at that time, and I was convinced it was a spur-of-the-moment idea concocted purely because of a railways promotional flyer received in the mail. I had, up to that point, perfectly followed my writing calendar. I was on schedule to finish what would become my first novel, and a week of disruption would mean the inability to finish it before school started. So I did what any enterprising young Steinbeck would do. I snuck into my mother's room, fished my train ticket out of her purse, and destroyed it.

She didn't handle it well. She called me insolent. Spoiled. A brat. She tried to make me feel guilty for not wanting to see my grandmother, for not wanting to spend time with my family. I didn't understand the obligation I had to a woman whom I'd only seen a handful of times. I didn't understand the ridiculous expectation that I should love her simply because she birthed my mother. I wasn't even sure, in that thirteen-year-old mindset, that I loved my *own* mother.

But I did love Bethany. Even when I screamed and ran away and ignored her—I loved her. I used to look at her and my heart would *hurt*. It would swell in my chest, and there would be a sudden flare of panic—a sharp prick of vulnerability. In that moment, I would fear losing her. Maybe it's a normal fear, one that every parent has. Or maybe, it was God's warning to me, the foreshadowing he was writing into my story.

I should have listened to it. I shouldn't have swallowed that fear. I should have been the right kind of mother, suppressed my instincts and selfishness, and put her first. I should have kept her a million miles from my mother, held her against me, and never let her go anywhere, do anything.

Keeping her prisoner would have been better than losing her.

On his front porch, the rocker I sit in wobbles, each forward roll creaking over bumpy boards. The blanket around my shoulders is soft, and I relax against it, the mug of hot chocolate cooling in my hands. Before us, there is a stretch of darkness, no fireflies in this space, the moon behind a cloud, the occasional click of nails giving away the dog's location.

"You tired?" Mark sits on the step, ignoring the other rocker, his shoulders hunched over as he lights a cigar. "It's been a long day. Gotta be past midnight."

I *am* tired. Too tired to even pull back the sleeve of my shirt and check the time. It doesn't matter. Out here, the chorus of crickets humming—we seem a hundred miles from civilization, in a place where clocks don't exist, deadlines don't matter, and basic needs are the only concerns. I can't imagine sitting on this porch and caring about bestseller ranks and end-cap placements. I'm shocked Mark even knows who I am, or has read my books. It had been easy to picture Marka in an expensive high rise, her fake nails tapping out nasty emails. But I can't fit Mark into that mold. I can't see those terrible words coming from this man.

"Your emails to me." I eye him, watching the muscles of his back as he straightens, setting the lighter to the side and rolling the cigar between his fingers. He turns his head and wisps of smoke frame his profile. "Why did you start emailing me?"

He looks down, and I watch the flex of his jaw as he eyes his cigar.

Bringing it to his mouth, he takes a long pull before turning to face me, his face a quiet mix of emotions. "*Memphis Bride*," he finally says, one leg crossing over another.

"Excuse me?" My medication makes me loopy, but I am fairly certain a fully rational person wouldn't be able to follow that answer.

"The name ring a bell?" He raises his eyebrows. "No?" There is a hint of accusation in his tone, and a pool of dread forms in my stomach. *I should know this.* For some reason, I am failing this test.

"No."

"It was my first book. My first *real* book." He waves a hand toward the house. "Not like all of the *trashy crap* that paid for this house, or for my wife's chemo treatments. It was a good book, one that took me three years to write and eighteen rejection letters to recover from before I got a publishing deal. My first publishing deal. It's a big deal, you know?" he shrugs, and brings the cigar to his lips. "No. You wouldn't know. You got one right out of the gate, right? I read that article. You had agents and publishers tripping all over your first novel. But not me. It's not easy to convince editors to read a male-written romance."

I already regret asking the question. I can see this train wreck, and the place it is leading to. *A blurb.* Had he requested one?

"I got a twenty-thousand dollar advance on that book. Half at signing, same as our deal." He smiles at me, but there is no warmth in the gesture. "I quit my job that day. Took Ellen and Maggie out, bought us all steak dinners. Life was good." He blows out a stream of smoke and the smell of the cigar inches closer, the hint of it stronger in the air. "How'd you celebrate your first advance?"

I don't answer. I only wait, for what is surely to come. He eyes me, and I don't move, don't look away, our dance finally interrupted by a shake of his head, his eyes moving past me and out into the darkness.

"The publisher wanted author blurbs. They reached out to authors with similar books, you had recently published *Garden Room.* It was a long shot, but you accepted the galley."

"I'm guessing I didn't like the book."

He coughs out a hard laugh. "Oh no, Helena. It's safe to say you *didn't like* the book. I'm surprised you've forgotten it, actually." He glances down, wiping a hand on his sweatpants before looking back out. "You wrote a four-page letter to my editor and were kind enough to CC me on it. You described every flaw in the novel, the root of your opinion being that my writing was flat and without talent. Childish, that was one word you used." He tilts a head toward the house. "You can read the letter if you'd like. It's framed in my office, right next to a *New York Times* list, the first one where I topped you."

"It wasn't malicious." I straighten in my seat. "I was probably trying to help."

"Help?" He snorts. "You scared my editor so badly she pulled the novel. It was never published, and I never got the rest of that advance. My writing career was done. Just like that." He snaps his fingers and looks over at me. "That easily. All because Helena Ross didn't like my book. You were hot shit and I was expendable."

I should apologize. The path is clear and obvious. But I push my lips together. If I took the time to write a letter, it must have been bad.

"I couldn't get my job back. Ellen… she worked at a farm up the road, and we limped along and I wrote anything and everything. Publishers weren't interested in any of it. Then she got sick and I got desperate. I started self-publishing, in a bunch of different genres. Erotica is the one that took off." He leans forward and spits out, into the darkness. "And Marka Vantly was born."

I've read Marka Vantly's bio fifty times. It's all flowers and champagne, a California party girl who stumbled onto publishing success after writing down her steamy exploits on the Beverly Hills dating scene. It doesn't say anything about a sick wife, or a grizzled cowboy, one who cooks a mean pot of chili but doesn't clean his baseboards.

I tried to do the math in my head. "How long did your wife… when did she—?"

"It started out ovarian cancer. She fought it four years before it took her. She left us three years ago. Three years and two months." He probably knows more. He probably knows the days and the hours, the timeframe clicking through his mind. In some ways, I recognize so much of his grief. In other ways, we are completely different.

I stand up. "I'd like to go to bed."

I am opening the screen door when he speaks.

"You asked why I started to email you."

I pause, not certain I still want the answer to that question.

"For a long time, I hated you. I emailed you out of that hatred. I wanted you to know who I was. But over the last seven years…" The dog approaches, and he puts out his hand, drawing the animal closer. "You made me a better writer. Knowing that you were reading my novels—that pushed me forward." He looks over at me. "So, thank you. For responding. I'm sure that you get a lot of mail."

I shift, and his forgiveness only makes me feel worse. "Okay."

I nod to him, an attempt at a parting gesture, and then, swinging the door open, I escape inside.

chapter 37

A baby. Impossibly chubby face, her eyes just slits that avoid my own, flitting over everything else. She cries all the time, a piercing shriek, a broken record on repeat. In some ways she's delicate, in others she's a battering ram.

I feel damaged every time I lift her. I feel wrong, void of instincts, lost at what to do with her. The insecurity grows every time I look into Simon's eyes and see his disappointment.

It's only been a week, but I think I hate her.

I wake up in the small guest room, the room hot. I kick off the blankets, my mouth cottony and metallic, my headache painfully strong. Rolling out of the twin bed, I move over to my bag, my limbs slow as I pull on my jeans and a fresh shirt, not bothering with clean underwear or a bra. The house is quiet and I brush my teeth, then head downstairs.

His house is an odd mix of clean and dirty. The bathrooms sparkle, the scent of bleach in the air, the mirrors spot-free, the grout freshly scrubbed. But in the main rooms, there is clutter—stacks of mail and odd items, a dead light bulb left out on the counter, oily fingertips along the edge of a table, filthy boots left by a chair. I walk down the staircase, my eyes moving over the framed photos, and I stop at a larger frame, a single page surrounded by a thick mat, a page of stationary, with the copy of a check below it. It's an acceptance letter, the publisher's seal at the top of the page, a flourished signature below two paragraphs of congratulatory communication. The book name is there. MEMPHIS BRIDE. He had framed it, or his wife had, like a proud parent with a certificate of achievement poster. Thousands of books were bought each year. Thousands of checks written, thousands of dreams begun. Probably thousands of framed items like this. *Was* it my fault his had temporarily died? Without my letter to his editor, would he be writing contemporary fiction? Creating books he actually respects?

I take another step and move past it. In our industry, the work speaks for us. It's not all my fault. I write scathing blurbs all of the time, for books that still end up published. If it had been a strong enough novel, my opinion wouldn't have mattered.

I continue down the staircase, following its curve into the foyer. There is a note stuck to the front door.

> *I'm at the barn. There's some food in the kitchen. Royce can get you over if you want to see the baby.*

I leave the note and move to the kitchen. I grab a banana from a bowl on the counter, peeling it back as I take a leisurely tour of the first floor. It's spacious, everything made for a giant. The wide leather couch straight out of an Architectural Digest catalogue. The thick coffee table made from a section of tree trunk. It's knick-knack-free, everything a mix of leather, wood, and photos. Someone in the family is a photographer. There is a huge print of a pasture, the vivid color of a setting sun giving warmth to the entire room. I wander into another room and see a series of black and white photos, close-ups of Mark's hands, a sway-back horse, and one of his daughter's smile. I look away, and realize I am in his office, a printer in one corner, a desk before me, filled with stacks of pages. Along the far wall, below a long window, there are bound manuscripts, over twenty of them, and I scan the titles, hunting for, and not finding, the doomed Memphis Bride. I don't look at the walls, to see if my framed letter is there. I believe him when he says it is brutal. I don't need proof of that.

The dining room and sunroom bore me, and I head back upstairs, skipping my guest room, and only giving his daughter's room a cursory glance. The next room is gold—a library, complete with floor to ceiling bookshelves, a rolling ladder, and inset lighting. There is a large chair and a couch, both the sort that you could sink into and never leave. I should have created a room like this in our house. We bought five thousand square feet and wasted it on Simon's larks. A workout room. A media room. Two guest rooms that were never used. A formal dining room. Why hadn't I taken a larger piece of it? Why hadn't I insisted on something like this? And later—once they were gone and I was alone, why hadn't I created it for myself? But I know the answer to that. I didn't create it afterwards because I hadn't deserved it. It would have felt tainted and selfish.

His books are organized by author, and all of the greats are here. I don't touch anything, the banana still in hand, my respect for his books greater than for door handles and light switches. I find my section, and am pleased to see all of my titles here, their spines creased from reading. Aside from me, there is little romance, his tastes tending to classics and contemporary fiction. I smile at a few of the names and lift my chin, my gaze moving up the shelves, itching in my desire to climb the ladder and properly peruse his collection. There is a sharp pain at the base of my neck and I carefully drop my head, stepping back. I'm overdue for a pain pill and abandon my snooping, heading downstairs and toward my medicine.

The meds taste terrible, the kind of chalky pills that instantly melt a little on your tongue, before you get a chance to drink any water. I take two, plus the anti-nausea, and glance out the window above the sink. Mark's Bronco is there, a thin man standing near it, a phone to his ear, cigarette in hand. It's the man from last night, the one who works for Mark. Royce.

Something bumps in the living room, and I turn, relaxing when I see his dog trotting toward me, his tail hitting everything he passes, a thump-thump-thump that could destroy an entire china shop. He smiles at me, his body sidling up and leaning against me, his tongue lolling out of the side of his mouth as he looks up. He swings his tail and his entire body flexes from the action. "Hey bud." I don't want to pet him. He looks dirty, and his trot through the house has left a path of wet paw prints. He rests his full weight against my shin, and lifts one paw as if I understand what that means. Simon once wanted an Akita, some giant bear-hunting dog that sheds like a cheap sweater and slobbers a gallon a day. I had refused, he had gotten belligerent, and somehow, two weeks and a dozen arguments later, we compromised and he had a new motorcycle. That was how most of our arguments worked. Part of me suspects he never even wanted a dog, the motorcycle his end goal, the entire thing a psychological game I'd lost.

A low whine comes and I look back down, his brown eyes minutely moving as he searches my face. Despite myself, I reach down and carefully pat his head. As an adult, I've always considered dogs in the same way that I did children: slobbery noise-machines that require an enormous amount of effort. I had been wrong about children. While Bethany, especially at the beginning, had been a nonstop drain of time and energy, she had been worth it. A million times worth it.

This dog wouldn't have been worth it. Now he is lying down, right on top of my shoes, his belly arched towards me, his paw still stretched up, hanging in the air. His mouth is open in a ridiculous expression of joy, as if this act—restricting my movement—is cause for celebration. I pry a foot out from his heavy body and step to one side, his head lifting to watch as I make my escape.

I am heading to the front door when I see the pages. They sit on the dining room table where we ate last night, a small plate on top of them, one with a muffin and banana on it. I pause, sidestepping until I am in front of the stack.

CHAPTER FIVE in bold letters on the top of the first page. New content. Before I had trudged up the stairs and into bed, I'd outlined a few chapters, had written a page or two of content and left it on the counter. He must have stayed up, read it over, and dove in. I move aside the plate, and think back over our conversations in that barn, my hand-written additions where those had left off—a lot of ground to cover. I flip through the pages. Twenty, if not more. It would have taken me two weeks, and he did it in hours. I pull back the chair and sit.

Moving the pages toward me, I barely notice the brush of the dog's body as he settles at my feet. The first pages cover Bethany's birth, and I mark up several passages, the muffin disappearing as I add in comments and move through the scene of bringing her home. Mark's writing is improving, and I can almost feel my nerves when we made it home, my hands shaking as I gripped the edge of her crib, Simon's enthusiasm annoying in its confidence. Why had I been the only one afraid? Why had I been the only one with regret?

I read further.

All of my emotions, they are on these pages. They are raw and real, and I regret my sexist opinion that—because he was a man—he wouldn't understand. A knot of anxiety worsens as I read, old emotions rushing back, all the conflict I had struggled with, along with the terrible spite I'd had for my daughter.

I push aside the muffin wrapper and force myself to turn the page.

chapter 38

I step out of the house an older woman. Reliving those first months with Bethany had been hard, yet nothing compared with what's to come. Royce gives me a ride to the barn, I pet a happy and healthy baby calf goodbye, and three hours later, I'm climbing back into the plane. I pause, one foot in, and take a moment to inhale the warm air, my muscles pleasantly tired from the exertions, my hair still carrying the scent of outdoors. There is part of me that doesn't want to go home. I can imagine settling into this world, watching the leaves fall from the trees, writing in the mornings and spending afternoons in Mark's library, working through his collection one hardcover at a time.

I sit down and close the airplane's door, struggling a little to lock it into place. When he steps in, the plane shifts, and I watch him go through a long process of flipping switches and checking off marks on a clipboard.

"I read the new pages," I say, once he is finished, the plane slowly easing forward, the propeller humming along.

"And?"

"And… they were good." The words seem too small. "Really good."

The corner of his mouth lifts a little, a deep dimple popping out amid all of his stubble. "I'm glad you liked them. I was worried it was too—"

"No." I look out the window, toward the hangar. "It was good."

He passes me a headset and pulls on his own, his voice deep and competent as he speaks to the traffic controller. I take the excuse and close my eyes, working through his new content in my mind. We are working in chronological fashion, a way which, on its own, will probably bore the reader. Later, Pridgen will restructure it, put in hints of the future, and change up the structure of the delivery. But for now, what's important is that Mark sees and tells the events in the way I experienced them. The reader needs to understand the emotions I felt, the catalysts and reasoning behind the decisions, and the mistakes I made.

They'll still judge me, despite the three hundred page explanation. But, maybe some of the millions of readers will understand me.

Once we are airborne, the wings leveling off, Mark's hands relaxing on the throttle, I pull out my laptop and start to write, picking up where Mark's last content had left off—Bethany's tenth month of life. And for an hour, Mark silent, the hum of the engine my backdrop… I dive deeper than just an intro. I relive a moment, and put it all on paper myself.

chapter 39

"I'm not your patient." I cross my arms so she can't see my hands shake. This is the problem with having a mother who's a shrink. You can't do anything without it being analyzed, criticized, and classified.

"You need to talk to someone you can trust, Helena. If you don't talk to me, then Simon will call another doctor. And I won't be able to protect you from their opinion."

I dig my nails into the flesh of my palm. "I don't need protection from an opinion. And Simon can't force me to speak to anyone. I am fine, everything is fine—and I'd like you to leave. Now." She has to go. I need her to. I can feel the buildup—the transition from irritability to anger to rage. The rage is almost here—and I fight the urge to physically shove her out the door.

"Explain to me what happened."

I look away. She won't understand. Not this woman, who is always so in control of everything. The woman who has never erred in her motherly duties, never skipped a beat over handling things, without the assistance of a man.

Meanwhile, I've fallen apart because of baby formula. Clumping baby formula. I'd moved it to a bowl, had gotten out the smallest whisk we had, and had beaten the mixture until my palms blistered. Still, clumps. Clumps and I DIDN'T HAVE TIME FOR THEM. When I'd tried to pour the formula into the bottle, it had clung to the lip of the bowl and dripped back, getting all over the counter, another waste of time. I'd taken out my frustration on my cell phone first, a forceful and intentional slam of iPhone against the kitchen floor, the job finished by the heel of my shoe. I'd stared down at the cracked screen and felt no relief. I'd gone for the glass bowl next—its crash much more satisfying, the noise delightfully loud until Bethany had reacted, her eyes pinching shut, her mouth opening, a shrill scream pealing out. I eyed her, her feet kicking, one sock missing, her body bucking against the high chair. Gripping the bottle of formula in my hand, I'd attempted to take a deep, uninterrupted breath.

It was clear what should be done. Crying babies should be picked up and soothed, rocked and fed and burped. The issue was that I wasn't the woman to do that job. I was a woman who hadn't written in four days, with a deadline looming, who had barely slept in the last forty-eight hours. And Bethany NEVER SLEEPS. She NEVER STOPS. She CONSTANTLY NEEDS, NEEDS, NEEDS. And I couldn't deal with it. Not when I had another family that needed me. John and Maria and their special-needs daughter, a beautiful autistic girl who hides a secret from them. Their story was waiting on me, needing a conclusion, one built from words that WOULDN'T COME because of my stupid pregnancy and screwed-up hormones and why did I do this for him? Why did I ruin everything for a man who waltzes off to a job that doesn't even cover our car payments? He doesn't even think about my work. My worlds. My sanity. And this—she—wouldn't stop crying, wouldn't stop chipping away at all of that.

"Bethany was fine." I don't want to explain myself to my mother. I should be able to run my own house without being questioned and judged. "Simon overreacted."

"She went to the hospital, Helena."

Frustration bulges at my seams. "He overreacted. She didn't need to go to the hospital." She hadn't. Even the doctor said so, though he'd couched it in the most evasive way possible. Bethany had been dehydrated. She had thrown the bottle of formula down on the floor and screamed out the moisture in her body. If she had just held the bottle, or stopped screaming—it would have all been fine. Instead, in those hours I had left her alone, she'd worked herself into a fit.

"How many words did you write?" The question is a cold accusation, spoken by a woman who knows me well. 3,008. The most in months. I couldn't stop once that started. It was impossible.

"I don't know," I lie, turning away, my eyes catching on the clock. An hour we've wasted on this discussion. An hour of piling blame, worsening my guilt, a waste of precious time I could have spent writing. This evening is a rare opportunity for productivity, Simon carting Bethany away with a glare, his face haughty, as if he is punishing me, as if this would teach me. HA. Please don't throw me in the briar patch, Briar Rabbit. Pretty, pretty, pretty please.

"It was four hours, Helena. Four. Hours." She sticks the final words as if she's a gymnast nailing a landing, as if those two syllables prove anything. She doesn't understand I was doing Bethany a favor, leaving her down in the kitchen while I went upstairs, my office door shut, music turned up to drown out her screams. I left so I wouldn't pick her up. I left so I wouldn't break her, like I had the phone, like I had the bowl. I left her to protect her.

"Helena." Something in her voice makes me turn back. "I think you need some time away."

Mark looks up from the laptop, his body relaxed in the kitchen chair, some of Debbie's chicken and rice ignored beside him. His face is calm, as if he didn't just read something painful, something that stamps UNFIT MOTHER in giant font across my forehead. "Some time away?" he asks.

I pull my hair up, twisting it into a knot, the skin on the back of my neck damp with sweat. "She meant a mental institution." Mother hadn't called it that, of course. She'd proposed it as a postpartum treatment center, the sleek brochure touting massage therapists, group classes, and non-stop counseling.

"Did you go?" Mark reaches forward, picking up a fork and casually scooping up a bit of rice, his face almost bored in its serenity. If he hadn't found success as a writer, he could have been a therapist. The calm tone, the lack of judgment… he's better than Mother ever was.

"I didn't fight her. I wanted to go. The idea of weeks away from Simon and Bethany—with no distractions—it sounded like heaven. And I thought…" My words drop off for a beat, and I try to find the right words. "I thought that maybe Simon would *understand*, once he had to deal with her all of the time." But he hadn't. Not perfect Simon. I came back eight weeks later to find a happy baby and husband, both of them working in seamless concert—no need for me at all. In those two months, my mother had also wormed herself into my home—her grocery lists tacked to the fridge, her magazines on my coffee table, new post-natal vitamins and organic foods stocked in our pantry.

In those eight weeks away, I finished my novel, but I lost them both. The next five years were a battle to regain my footing, my marriage, and our family.

A battle I lost.

MARK

She looks good, almost better than she did two weeks ago, when she'd first swung open her door and scowled at him. Part of it is the sun. Just those two days in Memphis, and she's got a bit of a tan, freckles dotting the surface of that pale skin, her nose a little pink. He hadn't thought to give her sunscreen, hadn't thought about the disease and how it changes your skin's fragility. But sunburnt or not, she looks better. Her shoulders have lost their hunch, her eyes burn with attitude, and she even—on rare occasions—laughs. With Ellen, he used to get a laugh just from smirking at her. But with Helena, each laugh is like the final line of a difficult chapter. Exhausting to get to, but worth the hours of headache when it finally comes.

They are so different, Ellen and Helena. Not only in their personalities, but in how they handled their prognosis. Ellen had fought it in every way she could. Helena… Helena doesn't seem to care that she is going to die. She doesn't seem to have fear, or dread, or any emotion whatsoever. The cancer, the medicine—it is all an annoyance to her, something to step over in her path to get to the next page, the next chapter, the next scene. Everything in her is focused on this book.

Her head droops against the office couch, and he considers the pillow, which has shifted out of place underneath her neck. She hadn't wanted a pillow. She had told him, in the sort of tone you'd use on a disobeying dog, that she wouldn't be sleeping. "We need to *work*," she had chided, shoving her laptop open, her settle into the couch almost defiant. "We have to catch up from this weekend. I'm not going to be *sleeping*."

He had grabbed the pillow anyway, ignoring her hostile glare when he'd stuffed it under her head. Now, a low snore drags through her open mouth, the sound waking her up, and she starts in her seat. "I'm not sleeping," she calls out loudly, though he sits just two feet away, hunched over the desk. "Oh-kay," he calls back, as if he can't care less, his pen moving across the crossword puzzle page, filling in the boxes with neat and careful letters. A-S-P-H-A-L-T. Before he finishes the next clue, she has fallen asleep again, another soft sound coming out of her open mouth.

He closes the crossword book and sits for a moment, watching her. Two weeks together, and they've finished the first seven chapters. She's refused to give him a full outline, so it's hard to tell how far into the story they've gone. At this pace, they should be fine, finishing the manuscript and submitting it to publishers before she gets too bad. He'll get paid and be back in Memphis by Thanksgiving, spending Christmas with Maggie while Helena—his chest grows tight, like it hasn't for a long time. There, in the recesses of his chest, the yearn for a drink. He reopens the crossword and stares at the rows of blocks and blanks, dark specks blurring as he struggles to focus.

Adult Insect. 12 across. Five letters.

I-M-A-G-O. Her, alone, bent over a bucket, vomiting. Snow outside, her struggling to walk, to fix herself something to eat.

He steels himself against the visual. She's a wealthy woman. She can afford nurses, twenty-four-hour care. Kate will come, Kate will be here, surely. It won't be like that.

One of her hands curls against the white fabric of her sweatshirt and he watches it, the thin fingers, the blue veins along its back. Such tiny hands to create such huge worlds.

He looks back down at the page, but his mind is blank.

I'm worse. I didn't think I could be worse, but my body is an asshole. When I roll over on the couch, I feel my stomach heave. When I close my eyes, the room spins. Everything aches. Everything tastes terrible. I am freezing, yet I can see the damp stains underneath Mark's armpits and the sweat dotting his forehead when he brings me hot tea. When I made it to the bathroom, I looked at the thermostat. It's eighty-three degrees in here. My teeth shouldn't be chattering. I shouldn't have goosebumps along my arms.

"Here." He moves in front of me, a blanket in hand. He covers my chest, and I watch a bead of sweat run down his neck. I don't need his help. I'm not an invalid. I am perfectly capable of getting my own blanket and tea. I can fight this bug, or whatever this is, without his help. He should be writing. One of the two of us should be productive right now. "Open up." He has a thermometer in hand, and he's forgotten the clear disposable cover, the one that keeps the tip free from germs.

"It needs a cover." I sound pathetic, the words scratchy and weak.

"We ran out. I'll grab some tomorrow."

I pin my lips together and he smiles in response. "Open your damn mouth."

Bethany, her lips in a tight line, eyes wide at Simon. The dental floss stretching out from her lips, the end of it in his fingers. Open up, Bethany. It won't hurt. Just a quick tug.

That night, their quiet slip into her room. Glitter dusted across her pillow. The silver dollar replacing the tiny tooth.

I open my mouth and close my eyes, trying to hold onto the memory, the sound of her squeal when she discovered the silver dollar, the way she had run into our bedroom and crawled in between us, glitter sparkling off her hair. She had laid back and held the coin up in the air. She had called it magic, and Simon had cut off my rebuttal with a warning look. "Yes," he'd agreed, his head settling on the pillow beside hers. "It's magic."

The dirty thermometer pokes at the underside of my tongue and I reach up, taking it from Mark and closing my mouth around it. I watch his hands as they move to his hips, hanging there. He needs to be writing, yet he has nothing to write. I have to tell him something, anything. I have to give him the next story, yet all I seem capable of is sleep.

It beeps and I relax my jaw, passing the stick over to Mark, who brings it up to his face. "Ninety-nine point nine."

"I told you I was fine."

"Your chills say otherwise."

"I'm *fine*." I say it louder, and he raises an eyebrow at me. I bet his wife handled her death better. I bet she wore makeup and cracked jokes and was one of those annoyingly happy individuals. She probably didn't sweat him out of the house or snap at him. "Go back to your hotel."

"I will in a bit." He's been saying that for two days. If I knew where my phone was, I'd call Kate and complain. I'd have her come, purely as an excuse to get him to leave. But I don't know where my phone is. I don't know, right now, much of anything. "Drink some water." He holds out a bottle and I take it. I take enough to wet my tongue, but little else. Nothing is staying down in my stomach. My body, like my mind, hates me.

My flu gives up, and two days later, I am able to eat a real meal. Kate comes to town, and brings a Scrabble board. We play in the kitchen, and I beat them handily. When they leave, it is together. I watch his hand on the small of her back, and feel a faint pull of longing. It's been so long since I was touched. Caressed. Cared about. There had been a kiss between Simon and I, the morning that he died—a brief peck on his way out the door. In that kiss, had there been love? It's hard to remember, my memories tainted by everything else that happened that day.

October comes, and I outline, write an intro, and tell Mark about Bethany's second year. It was better. Less crying. Less frustration. Her words grew from day to day, hesitant pronunciations, a wide grin flashing at our praise. Mark and I sit on the back porch and watch the last leaves fall off the trees, and I tell him about our walks, how Simon and I would take her hand, and swing her into the air, the toes of her sneakers flashing at us before she landed. Mark builds a fire in the living room and I describe the forts we built, all over the house, sheets stretched across dining room chairs, and tucked under couch legs, flashlights lighting the interiors, a sea of pillows inside.

I lie on the couch, watching the slow spin of the fan, and tell him about her singing, her tiny voice filling the bathroom, my fingers working berry shampoo into her hair. *Sing, Mommy.* She had held out an imaginary microphone and I had leaned in close, wiping away my hair with a sudsy hand. Paired with her voice, mine sounded huge and deep, our melodies echoing off the tiled walls. Before she'd get out, she'd draw smiley faces in the fogged glass of the shower door.

I wake up and hear Mark's hushed voice, his phone to his ear, his back to me as he paces through the hall. He says his daughter's name, and then laughs at something she says. I close my eyes and float back down into nothing.

The days blur in a mix of pills and mounting exhaustion, and when I wake up, he has written two more chapters, moving us into Bethany's happy days—her adorable time as a three-year-old. I read over his words, smile and nod, my pen scratching notes in the margins. I try to focus on those happy memories, those bright moments of her life, but I can't enjoy any of it, not when I know what is coming up next.

chapter 43

Do we all live in such oblivion? I thought he loved me. I thought the ring on his finger meant something, that my taking of his last name bound us in some way. I thought, when he smiled down at me, when he reached over and cupped my face, his lips lowering to mine... I thought all of that is brick, solid and strong, the building blocks of a lifetime together.

The letter, folded over and tucked into the back pocket of his jeans, rescued in the moment before they drop into the washing machine, changes all of that. In that letter, in the moment I read her words... everything pure and lovely between us implodes.

I should have left him, right then. Maybe then, no one would have died.

"Who was she?" Mark passed the hot cocoa over, and I took it cautiously, watching the creamy liquid almost slosh over the rim. I lifted it to my lips and stole enough off of the top to reduce the risk of spillage.

"I haven't had hot chocolate in forever," I remarked, lifting the giant can of whipped cream and carefully dispensing a giant mound of it into the cocoa.

"Helena." He leaned against the counter, his arms crossing. "Who *was* she?"

"I don't know." I pick up a handful of mini marshmallows and drop them into the cup. Picking up the concoction, I move through the empty dining room and to the living room, carefully settling down on the floor before the fire. "I never found out."

I'd always wondered about Simon's fidelity. A man that attractive, that funny, that kind… I knew how women looked at us, compared us, plotted against us. He was the husband they all wanted. I was the odd girl with the big ears and flat chest, the one who nagged, and scowled, and never let Simon have any fun.

"Did you try?" He follows me into the room, crouching before the fire and grabbing the poker from the hearth.

"No. I think…" I close my eyes and try to remember that day. "I think I was afraid of finding out too much. If she loved him, then maybe he loved her. And where would that leave us?"

"You were worried he'd leave you."

"Yes." I set down the mug and hug my knees to my chest. I had attacked Simon the moment he'd gotten home, screaming accusations, my insecurities raging. I'd swore to leave him, and he'd begged me to stay. I'd called him names, and he'd told me he loved me.

Standing before my husband, that note in hand, I'd considered a scenario where Simon and I parted. I'd thought of a life without him and Bethany. I'd thought of another woman, playing with my daughter before dinner, and spending the night in bed with my husband.

The thought had filled me with such fear, such despair, that when he'd pled innocence, I believed him. I caved and I accepted—and pushed aside the words of the note. *I love you. I want you to kiss me again.* I believed him when he swore he'd found the note, that it hadn't been his. *I want to be yours.*

I'd decided to believe him, but I'd never trusted him again. And that difference, that small tweak to our relationship… it started a crack in our armor that we never recovered from.

I tilt back the mug and avoid Mark's eyes.

The front door swings open, and I turn my head and watch Mark's boots trek inside and across the polished floor. He has firewood in hand and moves out of sight, to the left side of the house. When he reaches the living room, I hear the loud tumble of logs onto the tile, the clack of wood as he stacks it. The front door hasn't fully shut and I eye it, watching it slowly swing, just a little more open. Ridiculous of a man to bring in the cold while trying to warm the house. His boots clump back, the sound of him similar to an elephant, and I relax only slightly when he pushes the door shut and flips the lock. The housekeeper will have to come back. Mop the floors, clean up his mess. Another person. Another invasion. I stab at a piece of Debbie's reheated broccoli and lift it to my mouth.

He takes off his boots and comes into the kitchen, moving straight for the coffee pot.

"You need a refill?"

I shake my head and turn the page.

"Thought I'd build another fire tonight. We're supposed to get a cold front. Temperatures are dropping into the thirties."

"Okay." He's obsessed with the weather, his most frequently used app one that shows radar and dew points, as if anything outside will affect our writing progress. We have a thermostat, our heater works—I don't understand the dogged interest in what my front yard feels like. I cross through an unnecessary line and he settles into the other chair. "Kate's coming into town tonight. She's asking if you'd like to go to a movie."

My pen stops, halfway through an exclamation point. "A movie?" A familiar prickle, one of paranoia, moves through me. They've been talking about me. Together, alone. Comparing notes, making assumptions, calculations, assessments of my health and mental state. Perhaps they've decided that I am crazy. Perhaps they think this book is ridiculous, and I am throwing away my money. Perhaps Mark has told her everything—about my postpartum, about the hospital.

Maybe she thinks I should be committed. Maybe she is reviewing all of my contracts, and pulling the ones she doesn't like, ones she can reject for reasons of incompetency. I feel hot, for the first time in a week. I scoot back against my seat, and the pen drops from my fingers.

"What's wrong?"

"Don't talk to her." The words hiss, and he looks up at me, confused. Simon had once looked confused, his face an innocent mask that hid all of the scheming he had done with my mother.

"Who? Kate?"

"She's *my* agent." *She's my daughter. He's my husband. This is my family.* I shouted those words once, at my mother. She looked less confused than Mark.

"I'm not trying to steal her away."

I close my eyes and try to focus, my mind loose from the Vicodin and Klonopin cocktail, one that was supposed to relax me but only seems to make everything worse. Already I can't remember why I am upset. Something about Kate. Mark and Kate. I let out a breath and remind myself that they are not Simon and my mother, that their friendship is not an attempt to take my child away from me.

"You want to talk to her?" He sets his phone down in front of me. "Fine. Here's my phone. *You* talk to her."

My jaw clenches, a painful flex of muscle that didn't used to hurt. "I don't want to talk to her. Neither one of us needs to talk to her, or go to movies, or do anything except write. That is why you are here." I stab the pages before me and my finger slips a little on the page. "*This* is what we need to focus on."

He doesn't say anything, and I look up at him quickly, just in time to see the sympathy cross his face before it is gone. "Don't," I snarl. "Don't look at me that way."

Simon would have asked what I was talking about. My mother would have moved down a list of questions designed to uncover the root of my feelings. Bethany would have scrunched up her face and begun to cry. Mark only smiles. No wonder he has so many damned wrinkles. I'm surprised his teeth aren't bleached white from all the exposure.

"Relax, Helena." He picks up his coffee cup and stands, leaving his cell phone in front of me. "You're screwing this cat. I'm just holding its tail."

"That's disgusting." I stare at his phone, the screen dotted with fingerprints, and it has to be a cesspool of bacteria. I haven't seen him clean it once. He only washes his hands after the restroom. When I looked through his overnight bag, he didn't even pack floss.

"The movie's a comedy," he says from his place by the sink, speaking loudly over the running water. "Might be good to clear our heads."

He's talking about the movie like it's still a possibility. I'm not going to a movie. The last movie I saw was an animated one with Bethany. I checked her out of kindergarten and we played hooky and shared Twizzlers and an Icee, and Simon said I was setting a bad example.

"No movie." I use the end of my pen to push his phone away. Maybe the simple sentence structure will get through to him. Bad Author. No Movie. Write Now.

"Want to work through the next chapter?"

Another chapter? I'm still exhausted from the last, which had taken three days and left me emotionally drained. Up next, Bethany's fourth year and the square off of Me against Them. We are climbing the hill toward the climax, though Mark doesn't know that yet. He has no idea that all of these pieces, all of the stories, are blocks of dynamite, carefully placed and positioned for the eventual explosion.

"Helena?" Mark prods. "Want to do the next chapter?"

"I'm still editing this." He should know this, should see I still have a dozen pages to go.

"Then I'll head out. Do you need anything before I go?"

I can feel something lingering in the air, something he is hiding. He wants to leave, yet he never leaves early. I set down the pen and turn in the seat, really looking at him for the first time.

Mark

Suspicion is not a new look on Helena, but it still stabs when it hits. He shifts against the counter's edge and meets her stare. She seems to be calculating, eyeing puzzle pieces and moving them together. He helps her out, his words slow and unemotional, the sentences as clear as he can make it.

"I'm picking up Kate from the airport at seven. The movie starts at eight. Would you like to come with us?"

"No movie." The words are quick, an automatic response as she continues to think.

"Okay." He lets out a long breath. "Would you like to come to the airport with me to pick her up?"

"We need to work." She's stuck on this, her dedication impressive, if not exhausting.

"I can't write any more until you tell me what to say." This side of her is new, and he wants to ask questions, but doesn't want to start a fight. She's taking enough drugs to kill a small animal, and he's dealt with some of them before, handled the side effects of increased irritability, ones that had occasionally turned Ellen into a raging bitch.

"I'm sorry. I get paranoid about..." she sighs. "Things. I don't care if you and Kate are close, but I don't want you to tell Kate anything about *this*." She taps the top of the manuscript with her finger, and he sees the vulnerability in her eyes. A spark of understanding flares.

"I don't. We don't talk about anything like that." His conversations with Kate had been strictly Helena-focused, but never about *that.* They had been almost business-like in their execution, calls about groceries, doctor appointments, blood test results and travel arrangements. He'd expected, in every call, a question about the manuscript—but there had been none.

"I am a very private person."

"I don't talk to anyone about the things you tell me." She must read the truth on his face, her shoulders relaxing slightly, her voice dropping in intensity.

"I'm sorry." She looks down, her fingers lining up the pages, making them perfectly straight in their stack.

"No need to apologize."

"My mother and Simon…" her voice trails off and he crosses his arms over his chest, waiting her out. She presses her lips together, her eyes darting across the table. "I shouldn't assume that you are the same." She looks up and his hope disappears that a revelation is coming. Her face is closed, the expression one he's becoming increasingly familiar with. When she gets like this, there is no discovery to be had, no confessions of the past, no stories to record. When she gets like this, he can only retreat and wait. "Enjoy the movie." She smiles and there isn't a bit of sincerity behind the gesture.

He waits for more, but she picks the pen back up, and he loses her to the words, her head dipping, body relaxing, eyes moving. When he leaves, the house is quiet, his truck halfway to the motel before he realizes he never built her a fire.

My earnings have gotten excessive. Simon doesn't have to work, but he does. I don't have to write, but writing has never been about the money anyway. So I'm writing. He's working, and he's spending.

First, a new Jaguar coupé, one that Bethany's carseat wouldn't fit into, one that took up the only spot in a garage that was quickly filling with more and more things. It caused too many fights, and was quickly replaced by a Range Rover.

Then, a sailboat, my name emblazoned on the side as if that would make the terrible purchase okay. An expensive chore, that's what "The Helena" was. Simon wanted to spend a summer on it, talked about me writing out on the open sea, like it would be exciting to bathe in a gallon of water, and vomit from rough weather, and constantly be on the lookout to make sure that Bethany doesn't fall over the side. We paid marina rent on that boat for two years before it sold. Every month, I hated him when I wrote that check. Every month, a small dark part of me wished he would go out sailing, catch a storm, and never come back.

Then, skis. A SubZero fridge. Automated blinds that rose and fell with the click of a remote. Heated floors in our master bedroom. Season tickets and a skybox to some football team three hours away.

He won't stop spending, and I only watch and say nothing. Our house fills with things; I close the door to my office and write. The more I earn, the more he spends.

Maybe we're normal. Maybe every husband drives his wife crazy. Maybe every wife falls short.

But it doesn't feel normal. It feels like we are at war. A war I am losing.

I write, outline, then set aside the notepad and build a fire the way I was taught. A core of paper, finely shredded, set against the base of a log. A surrounding tee-pee of kindling. I strike the match and watch the flame, my hand shielding it as I take it to the base of the kindling, the first three matches burning out before anything catches fire.

Then, a glow of ignition, the crawl of the flame up one stick, then a second. The paper catches fire and there is a small WHOOSH of action, the warm crackle bringing a smile to my face. Simon hated fires, his stubborn chauvinism never allowing me to handle the task, his own attempts pitifully inept. Every winter, in this house, he had tried to build a fire. Every winter, there had been cursing, the lighter fluid grabbed from the garage, our living room reeking of failure and chemically-created warmth. Mark's fire was the first authentic fire in this fireplace. And now mine. I leave the grate open and scoot back until I reach the couch, leaning back against the leather as I watch the flames, their lick and spark, the jump of embers, smoke curling its way up the chimney. The warmth heats my legs, and I close my eyes, appreciating the moment.

When the knock sounds, I almost miss it.

I wrote my first novel about my mother. They say you should write what you know, but I didn't know her. I wrote about her to understand her. I built a world around a character so that I could live in her shoes, could think her thoughts, could understand her intentions. I wrote a hundred thousand words and barely understood any of them.

The readers didn't care. They loved the woman I didn't. They embraced her when her husband left. They rallied beside her when he reappeared. They never read the truth. I buried those pages in the back of one of my journals—my knowledge of the romance world advanced enough to understand the value of a happy ending. So I gave my mother one. When my father returned, they fell back in love. And when the daughter ran from him, he chased her, hugged her, loved her.

All of that second half was lies. When my father came back, I was eight, and my mother was bitter. There was no joyous reunion. There was a lot of shouting. When I ran from him, he called me a nerd. When I woke in the morning, he was gone. And I didn't, not in my third-grade uniform, nor as a college freshman, give a damn about it.

The last time I spoke to my mother, I was dressed in black and huddled against the wind, staring down at a fresh gravestone. She tried to hug me. She told me she loved me. In response, I told her the truth.

I told her I hated her for turning Bethany and Simon against me. For calling me unfit. For siding with him. For taking my daughter from me. All unforgiveable sins, ones that I could only punish her for with cruel silence, ignored calls, and spiteful words snarled beside a black hearse.

I vowed, in that graveyard, to never speak to her again unless she found a way to return my daughter to me.

I open the front door, and that threat scatters in the wind.

chapter 46

Any other night, Mark would be here. He would be the one to answer the door and deal with this. Instead, I am unprotected, exposed in the doorway, when I'm hit with her eyes.

"Mom." Just a single word, yet it burns on its way out.

"Helena!" Her head snaps back, and those eyes widen in alarm. "Are you all right? You look *terrible.*"

My eyes automatically drop, to the space beside her, to see if Bethany is there. It is out of habit, and my stomach clenches, my heart frustrated with my rote memory.

"I'm fine." I pull self-consciously at the neck of my sweatshirt, grateful for the bulky material that hides my thin frame. Her eyes move into the house, darting into the spaces behind me, and I fight the urge to turn, to see what she does.

"May I come in?" She is wearing a rust-colored sweater and her hair is shorter, now almost completely white. She has a scarf around her neck but no jacket, and she rubs her arms as if she is cold. It's an odd moment for her, preparedness being a skill she taught me early on. You make lists. You pack appropriately. You prepare for unknown situations. I was the child at school with a back-up set of clothes in my backpack. We had fire emergency routes in our home and first-aid kits in the car trunk. We attended CPR training courses on the weekends, and if I'm ever abandoned in the wilderness, I can create a flame from two sticks and determination. In some ways, I am exactly like my mother, and maybe that was always our problem.

She has to have a jacket. If this shivering routine is an attempt to gain entry, she should know me better than that. "No." I close the door until just a crack shows, enough for me to see everything and her to see nothing. "Go away."

"Helena—" she holds up a hand. "I'm here for a reason."

Oh goody. I can't think of anything I want to know less than her reason for coming.

"A woman came by the office today." The office. That sterile room where relationships are judged and families critiqued. It has been half a decade since I pushed open that door, but I bet my life it's exactly the same. A black tweed couch. A bowl of peppermints on her desk. A view of the city through streak-free windows. The click of her pen against her notebook. *Do you have feelings of love for Bethany?* My mother swallows and there are more wrinkles than before, the last four years unkind. She thinks *I* look terrible? Ditto, dear Mother. "She's a reporter—"

"Charlotte Blanton." I interrupt, anxious to get on with this exchange.

"Oh. Yes." She is surprised, and glances away. "So you know her."

"What did she want?" My mother is a professional, one who considers me to be more patient than daughter. I'm not worried about what she told Charlotte Blanton. Her professional standards wouldn't allow for idle gossip.

"She had questions, about Simon. About you." Her hand trembles as it reaches for the scarf, patting the silk into place. "And Bethany. She wanted to know about Bethany."

Any fear I had over Charlotte Blanton—it turns the corner into something deeper, and darker. It reaches the level where murders are plotted and mama-bear-instincts come out to brawl. It's a familiar place, and I fight to keep my face calm, my mouth still. I can't be distracted by Charlotte Blanton right now. I have to work. Mark and I need to write. And my mother—she needs to *leave*.

Headlights sweep across the dark porch and my mother turns, her hand lifting, shielding her face. A truck turns into the driveway, and it's Mark. Panic zips through me. She can't meet him. In the cab I see curls and color, and I open the front door and step onto the porch. "I've got to go. My friends are here to pick me up."

"Your *what?*" I jog down the steps and she scurries after me, the click of her heels slower as she tries to navigate the dark stairs. I am rounding the front hood of the truck, waving in false enthusiasm to Mark, when she calls out. "Helena, we need to *talk!*"

I open the passenger door and crawl over Kate's body, the time too short for her to unbuckle and move over, the truck's headlights illuminating my mother, and her chase. Pulling the door shut, I hit the door's lock, my knee bumping into Kate's midsection, her breath wheezing out in a painful huff. "Sorry," I mutter, my butt finally hitting the seat. "Go!" I elbow Mark and he only chuckles, shifting the truck into reverse, his elbow all in my personal space.

"Who's the crazy woman?" Kate stage-whispers, her body pressed away from the window, the scent of her perfume overwhelmingly sweet. My mom bangs on the glass and jogs with us as we roll backward, out of the driveway. She stops at the base of it, her eyes on mine, the connection broken by Kate's curls, her face turning to me, a smudge of lipstick against her front teeth.

"It's my mom." I say quietly, sitting back, my hands searching for the belt buckle. "You guys have good timing." I turn in the seat and look through the back window, her body shrinking as we pull away, and I suppose I should be grateful she doesn't chase us by car.

"Oh." Kate slumps against the vinyl. "I'm sorry. I didn't mean crazy in a *bad* way."

"It's fine." Crazy just defines a person you don't understand. "You can turn right up ahead, it makes a big loop and circles back."

"Circles back?" Mark glances at his watch. "The movie starts in thirty minutes."

"I'm not going to the movie." If this was a novel, I'd draw a big fact line through that statement, with the words REPETITIVE in angry text above their vowels. Next to Mark's character description, I'd add 'stupid-head', for no other reason than to make Bethany, wherever she may be, giggle.

"That's why we were coming," Kate pipes in, and if there was any perfume left in that bottle once she got done with it, I'd be shocked. "To pick you up!"

"And you're already here in the truck." Mark says the words gravely, as if my physical presence means absolutely anything at all. "I don't really have time to go *all* the way back to your house." He looks at me and winces, an overly dramatic gesture that conveys zero remorse.

"Oh please." I fold my arms across my chest. "This is ridiculous. We're barely out of the neighborhood and I'm in pajamas, for God's sake." *Bethany, sitting at her desk. Pajama onesie, a dinosaur print along the length of her leg.*

"And socks," Kate supplies unhelpfully.

"And socks," Mark repeats, in a tone designed to irritate.

"And socks." I intone. "Pajamas and socks. So I can't go anywhere but back to my house. No movie."

"It's got Matthew McConaughey in it." Kate digs around at her feet and produces a purse, one big enough to hold a bowling ball, should that activity also be on the agenda.

"Good for him."

"And action," Mark points out. "Very manly action."

"Anddddd…." Kate finds what she is looking for and pulls a handful of chocolate out of her purse. "I've got candy!"

"Illegal candy." I frown. "That's against the rules."

"What rules?" She stops, halfway through opening a bag of M&Ms, the foreshadow to a mess of dropped tiny melted chocolates inside her purse.

"The theater rules." I may not have been to a movie in five years, but I'm fairly certain that their business model hasn't changed. Ticket prices cover the movies. Profit comes from concessions. I tilt my head and see the edge of a Ziploc freezer bag. "What's that?"

"Nothing." Her hand closes on the top of the bag, clenching it shut. "Are you this way—your way, I mean—about *all* rules? I thought it was just your own."

"So you think I create rules but ignore everyone else's?" There is a word for that. An obvious word, one that I should be able to produce without an iota of effort. My mind clenches uselessly. Oh god. Is this the beginning of dying? How much worse will it get? If I can't think of *this* word, this simple, obvious word... Mark turns right, and Kate is saying something about ticket prices being a crime in themselves. Mark swerves around a slow car and her bag bumps against my leg. It's cold, enough so that I feel it through the thin flannel of my pants. I reach over and pull at the neck of her bag. "You have ice in there?" I can see in now, see the gallon-sized freezer bag full of ice cubes, two diet sodas peeking at me, one inside of a slightly squashed theater cup. "And a used cup?"

She flushes, pulling the bag away and pushing it into the floorboard, her jaw working at the M&Ms before she swallows. "It's a plastic cup, Helena. They can *be* reused." She says it the same way Simon used to speak. As if I'm the crazy one and her actions are perfectly normal.

"I'm not wearing shoes." It the only response I think of, and it doesn't really help my cause.

"We'll get you shoes," Kate beams, and I can tell right now they are going to try and make this experience FUN. I don't want fun. I want to be back in my living room, in front of my fire. I could be rereading Mark's pages. I could be outlining the next chapter, not that Mark will be writing tonight. He seems to have completely tossed aside our work, his focus switching to crap like this.

"The mall is open," Mark points to the giant complex, one which has grown since my last visit, the movie theater squished somewhere in its depths. "I can run in and grab a pair of shoes."

"*I'll* run in." Kate sounds offended, and I feel like a child, stuck between two parents. The fact that I don't *want* to go to the movie seems to be lost on both of them.

"Mark can go." I'll have better luck with Kate in the car, alone. I can order her to cancel this stupid field trip and have her drive me back home before Mark figures out the difference between ballet flats and Toms. I point to the west entrance. "Park there." He pulls into a spot and I try and remember the layout of the mall, in search of a store as far from us as possible. "I wear size nine. I want—"

"I'll find a pair." He turns the engine off and opens the door.

"You aren't going to leave the truck on?" I overdo my tone of concern, and he cocks a suspicious head at me. "It's cold out," I add, sinking back against the seat, in an attempt to look as pitiful as possible. He can't leave us in the cold. He won't. It'll go against every protective bone in that big body.

"I know what you're thinking, Helena."

I open my eyes wide, the innocent face one I haven't used in years, not since I was last questioned by police. He shakes his head at me, shrugging out of his jacket, and passing it to me. "Keep the doors closed and you'll be fine for the next ten minutes." He swings the door shut on my reply. I growl against the leather of his coat.

"You guys have kidnapped me, you realize that?" I turn my anger on Kate, who is halfway through unwrapping a Starburst.

She pushes the yellow square into her mouth. "You did…" she ventures, speaking around the candy, "get into the car with us and scream at us to drive away. I don't think you can call that kidnapping. Besides," she brightens. "It'll be fun! When's the last time you went to a movie?"

KATE

She doesn't know why, but it is the wrong thing to say. She *always* picks the wrong things to say. Last week, she made the horrific blunder of congratulating a pregnant woman who was, in fact, just a little chubby. And that was just one example. There have been a hundred more, all accompanied by the sinking feeling hitting her gut right now.

Helena deflates, her anger seeping into something else. Sadness? She looks away, toward the mall. Maybe she wishes that Kate had gone inside instead. There is a twist of jealousy at the easy relationship she seems to have with Mark, their interactions lacking the stiffness that Kate has always felt with the woman. It isn't fair. She's championed for Helena for thirteen years. She helped to make her famous and protected her against the publishers, the press, the readers.

Yet, Mark is the one who Helena has let in. When he argues with her, she doesn't blink. When he touches her shoulder, she doesn't move away. And this book... whatever it is... she is sharing it with him. Maybe that's why their relationship has grown so quickly. Maybe it's something between two artistic minds, the writing process a bonding one, a type of personal interaction that her contracts and deadlines can't compare to.

She abandons the question about movies. Maybe Helena's last movie was scary, some horrific slasher film that triggered a panic attack. Or it could have been one of those painful biopics, the kind that look great in trailers, and then end up boring the life out of you for a hundred and twenty painful minutes. She eases her hand into the space by the door and drops the Starbucks wrapper on the floor.

"I can't believe he left us out in the cold." Helena grumbles into the leather of Mark's jacket.

"Me too." Kate warms to the idea of an imperfect Mark. "What an asshole." Bonding over a common enemy, that strategy might work. "I mean," she continues, "why wouldn't he leave the truck *running*? No one's going to steal it with us inside."

Helena turns to her, the word IDIOT written across her features. "He didn't want *me* to steal it and drive myself home. Or for me to get you to drive me home."

"Oh." Kate shifts in the seat, Helena uncomfortably close, even though Mark's seat is now vacant. "Was that your intention?"

"Of course."

"You don't want to go to the movie?" It just doesn't make sense. It's not like Helena has other plans. And this movie is supposed to be hilarious. She could stand to laugh a little. Kate would be willing to bet that she hasn't laughed since… her mind instantly sobers. Since that little girl lived upstairs.

"No." Helena says shortly, turning to face the mall, her eyes on a passing couple. The man puts his arm around the woman and Helena looks away.

"It'll be funny," Kate says quietly. "I read that it's good, when writing, to clear your mind every once in a while."

"Thanks for the writing advice," Helena says tartly. "I've never done this before."

She's in rare form tonight. Kate *knew* they shouldn't have gone by her house. She tried to tell Mark that it was a waste of time, that Helena—if she had already turned down the movie invite—wouldn't change her mind. And now he is in the safety of the warm mall while she freezes her ass off with a possibly-kidnapped client. "How's it going with Mark? The book, I mean."

"It's fine. He's talented, which is a nice surprise."

"How much have you guys gotten done?" She quietly moves her hand inside her purse, stealing out another Starburst.

"The rule isn't against eating in the car, Kate."

"I know that," she says defensively. Except of course, that she sort of hadn't. Not when Helena glared at the slightest bit of wrapper noise, or chewing noise, or each time the ice shifted in her purse and made noise. Maybe she *shouldn't* have brought the ice. But no one had Diet Dr Pepper anymore. And she didn't want to go through an entire movie without a drink. And she'd assumed, while filling up the bag at the hotel's ice machine, that Helena wasn't coming, so why would it matter? Mark wouldn't care. Mark probably wouldn't even *notice*.

Now, she feels stupid and fat, unable to stop herself from eating during a chance to have a real conversation with her client. There is no way, in the theater, she'll be able to pull out the bag of ice and cup, assemble the contraband soda and pour in the first can. Not with Helena right next to her, all appalled and righteous, with her naturally thin body and—she stops herself. Helena is dying. If there is a pity party to be had, Kate is the wrong host.

"We're almost halfway done with the book." There isn't an ounce of cheer in Helena's voice, the words dull. If they had a smell, it would be of defeat.

"Halfway done with the novel?" She puzzles through the reply, her mind calculating the time frame. "That's ahead of schedule, isn't it?" She and Mark had been working… almost twenty-two days? Twenty-three maybe? And at least half of those had been days where—according to Mark—she did little more than sleep. It seems incredible that they would be so far along. They'd be done by Thanksgiving! Her final month could be spent… she put another Starburst in her mouth, unable to imagine Helena relaxing. What does a calm, peaceful Helena look like? What will she spend those final weeks doing? She glances at her. "Isn't that good?" Any author would be pleased to have forty thousand words completed in twenty-odd days. Any other author would be freakin' joyous right now.

Helena's face is anything but. "It is good. I'm glad we are sticking to the schedule."

"You don't *look* very happy about it," she ventures.

"We're approaching some difficult scenes. I'm just working through it in my head."

The urge to ask questions is almost painful, like holding in a secret that's ripping at you to come out. She knows she shouldn't, her mind screaming at her to *STOP* yet still one falls out. "What's the book about?"

There is an overall stiffening, one that ripples through Helena's body, as if the cold has finally seeped in and she has crystallized, from knee to forehead. When she turns her head to Kate, she almost expects to hear her shatter. "You don't know?" The question is slow and almost accusatory, as if *surely* Kate should know, as if this was part of her job description, and asking this question has proven her incompetence, once and for all.

"No," she says, almost helplessly. "I'm sorry." *I'm sorry.* What a weak thing to say. Ron Pilar has probably never apologized to his authors. Ron Pilar's authors probably apologize to *him.*

"Mark hasn't told you?" Helena isn't letting this go. She's insistent on embarrassing her, on dragging this out, the way Kate's mother used to do. *No date to prom? Really? You're joking. Tell me you're joking. No one asked you? NO one? Explain that to me.*

"No." She tries to find some backbone, to say the single word in a breezy, confident tone, as if she has other clients and books to worry about and this isn't the only thing on her tiny shaky plate.

Helena's eyes see through it all. She examines her as if to find a lie, as if Kate would lie about *this.* "Good."

Good? She can't tell if the word is uttered in sarcasm or sincerity. Helena leans forward, the leather jacket falling from her chest. "He's back."

Mark is a shadowy figure, coming across the lot, big and bulky, the sort that causes Kate to walk faster on the sidewalk, and grip her keys like she had been taught, one poking out between each finger. He pauses beside the door, eyeing them through the glass, then opens it. "You didn't lock the door." He glares at Helena, and she reaches an arm out.

"I know. And dammit, no one tried to steal us."

He smiles, and Helena smiles, just the edge of it visible to Kate, just the edge of it enough to knock her off guard. There is the rustle of plastic, Helena's head down, elbows sticking out as she rummages, like a scavenger squatting over its kill. She pulls out sweatpants and a long-sleeve t-shirt, then a pack of socks and a sneaker box. "Hmm," she says, and it's impossible to tell if she is pleased or irritated.

"We'll give you some privacy to change." Mark starts to close the door. "Kate?"

"Huh?" She looks from him to Helena, then realizes her mistake. "Oh!" She scrambles for her bag and jacket, pushing open the door awkwardly. "Just a minute." She's had ten minutes to be ready, yet doesn't even have shoes on. She works her feet into the boots, then steps out, making her way around the truck, Mark meeting her by the back.

"This'll be fun," he drawls, in a manner completely void of sarcasm.

"It'll be interesting," she counters. He's an idiot if he thinks this will be fun. Fun and Helena Ross… those two concepts don't intersect.

"Where's your sense of adventure?" He leans forward when he asks the question, and she gets a whiff of him, a mix of soap and masculinity—a masculinity that doesn't live on the streets of Manhattan. A masculinity that makes a forgotten part of her swoon.

Where *is* her sense of adventure? She probably lost it years ago. Regardless, a movie date with Helena is probably not the thing to bring it back.

chapter 48

"Why don't you like JayJay?" Bethany sits to my right, in an empty spot on the floor, pages spread out before her, a marker in hand. She carefully caps the marker and sets it down, solemnly staring at me.

"A variety of reasons. Probably because she attempted to squash my creative spirit. She never wanted me to write. She's perpetually irritated at me for my success, and for my general existence."

"Mommy doesn't dislike JayJay," Simon feels the need to interject, standing in the doorway, a kitchen towel in hand, his eyes stabbing me with little warnings that he should know I'll ignore. "She just gets frustrated by her sometimes."

"No," I say, rolling the phone over in my hand, "I don't like her. You were right the first time, Bethany."

"Helena..." Simon warns, leaning against the door's frame.

I squat before Bethany. "Sometimes people act a certain way that doesn't match the person that they are inside. There are two different things at play with all of us, at every moment in our life. There is the way we act versus the person that we are inside. The person that we are grows and develops at your age, Bethany. Right now, you are a clean slate. Your personality is growing and building with every interaction, with every decision you make. You may act stubborn, or ill-mannered in one instance, but that doesn't mean that you are stubborn or rude here." I place my hand on her chest, my palm firm against the soft cotton of her t-shirt, "or here." I move up my hand to her silky head, still damp from her bath. “Some people are just having a misfire of judgment or control. But other people are letting you see a bit of the rotten person inside. Their cruel or stupid behavior is a gift of sorts, because it lets you see the real person that they are beneath.”

“So how do you know?” Her forehead scrunches, and she lifts her hands in the exaggerated gesture of a child. “If it’s who they really are?” Her voice stumbles over the words, and I watch her carefully wet her lips before finishing the question.

“You watch everyone, very carefully.” I remove my hand from her chest. “You observe and you remember. JayJay’s shown me, for thirty years, the type of person that she is inside.”

“Which is what?”

“I’m going to let you figure that out yourself, from watching her.” I lean forward and lower my voice in excitement. “It’s like a game.” She nods, and I can see her brain filing away the information, adding another ‘to-do’ mark to her list. My daughter loves lists. And information. And tasks. She is very much like myself, though she and Simon don’t realize it. “But more important than watching her is watching yourself.” I look into her eyes, making sure that she is listening, her dark pupils fully focused saucers of intelligence. “You need to analyze your thoughts and motivations, Bethany. You need to think through your actions and pick up on the darker thoughts in your head. You can become anything,” I say to her. “Make sure that you don’t become selfish, unimaginative and dumb.”

“Jesus Christ, Helena.” Simon pushes off the doorframe, and I see the disgust on his face in the moment before he turns away.

I don’t care. Life is too short to not speak the truth.

"Coming back?" The voice startles me, and I look up at Mark, who smiles down at me. "I gotta tell you, abs are all over that big screen right now."

"Ha." I look down at the page, one begged from the ticket counter, my writing finished a good ten minutes ago. "I just wanted to write a scene." I scoot back a little, pressing my shoulder blades against the wall, the bones of my butt aching against the hallway's thin carpet floor.

"You finished?" He crouches before me, and there's a patched rip on the right knee of his jeans.

"Yes." I fold the page in half and hand it, and the pen, to him. "Hold onto it for me?"

"Certainly," he drawls and, if he had a hat on, he'd tip it. I roll my eyes, then take the hand he extends, letting him pull me to my feet.

I stand, and watch him carefully tuck the page into a front pocket of his shirt, the pen disappearing into another pocket, and follow him quietly back into the theater, greeted by the sound of laughter, a scene in full effect.

A small part of me misses life. The activity. The sounds. The energy of a crowd and their reactions. The friendly wave of Kate as she moves her feet and I squeeze by. The wink of Mark as he offers me illegal cubes of Snickers.

I shouldn't be here. I don't deserve any of this.

chapter 49

"You don't have to walk me up." I stop, halfway around the hood of the truck, and glare at him.

"Just let an old man use his Southern charms." He shuts the door and gestures for the steps. "After you."

I sigh, and he smiles. "You're a battering ram, you know that?"

"Best compliment I've gotten all evening."

I take the first step and he supports my arm, an annoyance that is, unfortunately, needed as I work my way up the four steps to the porch. When did they get so steep? When did I get so old? "You've got the new stuff I wrote?" I ask.

He pats his shirt pocket. "Right here. I'll work on it tonight."

"Give me an hour or so." I come to a stop before the front door. I never locked it behind me. In my mad sprint to Mark's car, I just pulled it tight. Anyone could have come in, be waiting for me behind the door, knife poised, ready to slash at my throat or rape me. I consider inviting Mark inside, then discard the thought.

"Give you an hour or so for what?" He watches me turn the knob and frowns.

"Before you start writing. I have another scene I want to write. I'll do it right now and send it over to you."

"It's late. Send it tomorrow morning."

"No." I shake my head, tonight's encounter with my mother still raw and fresh, a dozen memories pushing to the surface and begging for attention. I need to get them down on paper while my skin still bristles from her contact. "I'm itching to write." I try to smile, to ease some of the worry from his eyes. "I need to." Maybe putting some of the past on paper will expel it from my body, like bloodletting, the words a thousand leeches that will suck the impurities out and heal a little of my pain.

Though, in that analogy, if this is bloodletting… The Night It Happened will be a slaughter fest.

"Helena?"

I snap my eyes to his, and his face is wary, his stance protective.

"Are you okay?"

I nod, pushing the door open and stepping inside, swiveling to the front and swinging the door almost closed. "Goodnight, Mark. I'll email over the new stuff soon."

He wants to say something, I can see his jaw flexing, forehead squishing, mind churning. But he doesn't. He nods, steps back, and I close the door, flipping the deadbolt latch and lifting my head, listening to the empty house. In the air, there is the faint smell of ash and smoke. I remember my fire, and glance toward the hearth, a few embers still glowing red among the charred logs. I am turning away when I stop, my vision sluggish in its alert of my brain.

"Helena." My mother pushes off the couch and stands. "I was hoping that we could speak." Her voice wobbles and I have never, not even at the funeral, heard her cry.

"Mother." I don't have the energy for this. It's already been too long of a day for me, the hours too far since my last pain pill, my exhaustion at war with the pain. "Please go home."

She comes closer, and at this distance, I can't hide. Her gaze travels critically over my face, and I wait for clarity, for the *aha* moment of understanding, but it isn't there. She isn't surprised, because she already knew, probably discovered it in her last three hours of snooping. I curse the unlocked door and drop the bag with my pajamas on the floor.

"What are these for?" She holds out a bottle of pills, and it's the *Phenergan*, the one I left beside the couch.

I take it from her, my eyes dropping to the label. "Anti-nausea."

She sighs. "I *know* what Phenergan is for, Helena. Why do you have so much medicine? Why do you look so terrible?"

If I walk outside, will Mark still be here? Was her car in the cul-de-sac and I somehow missed it? I step backward and feel myself sway.

Her arm closes around my forearm, and I am half-pushed, half-guided toward the couch. I sink into it, almost knocking over the water bottle when I reach for it. She sits next to me, silently, and watches me shake out a pill.

One pill. Ten minutes, then I'll be nodding off. No more Mother. No more conversation. No more pain.

"There's some medicine on the kitchen counter." I take the pill and settle back into the couch. "The Vicodin. I need two."

I expect her to argue, to force me to answer her question first, but she only stands, and walks to the kitchen. I watch the embers of the fire glow through half-closed eyes, and try to envision her waiting three hours for me. A long time to be alone in this house. A long time for a woman who liked to open drawers, root around in emotions, and pry into lives. She wouldn't have wasted time. She would have tried Bethany's door, found it locked. Seen the empty rooms, my sterile bedroom. Would she have wondered why the media room was locked? Would she have entered my office, sat at my desk, and criticized my life?

She blocks my view of the fire, her hand outstretched, two large white pills in her palm. "Here."

I sit up, and it feels strange when I touch her hand, when my fingers scrape over her palm. I think of the scene I was going to write, the one for Mark, and sigh. Now, my brain will be mush. Nausea pill mush. I put the pills on my tongue and tilt back the water bottle, the chalky taste registering for a moment before the water flushes it down. "Cancer." I say it quietly, but she hears me, her body lowering onto the couch beside me, her hands coming together on her lap.

"I figured it was something serious. Is it breast? Your grandmother had breast cancer, when she was—"

"No. Brain."

"Oh." She looks down at her hands. "I'm so sorry, Helena." *I'm so sorry, Helena.* She said the same words at the funeral. Then, they caused me to break, my hands to whip out, words screamed in the quiet of a thousand onlookers. Now, with the words uttered for a completely different reason, I search for sadness in her voice.

Is there some? Is that faint wobble from before catching on the end of my name?

It doesn't matter. It doesn't matter if she will miss me when I'm gone. I died four years ago, and she's had four years to recover from that. *I'm so sorry, Helena.*

"I'm not." I settle back in the couch, pulling at the blanket, covering my body. "Why are you still here, Mother?" It can't be about that reporter. There must be something else.

"Why do you hate me so much, Helena?"

I groan. She came here, staked out in my home, listened to my diagnosis, yet she wants her own pity party, one that starts with an accusatory question and ends with a clinical diagnosis, one where *I* am to blame, and *she* is the victim.

"I only had Bethany's best interests at heart. That day, I—"

"This isn't about that day," I interrupt, and the tone in my voice shuts down the topic. "Our problems were about you undermining my parenting and siding with Simon." I force my jaw to relax, my breath to flow, my hands to unclench from the blanket.

"Okay." She sighs. "Okay. Talking about this is good. Just tell me *how you feel.*"

I turn my head. "Why? So you can *forgive* yourself? So, after I'm gone, you can feel closure?" I shouldn't have told her about the cancer. I can't afford her to park herself in my life and pick the last bits of energy and peace from my bones. "A dying woman should be afforded one wish." I lift my chin and eye her as squarely as I can. "I want you to leave me alone. Go back to wherever you've been for four years. Reinvent history and paint it however you want. You were the perfect grandmother, Simon was the perfect father. I was the terrible beast you both kept Bethany safe from."

"Helena, I—"

"I. Want. You. To. *Leave.*"

"I was wrong in how I raised you." She stands, and I pray for her to turn, to exit, to not open up that pinched mouth and say another word. "I should have been different with you. I know that. Parents should adapt to fit their children. You were different from me, and I failed to adapt. I'm sorry for that."

It's not an apology. It's a point. It's a monologue, where the parent in this example is me, and the child is Bethany. She wants me to accept her apology, to agree with her, so that she can then whip around and spear me with the same logic.

I turn my head to the side, pull at the pillow, getting it into position and then lowering myself onto my side. "Goodnight, Mother."

In the dim light, I see her silhouette move in front of the fire. She bends over, and when she straightens, she's holding a stack of papers. I close my eyes and think through the content I was reviewing before the movie. Bethany's third year of life. Simon's overspending. The tension in our marriage. The love letter in his pocket.

"I read this." Her voice has lost some of its self-righteousness.

"Good for you."

"You're writing about us."

"Yes."

"Why?"

"Maybe it's cathartic."

"You plan to publish this?"

I tilt my head and look at her. "Are you worried it will be bad for business?"

She shakes her head tightly, and her earrings make a rustling sound. "I retired a few years ago. When… well. You know."

Oh yes. I know.

"I want you to be happy, Helena. That's all I've ever wanted."

Happy. I can't think of the last time I was happy. Riding on the back of that four-wheeler, I'd felt a burst of something. Finishing a novel always filled me with a strong sense of accomplishment. In the movie tonight, there'd been a moment when I hadn't been able to stop myself and had laughed. But happy? Happiness wasn't possible anymore. Happiness left when Bethany did.

I think of my daughter. I wasn't the perfect mother. In some ways, I failed her as often as this woman failed me. In other ways, I failed her a million times worse. I roll over, curling away from her and onto my side, my back to the fire.

"I'm happy." The lie spreads as smoothly as butter. "And I forgive you."

It isn't a lie for her. The lie is for Bethany, a deposit into the bank of karma, an offering to the gods, an understanding that—if I ever had a last moment with Bethany, I'd need her forgiveness, I'd need her acceptance, I'd need her love.

"Goodbye, Mother." I don't tell her that I love her. I can't.

I wait, listening to the crackle of the fire, and stiffen when her hand brushes over my shoulder, her mouth lowering to my head, a stiff kiss deposited there.

"Goodbye, Helena. Sleep tight."

I don't move, and when the front door creaks open, I close my eyes. When it pulls tightly shut, I let out my breath and throw off the blanket.

I take my time on the stairs, moving carefully to the hall, and unlock Bethany's bedroom door. I lower myself to the floor and crawl onto the sleeping bag, my eyes on her desk, on the crude artwork pinned to the wall above it. A family, four bodies together, a giant heart encircling us all.

She had wanted it. Happiness. Togetherness.

But putting things on paper don't make them so.

Simon hunches over the steering wheel, his knuckles white, jaw clenched. A dinner at my mother's, ruined. All because Oscar Wilde had anal sex.

"I can't believe you talked to her about keeping Bethany." I slump against the seat. A family should be a fortress. We should stand together, fight together, protect each other. Instead they've been scheming—comparing notes on my parenting, bringing up all my little mistakes, and making their own decisions about what's best for my daughter.

"I can't believe you talked to Bethany about that."

THAT. As if it was unspeakable. "The trials were a major part of his life. It's an important lesson to teach her. You expected me to teach her about Oscar Wilde and not—"

"She's a CHILD!" He screams the word loud enough that I stop. "She shouldn't know the details of anal sex!"

"I didn't go into great detail," I point out. "I simply answered her questions." Of which she had had a lot. I don't blame her, the appeal of the act confuses me too.

"I don't want to talk about any of it now." Liar. He doesn't want to talk about it in front of Bethany. "We can discuss her care closer to school starting."

"No. I feel like Bethany should be included in this." I twist in the seat, and look back at her.

"Included in what?" Bethany pipes in, setting down her block with interest.

"Nothing." Simon reaches over and grabs my hand, squeezing it tightly in warning.

I yank it away, my wrist twisting painfully in the action. "We're discussing you staying with JayJay during the day when Daddy starts teaching this fall." Teaching. A strong word for the fluffy crap of fourth-grade curriculum.

"Why?" Her favorite word.

"Yes, why Simon?" I raise my eyebrows at him and the car shakes as he passes a car unnecessarily closely, the jerk back into our lane done with spite. "Why do you think Bethany would be better with Janice than with me?" In another scenario, I might not have cared if Bethany spent her days with my mother. Mother should have approached me from the stance of offering to help. Instead, she and Simon had come at me offensively, citing Bethany's well-being as the reason she shouldn't stay with me.

"You're busy with writing and we aren't discussing this now." He looks up, into the rearview mirror. "Bethany, go back to your toy."

"I'm not busy with writing, I'll be fine." I clap my hands and smile at my daughter. "Good! Glad we settled that."

She smiles at me, an automatic movement, but I see the look in her eyes. The hesitation. I think, in that moment, she sees my fear.

Simon doesn't. He only sees an escalation of The Problem. Me.

"I feel like we're jumping a bit." Mark flips over a fresh page and draws a line, his pen sketching out a familiar shape. An outline. A year ago, it would have filled my heart with joy. Now, I close my eyes. "You and Simon meet." He adds the items to the page. "You marry. You get pregnant. You have Bethany. You go away for treatment. You come back. You have two seemingly happy years that we buzz through—with the obvious exception being the letter you found." He looks up at me. "And now you're focusing on her at four years old."

"That was when my mother and Simon started to really team up against me."

"Was this the beginning? Her not wanting Bethany to stay with you during the day?" He looks up at me, and I hate the calm way he asks the question. It is textbook psychology, the way my mother used to broach subjects, the way the postpartum shrink spoke when he asked if I ever thought about harming my child.

"No." I scratch a dry spot on my forearm. "That wasn't the beginning." The beginning… I can't even pinpoint it. It was always them against me. I believed in full disclosure when parenting my child. They believed in half-truths and sheltering. I believed that they were out to get me. They believed I was unfit, a terrible mother. Careless. Incompetent. My chest tightens. In some ways, they were right. I think of her, of her stiff posture and carefully chosen words, beside me on the couch. She *still* sides with him. He is dead, he was the cause of it all, and she still sides with him. Maybe I should have told her the truth, and let her sink her psychological teeth into that. *Your son-in-law is a liar. I killed him.*

"Helena?" Mark leans forward and I stand quickly, my hip colliding with the edge of the desk, my eyes flooding with tears. I barely make it to the office door before a sob wheezes out.

MARK

She is keeping something from him. It's like reading one of her books. The clues are there. He just, for the life of him, can't figure them out.

It's maddening. He can deal with it in her books. The pages can turn faster, life can be put on hold as he furiously burns through the novel. At most, it takes a day, a day to find out everything. But, it's been five weeks now. Five weeks where he has written as quickly as he can. Five weeks where he has wanted nothing more than to tie her in place and force her to tell him everything. He doesn't know how much longer he can stand it.

He pushes to his feet and steps out into the hall. Following the sounds of her sobs, he stops at a closed door, the one at the end of the hall. Putting his hands against the wood, he lowers his ear to it and listens.

HELENA

I take short breaths, my nose running, the sleeve of my sweatshirt now smeared in yellow mucus, the sobs not stopping, not easing, each hiccupping inhale only pushing my hysteria further. I press my fingers to my eyes and fight to hold out the memories. *I did it. I killed. I destroyed. I am the reason they are both gone and I'm alone.* I did all of that. Not Simon, and his mountain of sins. Not my Mother, and her fucking judgments and opinions. I did. I should be in jail. I shouldn't be in this house, in this bedroom, breathing in the scents and colors of my child. I sag, my arms buckling, my chest colliding with the door, and turn, sinking against the wood, and slowly sliding down its surface, my ankle painfully turning before I make it to the floor.

Had I been a terrible mother? I think I had been. I think I had been, and I think I'd known it, and I think I was almost *happy* that day. I think, when my arms were pumping, and I was sprinting through those neighborhoods, and thinking of Simon dying—I think I was fucking *happy*. Because yes, I would be the hero of this story. And yes, she would love me. And yes, they would all say that I was wonderful, and he was crazy, and we would live *happily ever after*.

I choke on a sob and lean back my head and *scream*.

chapter 51

MARK

The scream is one animals make as they die, one that comes from within and is filled with such despair that it drops you to your knees. A scream that makes you question every second left in life. The scream vibrates through the door, and he pulls at the locked knob, then bangs on it, calling out her name. She can't be alone like this. She can't make that sound and be okay. She can't go through *this*, whatever *this* is, and survive.

"Helena!" He sinks to his knees and presses his ear to the floor, another scream radiating, the sound so wracked with emotion it almost feels tangible. It dies and there is a gasp, then a sob, then the rattle of something against the door, and it takes a minute to understand that it's the shudder of shoulders against wood, of her body shaking as she breaks. He had wondered what it would take for her to come apart, he just hadn't realized she was so close.

"Helena," he whispers. "Please open the door."

The rattle stops, and for almost a minute, there is only the soft sound of sobs. When she finally speaks, he has to strain to hear the words.

"I can't do it." She whispers. "I thought I could tell you, but I can't."

There is fear in those words, as if he will judge her. Guilt in her sob, as if she is ashamed. If she opens the door, what will her face show? He closes his eyes and searches for the right words, something to bridge the gap between them. Words had never been kind to him, not when they came from his mouth. It was only through writing, that he had been able to really speak his mind. He stiffens. "Then don't tell me. Write it. Maybe this piece of the book… it needs to come from you." Such a simple concept, painfully obvious once stated. Why had they ever planned on him telling that portion of the story? Everything was building to, everything was centered around an event so personal it should *only* come from her. Another writer could never describe how he felt when Ellen's last breath wheezed out. Another writer could never describe the depth of emptiness, the hollow absence of life, that came when she passed. There were days he had looked at his daughter and hated her. There were moments, alone with a bottle, that he had caressed the trigger of his gun and contemplated ending it all. No one else could ever tell that story, unless they had lived that life. How was Helena's any different? Why had they ever thought that he would have the ability to tell it—to take that piece of her heart and mold it into his words?

He stands, his knees creaking, his back flaring as he moves too quickly, long strides that take him to the office, his hands fumbling through her drawers and to the stack of notepads. He grabs one, along with a pencil and pen, and makes his way back to the door, no sound coming from the other side. From the thin opening at the bottom, he can see her shadow, her thin body tucked against the frame. He pushes the first notepad through, feeding the pen and pencil next, the shadow shifting against the light.

"I'm not doing it." The words have a spine, and he wants to hug her for saying them, for coming out of that shell long enough to snarl.

"Just try." The same words he said to Maggie on the morning of Ellen's funeral. *Just try.* Just try to get dressed. Just try to eat. Just try to remember all of the good, all of her smiles, all of the memories. Just try to continue living. "Just whatever part is hardest for you to share."

She says nothing. She doesn't move, there is no sound. He sits back on his knees and eyes the pink end of the pencil's eraser. It doesn't move. Minutes pass, and after ten, he shifts his weight, settling against the wall, his feet stretched out in front of him. Surely, she will write. To put pen and paper in front of an artist is bait. She won't be able to resist its draw. She won't be able, with all of that ripping apart of her emotions, to stop its bleed onto the page.

If there is a story inside of her, it will come out. In their world, nothing else makes sense.

Then, her voice faint and muffled, she speaks.

"Would you trust me with your daughter?" I say the words quietly, my cheek resting against the door, my body now curled into a wilted ball against the wood.

"In what way?"

"Would you leave me alone with her?"

"Yes." Mark sounds sure of himself, but then again, his daughter is nineteen. I'm a decrepit skeleton, barely about to lift up a dictionary. What harm could I do? Physically I am weak. Emotionally—she wouldn't listen to anything I'd say.

Not like Bethany. Bethany was so fragile, so tiny. Her mind was so pliable, so easily influenced by Simon and me. Would Mark have trusted me with his daughter as a child? Probably not. I'm too cynical to even ask that question.

"I spoke to an attorney once. After Mother brought up keeping Bethany during the day."

"It's inappropriate, Helena. It's all..." my mother waved her hand in a dismissive gesture that encompasses my entire life. "It's all inappropriate. How you raise her. What you teach her. You can't have her going off to school and telling everyone all of the things that you've filled her mind with."

"I can do whatever I want to. I can raise her however I want to. She's my daughter."

"She's also Simon's. And he agrees with me. We think it'll be best if she stays with me during the day. You can come visit if you like, have lunch with us." She offered the statement with a smile, as if she was granting me something special, as if she wasn't trying to yank my daughter away and rip her individuality to shreds.

I knew what a semester in her house would do. I lived in that house. My mind almost died in that house.

Mark says nothing, and I think of the attorney, a short stumpy bald man, his pen tapping against the page, dots of sweat beading along his brow. A man. I should have waited longer, been more patient, and gotten a female attorney. I swallow. "It was preemptive. I just wanted to know, if things got worse, if they could actually *take* Bethany away from me."

"What did the attorney say?"

"He said that because I was a woman, that it would be hard. But that I could be determined to be unfit. He asked a lot of questions. If there was anything Simon could use against me. If I'd ever been arrested. Or harmed myself. Done drugs. Things like that." I close my eyes, thinking of the way his head had tilted at me, his eyes examining. Judging. He had judged me from the minute I had sat down, and his questions had only gotten worse.

When he'd asked if I'd ever harmed Bethany, I shook my head, and flatly denied it. *"But…"* The word had lingered on the roof of my mouth, ready to jump onto my tongue. *But…* I did leave her unattended while I locked myself into my office. *But…* I did shove her into the neighbor's arms and scream at the woman to just take her. It hadn't been right. It hadn't even been particularly sane behavior. The woman had filed a police report. She'd called me an unfit parent. She'd said, her perfectly neat script filling up every line of that report, that I often appeared unhinged. Also that I looked unkept. I think she'd meant unkempt. I'd told that to the social worker that had shown up a week later, the neatly written report in hand. The woman had merely blinked at me, as if misuse of a word was secondary to misuse of my child. Which, I agree, in a normal scenario, would be. But I didn't mistreat my child. Bethany had been a happy baby. She'd been a loved baby. That had been just *one* bad day. One bad day… among a few more.

"I told myself I was worrying over nothing." I wet my lips, and hate how weak and wobbly my voice is. "I was married to him. She was my mother. I shouldn't have had to worry about them taking my child—" My voice breaks, and I inhale sharply.

It takes me a few minutes to recover, for my body to relax, my breathing to calm, my tears to stop. I wait for him to ask questions, but he says nothing. I move, changing positions, and lower my head to the floor. From this angle, I can tilt my chin and see Bethany's stars. From this spot, I can see a forgotten crayon underneath her desk. Dust has formed under the eaves of her doll house. The dirty pink sock, over by the bookshelf, has a dead spider curled up beside it. This is the only room of the house that hasn't been cleaned. The only room that, in the last four years, has remained the same.

I reach out, running my palms across the blank surface of the notepad, the one that Mark slid under the door.

I think I have known, from the beginning, that it would come to this. Mark's right. *I* need to be the one to write the end of this story. The events of that day… I can't speak them aloud. I won't be able to explain my thoughts, the frantic rush of emotions. I might try to earn his understanding, to justify my actions, instead of just telling what happened.

But can I do it? Can I pick up this pen and write down that day? Can I walk back through my actions without breaking?

Just try. His stupid words echo in my head, the type of thing inspirational speakers scribble on the top of white boards. *Try harder.* That's what I need to do. *Try until it's done.*

I slowly sit up, my fingers tightening over the spiral bound end of it, pulling it onto my lap.

Just try.

If I'm going to relive it, to put that day into words, my feelings, my reactions… I need to go to the place where it began. I need to see the video that changed everything.

I pick up the notepad and pen, and carefully rise to my feet, the action still too quick, dizziness stabbing at me for a brief spell of time. I close my eyes, reset my equilibrium, and then open the bedroom door.

Mark looks up from his spot on the floor, his head lifting off of the wall, and our eyes meet. I speak quickly, before the urge leaves me.

"I'll write it. But I need you to leave me alone to do it."

He nods, and I can feel his eyes on me as I move down the hall and to the office, my hands shaking as I yank open the desk drawer, shoving aside bookmarks, note pads, pens and candy, my fingers picking their way to the back and to the single gold Schlage key.

I haven't touched this key in years. When the police came, after the ambulance left, they went through the entire house. I had held my breath, wondering what they would find, what conclusions they would pull, what suspicions they would have. But they hadn't blinked at the room or the duffel bag that sat beside its door. After they left, I had locked the door and never walked back in.

I've spent four years trying my best to forget everything inside.

I turn the key over in my hand. I haven't even unlocked the door and already I can feel my chest tighten. Maybe I shouldn't. Do I really need to walk back through the past? Do I *have* to see it again?

I don't. I could take the easy route and just remember that day, recapture that feeling from the safety of this office, or Bethany's room.

But it won't be the same. The memory will be muted, the emotions not as crisp. I need to relive it. She deserves that.

I close my palm around the key and stand up, back into the hall, stepping past Mark and toward the room that changed everything.

The media room.

the day it happened

I step into the media room and yawn. The heavy curtains are closed, blocking out the sun, the room cozy in the dark. We'd painted the walls a deep midnight blue, one that paired well with the cream carpet and the dark leather theater seating. I eye the closest recliner and consider taking a break, curling up under a blanket and reading for a bit. Maybe I'll take a short nap.

I discard the idea and move to the wall, the one dominated by a giant projector screen. Opening the built-in cabinet, I eye the rows of VHS tapes, moving past Simon's childhood videos and onto the sports videos, all of games played decades ago. My current scene needs a football backdrop. I need inspiration, and enough game lingo to sound authentic. Watching a few old games will do the trick.

My husband is addicted to videotaping things. In one cabinet are a hundred slim DVD cases with Bethany's first steps, her birthdays, her play dates with friends. In another cabinet are videos of our wedding, honeymoon, the day we moved into this house. Sometimes I wake in the middle of the night and hear him watching them, muted sounds barely audible through the wall. It's odd, but so am I. I'd rather him over-document things than not document them at all.

I move to the sports section, and grab one at random—Packers vs Vikings 1998 Superbowl—and push the VHS tape in, switching the input on the remote and waiting.

Hopefully, the video would have his walk into the stadium, some behind-the-scenes glimpses at the hallways, crowd, and vendors.

The screen flickers to life and I settle back against the couch.

The video is mislabeled. It's of a girl, one who can't be older than twelve. She runs through a yard, her blonde hair bouncing, curls flying, spinning, colliding. She skids to a stop, and her smile fades.

I don't recognize the scuffed Nikes that come down those steps. The camera video is poor quality, the action jerky, the yard unfamiliar. I also don't recognize the girl, her lips chapped, her face flushed. But I recognize the voice when it comes, when it says her name in a way that twists my stomach. Simon.

The camera bounces, then is set on the step, its elevated position giving me a clear view of him as he approaches her. He wears faded jeans, ones that are tight, the style of the eighties, his T-shirt sleeves cut off, and sunglasses perched on his head. He's young—maybe sixteen or seventeen, and when the girl steps away, his hand reaches out and grabs her wrist.

He looks so confident. Had he been that confident when he'd approached me at the fair? Had he been that aggressive when he'd kissed me for the first time? Dread closes my throat, and my palm is suddenly sweaty around the remote. I drop it, and watch in horror as a giant version of Simon pulls her to the ground.

The sounds are muffled. There is a crunch of leaves as her legs thrash against the ground. The yelp of her voice right before he clamps his hand over her mouth. I swallow my own scream when I see her head turn to the side, her eyes wide, his voice in her ear, whispers that don't reach the camera. My stomach cramps as I watch the loose flop of her shoes, her legs pinned by his thighs, her struggle useless. He presses a kiss against her cheek in the same moment that his hips thrust and her eyes clamp shut.

I reach out and stop the tape. I try to stand, and can't. I sit there, in front of that hundred-inch screen and don't move.

I can't think. I can't do. I stare at the blue screen and relive every minute of that tape. His excited grunt. His whisper against her ear. My eyes drag off the screen and over to the cabinet, to all of the other VHS tapes, all labeled in Simon's neat font. My stupid husband had assembled enough brain cells to hide his hellish past in clear sight. Football. A label I was guaranteed to never reach for. There are so many others. Golf Tournaments. Hockey matches. Baseball. How many of them are like this one? How truly terrible is the father of my child?

Something in me lurches, a panic, the realization that time is ticking, and I am wasting it. I glance at the blackout curtains, and wonder how low the sun is, trying to remember the last time I looked at a clock. It's afternoon, probably at least three. Hopefully not four. He will be home soon, may be driving here right now from the school, his SUV eating up the miles.

I push to my feet and stagger out of the room, my shoulder catching on the doorjamb, my eyes blurry as I make it to the hall, Bethany's door closed, the distance so far, the time too short, my heart galloping in my chest. I am having a panic attack. All of the signs are here. I wipe at my forehead and my fingers come away wet. My chest aches, breath labored, tingling in my fingertips. I need to find a clock, to see how little time we have. I can't be here when he gets home. Just one look at me, and he'll know. I push open Bethany's bedroom door and catch a piece of my heart when I see her at her desk.

Blonde hair. Not long enough to be braided. Pajama pant leggings, a dinosaur print repeating along the length of her leg. Would a man ever grab her in that way? Would a teenage boy whisper threats and promises against the soft skin of her forehead? Would her innocence be lost on grass and dead leaves?

I close my eyes and set down the pen, moving the notepad off my lap and taking a deep breath, trying to calm the anxiety building in my chest. It's been four years, yet this room is just the same. The smell of leather in the air. The expensive drapes, recliners, framed movie paraphernalia. Simon's gaming desk. The giant projector screen and surround-sound speakers. Now, at my spot on the floor, my back against a couch—I am in reach of the duffel bag, the one that still sits, just inside the door. I pull it toward me, remembering how quickly I had packed it, the inside still an unorganized mess of VHS tapes. I carefully sift through them, digging to the bottom and finally finding the one—Packers vs Vikings 1998 Superbowl—that I watched that day.

I came into this room planning to watch it first, before writing, but stepping inside, feeling the swell of emotions rise in my throat—I didn't need any further trigger, didn't think I could manage to see it again, to hear those muffled screams magnified through the extensive surround sound system. I shut the door, made it to the floor, and started to write, the memories as fresh and painful as if they just happened.

Now, I look down at the damn tape. It's heavier than I remember, and I turn it over in my hand, taking a good look at it for the first time. The label is worn, as if it was handled often, and there is tiny writing on the front sticker that I hadn't noticed before. I turn my head and read it. *Jess.* I pick up a second tape, looking at the same place. This one has an initial after the name. *Beth S.* I rummage through another five or six, my mind straining to recall any of the names from Simon's stories or past. None of them ring a bell. Then, a name that gives me pause. *Charlotte B.* A pain in my chest, one that started with the first name and grew with each new spotting—flares. *Charlotte B.* I shove aside the notebook and push myself up. Fumbling with the door, I rush into the hall and startle Mark when I burst into the office. "Call Charlotte Blanton." I pant out the words, my heart beating rapidly. "She works for the New York Post. Ask her if she is from North Virginia."

The woman I've run from, avoided. *I have some questions about your husband.* I thought she was suspicious of me, of Simon's death. Now, I see her question, her email, her pursuit, in an entirely different light. *A victim.*

I close the office door and return to the media room, stepping over the pile of tapes, of all of the names I have yet to read. I grab the notepad, my eyes dragging back to the videotape, to the neat print and the simple name. *Jess.*

I've told myself, for four years, that she doesn't matter, that Simon is dead and can't hurt her anymore. I've told myself that what happened on this tape is fifteen years old, and that she's a grown woman now, the scars of her past healed. I've told myself—I've *convinced* myself, that because I killed him, that I didn't owe her anything else.

Something stops in my chest, and the guilt is almost impossible to breathe through. I tighten my fingers around the pen and force myself to lower it to the page..

chapter 54

"Bethany."

My daughter stops, her head turning, one faint eyebrow rising at the urgent way I've said her name. Something in my stance, in the way I cling to the door, gives her additional pause. I must look crazy. Surely, the panic bolting through my chest is showing in my eyes. My eyes catch on her bed, the piles of stuffed animals, and I think of the prior weekend, of the two girls who spent the night with her. They'd been Bethany's age, just five or six. Surely too young, half the age of the girl on the video. Still, my stomach seizes. "Pack your backpack with your favorite things. Whatever you can fit inside it. Be quick."

I need to go to the police. I need to take the tapes, all of the tapes... my mind bounces to the attic, to the boxes and boxes of Simon's high school days, yearbooks and letterman jackets and awards. I came into our marriage with a stack of notebooks and my computer. He came with a storage facility worth of past. How much of it is tainted? How many secrets are packed in these walls?

I am suddenly frantic with the need to know everything. His computer history. His student's names. Simon teaches sixth grade, could he have... I push through Bethany's room and into her private bath, my knees hitting the hard tile in the moment before I vomit.

I've been a terrible wife, a terrible mother. I've let a monster run free.

Another surge of matter comes up my throat and I grip the

cool porcelain, my stomach contracting, breasts painfully pinned to the bowl as my lunch—spaghetti with bits of broccoli—comes up. Dirty water speckles my face from the impact of vomit, and I wipe at my cheek, Bethany's voice timid and scared from her new place at the door. "Are you oh-kay?" she whispers.

"I'm fine," I croak, and I wait a moment to see if my stomach is done. "Pack, Bethany."

"Where are we going?"

A great question. First, the police station. Then? After they arrest Simon? I can't return here. I can't live in a house that's housed so many lies. Maybe Bethany and I should go on a vacation. Come back and move to a new house, maybe a new city. One away from my Mother, from Simon's incarceration. Yes. I warm to the idea instantly. Maybe Florida.

I push carefully to my feet, letting my equilibrium adjust before I move to the sink and wash out my mouth, my mind quickly flipping through the things I need to do.
Grab every tape I can find.
Empty the safe.
Put Bethany in the car and drive straight to the police.

Downstairs, there is the loud scrape of the front door as it swings open and someone steps inside. I freeze, my hand jerking out and turning off the water, my ears straining for sound. Simon.

"Helena?" My name bounces up the stairs, and I almost collapse with relief.

"Mother?" I bump the edge of the doorframe on my way out of Bethany's room, and run to the top of the stairs.

"Helena, can I borrow your hot glue gun? I've got to—" she peers up at me, her hands clasped on the banister, her head craning in an unnatural fashion. "Are you okay? What's wrong?" The question is a mix of accusation and worry. I can feel the mix of judgment and superiority before she even rounds the stairs.

"Nothing's wrong." The lie falls out as easily as breathing, and my mind immediately questions the deceit. Maybe I should tell her. I could show her what sits in that VCR just down the hall. I could tell her that her stupid golden boy, the man who she sided with over her daughter, is a fucking pedophile. I open my mouth, then swallow it all when Bethany bolts past me. "JayJay!!!!" My daughter bounds down the stairs, and I rapidly run through my options. I think of the feeling that had cut through me when that front door opened. I think of what time it must be, and what I still need to do, and what will happen if Simon comes home and Bethany and I are still here.

In that split second, I make a decision, one that removes any risk to Bethany from the equation.

"Can you take Bethany?" I turn, and enter her room, opening her closet and grabbing the first shoes I find, sprinting back to the hall and down the steps—almost colliding with my mother, who is headed up.

"Take Bethany where?"

"To your house. Just for an hour or two. I'll come by and pick her up."

"Let me guess. Struck with *inspiration*?" There is that plaintive tone in her voice, the one that thinks my stories are childish, and family should always come first.

I grit my teeth and take advantage of the accusation, one that won't broach new questions. "Yes. Just for an hour or two. I'll come by and pick her up from your house."

"You know I always love to watch her." She smiles tightly. "But I *would* like that glue gun if you have..."

"I'll bring it with me. I need to find it." I hold out Bethany's shoes and can't stop the tremble in my hands. "I'll be there soon."

"With the glue gun," she prods. I'm not bringing her my freaking glue gun. I am going to collect every shred of evidence I can find, pick up my daughter, and run. I'm going to keep Bethany by my side until I know that he is in handcuffs, and then we will move far away. Far away from this woman and her judgments. Far away from this house and that media room. Far away from the man who will never, ever, look at my daughter in that way.

"Yes." I smile and all but push her down the stairs. "I promise I'll bring the glue gun." Bethany flies by in her dinosaur pajamas and I call out her name. She turns, her arms obediently reaching up and wrapping around my neck, a quick grip of messy fingers and peanut butter breath. I hug her tightly, her body squirming, her patience gone by the time I release her. "I love you." I whisper against her hair. "Be safe."

"Love you Mama." She brings a hand to her mouth and blows a kiss, the dramatic gesture one learned from a recent movie, the act practiced on every person she comes in contact with. She zigs to the right and then the front door is open and she is out into the sun, my mother looking after her disapprovingly. "She's wearing pajamas," she states, as if it mattered, as if tiny dinosaurs affect a child's day. I myself am still in pajamas, though mine are boring and navy, the same ones from yesterday. She glances at my top, at its big fabric buttons, and sniffs.

Everything in my life suddenly rests on bus duty. Would Simon have it? Would I have an extra forty-five minutes or is he in his car, right now, pulling into our neighborhood? If he gets here before she leaves, everything will be ruined. If he passes her in the neighborhood, he might flag her down and ask questions. My panic rises. "Mother, please go." I feel faint with panic and I grip the banister, almost sinking down to sit on the first step.

"Okay, oh-kay." She tilts her head, her eyes narrowing. "You really don't look well, Helena. Next week, I'm getting you in at my acupuncturist. No arguing about it. I'm putting my foot down."

"Fine." I lick my lips and can taste the salt of my sweat. "Next week."

She pats my arm and her self-satisfaction hangs in the air.

"Good girl." When she walks out the door, it is as slow as a pallbearer. When she shuts the door, I bolt back up the stairs.

There are so many tapes. I don't have time to determine which are real memories and which are horrific moments. Half of them are small cassettes, the kind that fit inside a standard-size VHS. I've been stupid. All of these sporting events, recorded in person? Simon hadn't been jetting around the country at sixteen, eighteen, twenty—a camcorder in hand, shooting pro football games. He had been in that town in Virginia, living in that farmhouse, wowing the local residents with his dimples and spiral pass. I grab a duffel bag from our closet and fill it with tapes. I eye the DVDs, our movie collection impressive, and consider adding them to the bag. Could a homemade DVD be tucked inside that Friday the 13th sleeve? Or inside the Madden 2016 case? I step away from the entertainment tower without grabbing them, the duffel bag too heavy already. I am lifting it over my shoulder when my gaze catches on the giant desk, one that took three men to carry upstairs, custom-designed to hold two monitors, a Mac Pro tower, and every possible upgrade. His computer. It is a convenient babysitter, one that keeps Simon busy for hours every evening while Bethany sleeps and I write. I don't know the passwords, haven't touched the thing in years. My stomach turns at what it might hold, at what websites he must visit.

The media room door swings open, and I look up into Simon's face.

"Helena." He studies my face, and I know what he must see.

The blotchy skin, the sweat, panic in my eyes, the tremble of my lips. I lie well, but will fail terribly with a man who knows all my tells. His eyes drop to the duffel bag, then dart behind me. I don't have to turn my head to picture the open cabinets, tapes missing, the mess there must be. "What's in the bag?" He is good. There isn't a shaky note in his voice, no crack in his composure. He looks at me, and isn't even afraid. He should be afraid. He should be terrified. He should drop to his knees, full of explanations.

Instead, he steps closer, and I think of his confident stroll toward the young blonde.

I remember how much I used to love his height, his build, the strong lean muscles that line his body. He was so opposite of anything I'd ever expected to end up with. Beautiful where I was plain. Strong where I was weak. Now? Evil where I am innocent.

My plain weak innocence fails me when his fingers wrap around my bicep, his short fingernails digging painfully into the skin, and I whimper in pain as he yanks me forward. It's the first time, in our years together, he has ever touched me like that. A week ago, I would have said he wasn't capable of violence. A week ago, I would have said he wasn't capable of rape. Now, the man before me is a stranger and I am suddenly very, very afraid.

"Let me go." I'm against his chest, the duffel bag still clutched in my left hand, and I can't release it, won't release it.

"Oh Helena." He looks down at me, with eyes that sag with disappointment. "Why?"

"Why?" I cough out the word, and spittle flies from my mouth, tiny white dots of saliva peppering the neck of his navy button-up shirt. So proper, my husband. Three-time Teacher of the Year. Loving Father of Bethany. Sickly-Sweet Rapist of Girls. I think of the blonde on the tape, her face as it changed from trust to fear. How many of them have there been? How many still exist? How many are here, in this town, in his classes? Is there a girl, right now, whose life he's destroying?

"Yes, Helena." He steps into the hall, and drags me forward, the loose skin of my arm pinched in his grasp, the look in his eyes hard and unfocused. "Why did you have to snoop?"

"I don't know what you're talking about." I scramble along behind him, trying to stand, to get my feet underneath me. Snoop. Has he ever used that word before? My brain shuffles for a better adjective. I hadn't been snooping. I had been doing research. I trip over a transition piece in the floor. "What are you doing?" I get one foot in place and try to plant my feet, to stop the forward movement. One of his hands comes loose and he grabs a handful of my hair. The pain, when he yanks, is blinding. I scream, and he drags me forward, his hand so tight on my bicep he must be leaving bruises. We come to the top of the stairs and he stops. "What are you doing?" I gasp, my neck bent, head almost sideways, in an attempt to relieve the pain against my scalp. If he jerks his hand to the right, my head will collide with the banister's marble pillar. I close my eyes and try to think.

Simon is not a planner. He doesn't think of details. He often forgets necessary items and skips instruction manual steps. He embarks on projects, then changes his mind. Right now, I can feel his brain working, the frantic search for a solution. The chances are high that he kills me right now—smashing my head against the banister, or tossing me down the stairs. He might make that snap decision without thinking through the consequences, without thinking of how he will dispose of me and his alibi and the hundred tiny details that murderers are responsible for.

"Where's Bethany?" He turns his head toward her door, which stands open, the room still and quiet. Had Bethany been home, she would have heard him come in, squealed with happiness and thundered down the hall. That, I might have heard from the media room. That might have given me time to hide the evidence and return to my office. That might have saved me from whatever terrible plan he is about to come up with. But that would have put her in danger, and I'd rather die than have risked that.

He yanks at my hair and I can't stop the sob in my throat. My knees hit the floor and part of the pain in my neck ceases. "Where is she?"

I can't think of a lie quickly enough. "My mom has her." If he goes to her, I can steal the tapes. I can steal the tapes, and go to the police, and they will hunt him down. He won't hurt Bethany, and certainly not in the brief time it will take to catch him. And they will catch him. He isn't smart enough to hide, and is stupid enough to think that he can.

"Did you tell your mother?" He leans down until our faces are just inches apart. He bites his top lip, and I can smell the coffee on his breath. Mr. Parks, Teacher of the Year.

He grabs my face, his thumb and forefinger straddling my mouth, digging painfully into my jaw. "Did you tell her?" He stares into my eyes, and I truly hate this man. It isn't even about the videos. I think I've hated him for years. I used to think him stupid, but he isn't. He's evil. He's manipulative. He's a liar. He glares at me, and I don't think there is anything to stop him, right now, from killing me. Has he ever loved me? I look into his eyes and try to find the man—the boy—I fell in love with. The one who had blushed when I called him sexy. The one who had cried when his mother died. The one who held my pregnant belly in his hand and beamed at me as if I was incredible. Somehow that man had filmed all of those tapes. He had whispered in children's ears. He had pulled up their skirts. If I could kill him right now, if I wasn't this pathetic, blubbering mess of pain and emotions—I would. I try to pull myself together, I try to look into his eyes and speak, but I can't. He sees the truth before I even open my mouth to lie.

"You haven't." He releases my jaw. "You haven't told anyone." He reaches down, his hand rough as it passes over the front pocket of my pajama shirt, then crudely gropes the sides of my pants. There are no pockets on the drawstring pants, no place to put a phone, though I rarely carry mine around. He pinches the back of my thigh and I squeeze my eyes shut from the pain. I can't cry. I need to pull myself together and reason with him.

"It wouldn't matter if you had." He straightens. "No one would believe you. Not without evidence, not with your history." He reaches for my face and I wince, surprised when his fingers are almost gentle in their caress of my cheek. "My crazy girl," he says. "That's what they say." Something in his eyes spark, as if he has an idea, and my stomach drops. "My depressed, crazy, girl." He almost whispers the words.

"She's bringing her back," I blurt out the lie, my mind frantically trying to work through a scenario where he won't, right now, hurt me. "They went to a movie. They'll be back in an hour." Would an hour be enough time to reason with him? To calm him down until the moment when I could run away? I let out a silent prayer of thanks that my mother never answers her phone, her hearing too eroded to pick up on the tinny chirp of the cell phone she often forgets to charge.

He steps down the first step and then the second, yanking at my hair, my hands scrambling to grip the spindles of the stairs before I am dragged down them.

"Get up." He orders. "Walk."

I get up. I get up and allow him to drag me forward, my bare feet stumbling on the steps, the kitchen slowly appearing through the haze of my tears. What is he doing? Where is he taking me? What is his plan?

We make it to the garage, the door shoved open, the concrete cold against my bare feet, and I understand when he reaches the utility room. The panic room. We had laughed when we saw the real estate listing. Who really needed a panic room? And in the garage? Why wouldn't someone just get in their car and drive away? Also strange was what had been inside the so-called "Panic Room". The hot water heater, washer and dryer. "It's a utility room," Simon had argued with the real estate agent. A utility room with an impossible-to-break-through door. It used to have a code. We used to be able to step into our utility room and arm the door. It would lock, and nothing could get in. Not fire, nor toxic gas, nor an army of home invaders.

But a punch code had been too risky. If Bethany had wandered down there and locked herself in... we would have had to tear down the walls to get her out. So we'd removed the punch code and put a normal lock on the door—one with keyed access on both sides, one impossible for Bethany to accidentally (or purposely) lock. The key is hung on a nail high above the light switches, and we lock and unlock the room when it isn't in use. The impenetrability of the room has come in handy. We had all of our files inside that room, the left wall a line of cabinets. All of our photos. Our passports and stock certificates—anything deemed irreplaceable. Now, he shoves me inside, and I stagger to my feet, all of my manuscripts coming into focus, the original pages that I sweated and cried over, in neat stacks on the shelves. Will I die in here? The possibility hammers at my subconscious, and all I can think about is Bethany. Growing older and never knowing. Developing curves under his watchful eye. Unprotected. Unaware. Until it is too late. I fling myself at the doorway and collide with steel, Simon slamming the door closed.

I don't hear the rustle of his keys.
I don't know if he said something else to me.
I don't hear anything through the six-inch steel walls. But I can feel the shudder of the knob in my hand. I can feel the resistance as I try to twist it. Locked. I step back from the door; the scream fading before it even hits my throat. The room is completely soundproof. It's the place we put chirping fire detectors that won't shut up. Bethany once called it magic, its ability to completely shut off noise. I called it creepy. Right now, it is terrifying. I open my mouth and force breath in and out.

I lift my head, my eyes tired from reading, my hand aching from writing. Inside my chest, my heart hammers, and I am torn between the urge to walk away and the need to finish this. Can I go through this all in one sitting? Can I relive this horrible day all at one time?

Part of me is afraid.

The other half of me knows that this is the only way. I have fallen into the snake pit, and I can't rest, can't stop. I have to fight my way through all of the memories, before the poison in them kills me.

I flex my fingers, working the muscles in them, popping my knuckles and stretching back the phalanges, one at a time, until the blood flow returns. I get off the floor and move to Simon's desk, stretching to the right, and then to the left, before settling down on his chair. Turning to a fresh page in the notebook, I return to hell.

Mark

"Call Charlotte Blanton. Find out if she's from North Virginia."

He remembers the tight pinch of her features, the panic in her eyes. He thinks back, through all their chapters, and tries to connect this strange new name to their story.

He opens a web browser and types in her name, adding in the New York Post and submitting the search. The screen goes blank, then her profile appears. He clicks on the link and, within thirty seconds, has a phone number and email address.

Settling back in his seat, he pulls his cell phone from his breast pocket and opens the flip phone, one that makes his daughter roll her eyes and officially brands him as technologically-inept. Pressing in the number, he lifts the phone to his ear.

"Charlotte Blanton." A crisp efficient voice, yet still one dipped in youth.

"Charlotte, my name is Mark Fortune. That name probably doesn't mean anything to you, but I'm calling on behalf of a friend. Helena Ross."

Silence. A long pause. Clearing of a throat. "Yes?"

"She had a rather odd question for you. She wanted to know if you are from North Virginia."

Another long pause. "May I speak to her?"

Mark glances in the direction of the room Helena had disappeared into. "She's in the middle of something right now. I can't interrupt her."

"Huh." The woman sounds as if she doesn't believe him, as if he's intentionally keeping her away.

"She's a writer," he tries to explain. "It's hard to—"

"I know what she is." Her voice was so cold, so cruel, that he blinked. *"I know what she is."* What. What was Helena? A writer. Or was the woman referring to something else?

"*Are* you from Virginia?"

"I'm from Tennessee, Mr. Fortune." She pauses. "But my family lived in Wilmont, Virginia for two years when I was ten. That's what Mrs. *Parks* is referring to."

Parks. Her married name, though she didn't now use it. But something in the sneer of Charlotte's voice… there is a history between the two women, that much is suddenly clear. He backtracks, wanting to be out of this conversation, before he says or does the wrong thing, before he stumbles onto a bed of fire ants and causes an issue. "I appreciate your time. Thank you."

"I'd like to speak to her." She speaks before he has a chance to end the connection. "Can you make sure she calls me?"

"I'm not sure anyone can *make* Helena do much of anything," he admits. "Especially not me."

"At least ask her. It's very important that I get her side of things. Before my article."

An article. The threat flares his protective instincts, and he straightens in his seat. "An article," he says slowly. "About what?"

"That's what I'd like to talk to her about. Please ask her to call me."

She ends the connection and he slowly closes the phone, spinning the chair toward the door, and thinking.

He is destroying the evidence. Or hiding it. He could put it all in his car and drive anywhere, throw it in a hundred dumpsters, or bury it in fifty different places. There is that land we own, two hundred acres up in New York—the place he goes on hunting weekends. He could hide it there, or rent a storage unit or burn it all.

Once the evidence is gone, it will be my word against his. I stop pacing, the scenario so bleak that it hurts, my stomach cramping, my breath catching. I push my fingers into my side and try to calm my breathing, slow my heartbeat, to think. No one will believe me. My own mother won't. And with the recent events—especially my visit to the divorce attorney—all of it will be suspect to the timing of my "discovery". My discovery with no evidence. The discovery of a woman ill-fit to be a mother.

If we get a divorce, I could lose her.

If we stay together, I will kill him. I can't live with him. And he won't let me. He won't let his loose thread of a wife dangle. My knowledge is too dangerous, my will too strong. If he doesn't kill me today, tonight, this week... he will soon.

A second possibility emerges, the idea that he will take Bethany and run. When I had considered this inside the house, his hand in my hair, I had thought—rather stupidly—that he would leave me at the house, unattended and free, while he took her. I had thought that the police would catch him before he got too far. But with me locked up, he can take his time. He can destroy evidence, pack bags, and visit the bank. His name is on every account, he could withdraw it all. There is easily thirty, forty thousand in our checking account. A hundred more in savings. He could pick Bethany up from my mother's and take off, be in Canada in six hours. Disappear in twelve. By the time I was found, if I was still alive, they could both be gone.

I can't let him do that, do either of those possibilities. I slowly turn, my feet moving over the bare concrete, and take in my prison.

By the door, a phone jack. At one point, a cheap corded phone had hung from its stand. We'd borrowed it, put it in the upstairs guest bedroom, and never returned it. Useless.

An electrical panel, one that controls the garage, utility room, water filtration and irrigation systems. I could turn off power to the sprinklers. Same with the five thousand dollar water purification tank that Simon had insisted we needed. Take that, my pedophile of a husband. You think you're drinking filtered water? Think again. Useless.

Our washer, a red LG behemoth with enough buttons to power a space station. Useless.

Our dryer, the second part of a matching set. Simon had been talked into paying an extra seven hundred dollars for the red color. I had gone out to the car and outlined my next scene. Useless.

Two hot water heaters, side by side. Overkill for two adults, even with Simon's thirty-minute showers. Useless.

I turn further left, the mental task calming, my heartbeat slowing, the shake in my hands subsiding. If there is a solution in this room, I will find it.

A skinny shelving unit, one that holds our laundry detergents, cleaning supplies, and iron. A toolbox sits on the bottom shelf, alongside a flashlight. The flashlight is long and heavy, the type that, if swung properly, could act as a club. I crouch and pull it out, the weight of it reassuring in my hand. Worst-case scenario, at least I am somewhat armed. Before I stand, I look through the toolbox. Basic items. Screwdriver. Hammer. A wrench. I eye the hammer. Another possible weapon. I start to stand, then stop, thinking of something.

The wrench. I turn back and look at it. It's not the big heavy sort. This one is more delicate, the sort that fits into a small hand like mine, its nimble pinchers designed for household screws and bolts. In a battle of strengths, it'd be as useless as a pillow. In a battle of wits... I bite at my bottom lip, an idea forming.

The Terrace. It's a book of mine that no one has heard of. If I move three gigantic steps to the left, it will be there, among the stack of manuscripts. It is one of the eight Unpublishables, eight novels no one will ever read. They range from uninteresting to terrible. One is about a talking cricket. One is about a menopausal woman who talks to herself for four hundred pages. One is about a lonely teenager who reads on her terrace while her mother dies from carbon monoxide poisoning. The twist? She's responsible. Carbon monoxide was the fourth attempt on her mother's life, and the first successful one. Somehow, the book managed to be boring, while also... I purse my lips and attempt to remember the carefully worded rejection. Disturbing. Psychologically disturbing. Boring while also psychologically disturbing. I had agreed with the editor. It was boring. And disturbing. If my mother had ever read it, she would have shipped me off to the closest mental health facility and locked me away forever.

In The Terrace, the girl floods the home with carbon monoxide. Her tools of death were simple: a wrench and a hot water heater.

I turn to the two eighty-gallon hot water heaters. I have everything I needed. Two huge water heaters and a toolbox. I turn and look at the stacks of manuscripts. A meticulously researched instruction manual of death. And, somewhere in those cabinets, I probably have the hot water heater's manual.

Can I do it?

Will I?

I slide my hand around the wrench, then drop it back into the toolbox.

I don't even know if Simon is still home. How long has it been since he locked me in—ten, fifteen minutes? It is hard to tell, the seconds stretching before me, my manic mind either moving extremely fast or ridiculously slow. If he has already left, if he is already on the way to dispose of evidence, or pick up Bethany, then I will accomplish nothing by turning the house into a poison-filled capsule. If anything, I'll only endanger my eventual rescue party, assuming one ever comes.

I step away from the toolbox and lean against the door, my back sliding down the metal until my butt hits the floor. Lowering my head against my knees, I fight against the panic.

Then, as if a gift from God, the hot water heater comes to life.

I lift my head and stare at it, the machine humming, the sound of water flowing, and I hold my breath, wondering if my husband is simply washing his hands, or has turned on the shower.

Part of me is shocked that, right now, he would think that a shower is appropriate. The other half of me understands it completely, especially if he is going to run away with her. Simon abhors the scent of the school on him, the smell of cafeteria and teenage sweat and the exhaust from the bus pickup. His first step—once home from work—is typically the shower. And he takes his dear time in there. I once asked him what he did for thirty or forty minutes, just standing there, under the spray. He said he thought about things, that it was where he got his best ideas. I never understood what great ideas he was coming up with. Fantasy Football projections? A more efficient way to stack his beer in the fridge? Now, with my newfound knowledge, my thoughts turn dark, his "ideas"—much more sinister in their possibilities.

The water continues, and it's been thirty or forty seconds now, definitely past the half-ass motion that he considers hand washing. If he is in the shower, I have a guaranteed half-hour where he will be at home. Add time for him to get dressed and pack up some items... probably more like an hour. He won't rush. Why would he? I am locked away, giving him all of the time in the world.

I spring to my feet and turn to the shelving, to the stacks of manuscripts there, my mind almost spasming with my next decision. Stay here and wait? Sit on my bony ass and do nothing? Or flood the house with carbon monoxide and kill him? Kill him and the possibility that he will ever hurt another girl again; kill him and ensure that Bethany's innocence will forever be protected?

I close my eyes and work through the process. The time it would take for the carbon monoxide to fill the house. Simon growing sleepy. Lying down on the bed. Death. When I don't show up to pick up Bethany. Mom will call. Grow worried. Come by. She will find Simon and call the police. She won't want Bethany to see the body. She'll take her into the backyard. The police will come. Search the house. I will be found.

I will have to tell them the truth. There's no way they'll believe the hot water heater malfunctioned on its own, not when I'd been locked inside the room with it.

Will the police understand? Will they consider it an act of self-defense? Or will they arrest me for murder? Even if found innocent, I might lose custody of Bethany in the process.

It's worth it. I would rather my mother have custody of her than <u>him</u>. I would rather risk my own incarceration than him ever touch her, or another child. Am I too late? Has he already... I almost vomit at the thought. Surely not. Surely she is too young, surely his tastes aren't that twisted. I close my eyes and think of every child at his school. The neighborhood full of kids that have sprinted across our lawn and dove down our slip-n-slide. Every smiling face we've welcomed into our home on Halloween or Easter. When she is older, we would have hosted sleepovers and movie nights. I would have gone up to my office to write. I would have left them alone with a monster and never been the wiser.

Imprisonment, losing custody… all risks I have to take. If I have the opportunity, right now, to stop him from getting to my daughter, or to any other child, I have to act.

I move aside five manuscripts before I find The Terrace. I rapidly flip through the pages, the first eighty percent of the book detailing the girl's failed attempts. Skimming over the scenes, I realize exactly how screwed up my sixteen-year-old self was. Had I really hated my mother this much? Had I felt this detached? How many of these emotions had been fiction, and how much reality? I'd blamed my stiffness with my mother on her disapproval of my parenting, on her attempts to separate me from my child. But now, reading through my teenage thoughts, I am reminded of how different we have always been. In my upbringing, there had been no cuddly moments, no friendly lunches or the sharing of feelings. Any discussions had been examined through her psychiatrist magnifying glass, my emotions and motivations picked apart and analyzed to death. I learned, early on, to hide everything from her.

The plot progresses and I slow my reading, bending the page over at the section where Helen (such an original name) did her research. The detail, as in all of my early novels, borders on excessive—an insecure need to show my thorough research. And I remember the research well. The Internet hadn't been as all-encompassing back then. I'd had to hunt down a local plumber and get my information from him. He'd found me strange, and had asked a lot of his own questions. What I planned to do with the information. If my parents were aware of my interest in killing someone via carbon monoxide. All of those suspicions had been overcome with a crisp hundred-dollar bill and a promise to mention him in the book's acknowledgements. I hold my place with my finger and flip to the back, using a precious moment to verify that I had, in fact, acknowledged him. And sure enough, on the second to last page, on the book never published, there was his name. Spencer Wilton. I let out a sigh of relief, that debt paid. I return to the meat of the document, skimming over the content quickly, then a second time, my eyes darting occasionally to the tall metal tanks, as I verify the facts.

The good news is, water heaters haven't changed in the last fifteen years.
The bad news is, I'm about to kill Simon.

I can do it. I can follow these instructions and pump our home full of deadly gas. In this airtight room, I will be protected. I could kill him and wait for rescue.

I scoot forward on my butt, toward the toolbox, and pick up the wrench.

I can do this.
I will do this.
I set down the manuscript and lean forward, toward the first hot water heater..

CHARLOTTE

Charlotte opens the manila folder, pulling out the printout and sliding it gently across the polished wood table. It is a front-page piece, four years old. In the photo, Janice Ross stares directly into the camera, despair radiating from the image. Above her picture, the title in big thick font: *"IT WAS* MY *FAULT."*

The woman's eyes are the only thing that moves. They dart to the page, to the photo, to Charlotte's face, then back to the page. A bit of tongue peeks from her lips, then disappears. "That's an old article."

"Not that old," Charlotte replies. "Do you still remember the day it happened?"

Her stare returns to Charlotte and she shakes her head minutely, a scornful sigh wheezing through her clenched mouth. "Of course I do. But like I told you before, I can't—"

"I'm not asking about Helena or Simon." Charlotte digs a fingernail into the eraser of her pencil and wills her voice to soften. "I'm just asking about you. About what happened that day."

"Why? You want to make me feel guilty?" Her arms cross over her thin chest, and there is a sharpening of the features, a straightening of the back. Suddenly, she looks more like the woman of three weeks ago, the one who had stood in her office's doorway and politely refused every one of Charlotte's questions. Of course, those questions had all been about Simon and his behavior with Bethany. She had been barking up the wrong tree with a woman who had all but thrown the Psychiatrist's Code of Ethics at her.

"I just want to understand the facts." She carefully sets the pencil down, next to her notepad. "Can you walk me through the day?"

"There isn't much to tell." Janice Ross's eyes drop to the article and she picks it up, her fingers tracing over the edges of the page. "I haven't thought about that day in a long time. I mean—" she corrects herself. "I haven't *relived* it in a long time." She glances up at Charlotte. "Are you sure you want to hear it?"

"Yes." She nods, and her fingers itch for the pencil, for the recorder that sits in her bag. But reaching for either, right now, might scare the woman away, might stop the story she seems so reluctant to tell. "Please." *Maybe this will be the break that she needs.* Maybe something in Janice's story will give her some closure.

A long sigh tumbles out, the sort that carries more than just breath. Janice Ross wets her lips and then, her eyes returning to the photo, she speaks.

"Sometimes, as a parent, you just know when you are needed. That's how it was that day. I was driving home and something just *told* me to stop by Helena's. It was as clear as if God had pulled my steering wheel to the right." She lifts her shoulders in a small shrug. "So I did. I swung by and came in. I made some excuse up about borrowing something—I can't remember what—but I was really just checking on things. And Helena—" she stops herself and there is a moment of inner conflict, some secret that she wars over. "Helena was there," she finally continues. "With Bethany."

"Was everything alright?" Charlotte thinks of the police photos, the autopsy report, the diagram of the home and the path that the gas had taken.

"Everything was fine." She gives a helpless laugh, her shoulders lifting. "I felt crazy, leaving the house. Bethany was fine, Helena was relatively fine…" *Relatively fine.* An odd choice of words. Charlotte mentally bookmarks the phrase.

"But you took Bethany with you." She risks a look at her notepad, where the timeline of events was summarized. "What time was that?"

"Yes. I took Bethany with me." She blinks, and her eyes glisten. "It—ah." She wipes at her eyes and a line of moisture smears across her cheek. "I guess it was a little before four."

Charlotte waits for more.

"Bethany was such a happy child. She was in the back, in her car seat. I remember her talking about her day, about a frog that they had found in the backyard. She wanted to keep him, but Helena had told her no." She reaches out, to the edge of the round table, and pulls a napkin free from its holder. She swallows, and her voice is stronger when she continues. "The traffic was terrible and it took me twenty minutes just to get back to my part of town. We were passing the north plaza when Bethany asked for ice cream. There was a fudge shop there, in the shopping center, and it had a few flavors. I had taken Bethany there before. I guess she looked out the window and saw the sign." She looks to the side, out the large dining room window, the light highlighting the tight lines of her throat. "I shouldn't have stopped. But I did. I stopped, and I went around to her side of the car. I opened the door…" her face crumples, her hand trembling around the napkin. "That was when I noticed her shoes."

"Her shoes?" Charlotte leans forward.

"She had been barefoot when I picked her up. Still in her pajamas, despite the time of day." Janice straightens, and carefully spreads the napkin, folding it in half and then dabbing at the wet underside of each eye. "Helena had passed me her shoes before we left, but I hadn't looked at them. I hadn't realized," she pauses, her lips pressed together for a moment. "I hadn't realized that they were mis-matched. Both Converses—Bethany loved pink Converses—but they were both for the left foot." She spreads her hands. "So I went back." She looks up at Charlotte with a hopeless expression of defeat.

"I went ...." She almost chokes on the words. *"Back."*

chapter 58

I feel a misguided sense of accomplishment when finished, the hiss of gas rerouted from its safe route and into our home's air vents. It was almost alarming how simple it was, how innocent I could engineer the look of the damage. I sit back on my heels and sniff the air, unable to smell anything new. It is a futile act, given the odorless nature of carbon monoxide. Simon will never know the cause of his death. He won't even know he's dying. He will lie down and drift off to sleep. The end.

It's too kind for him.

Still, it's hard for me. My hands tremble when I tighten the final nut. At one point in the process, I cried. Even now, I can feel the swell of emotions pushing at the back of my throat. For all that is broken in him, he gave me my daughter. Even if he did threaten to take her away. He is still half of her whole. She has his eyes, his smirk. By doing this, I am killing her father. When she finds out, will she hate me for it? Will she forgive me for it?

I slide back on the floor until my back hits the metal face of a file cabinet. Has the gas already reached the upstairs? How long will it take to fill the house? How long will it take to kill him? In my novel, it took fifteen minutes to fill the three-bedroom apartment. Our house is bigger, but so are these water heaters, both set on the maximum output. Fifteen minutes seems a reasonable estimate.

I reach back and rub my head, my scalp still sore from Simon's grip. My gaze travels over the floor before me, the concrete dotted with my instruments. I carefully move to my feet, dipping down to grab the screwdriver, box cutters, and wrench. Evidence. I open the lid to the washing machine and uncap the bleach, pouring the solution over the items, snagging a paper towel from the shelf above the appliances and wiping down each item. I return them to the toolbox, and shut the lid, pushing the paper towel down into the trash. It seems silly to destroy the evidence, yet feels cleansing, as if I am clearing the sin off my heart.

I always thought I'd make a great criminal. I'm very clean, very organized, and—apparently—able to take decisive action. My fingers tremble when I pick up the manuscript, and I almost drop it. Maybe I'm not so stone cold. I carefully align the pages and re-clip the gem clip onto the top, my hand resting on the cover page for a moment of reverence. It was one of my firsts, created on a cheap Dell desktop in the corner of my bedroom, illegal music downloading in the background, the Napster logo blinking from my status bar. Marilyn Manson and Nine Inch Nails had dominated that year of my life. When I'd finally finished it, I'd felt invincible.

Now, I feel anything but. I feel weak and foolish. I feel terrified. A reality where I kill my husband—what does that look like? A reality where my husband is a monster—how long had I ignored the signs? How many clues had I missed?

I put The Terrace back where I found it, deep in the stack. I turn and pick up the last piece of the puzzle, the manual for the hot water heater. I move to the far file cabinet, and open the top drawer, flipping back through the files to find the right one. They are all perfectly labeled, white stickers with the title printed on them, organized by category. Ten minutes ago, I'd skipped right to the file, my seamless organization proving its effectiveness. Now, with hours of waiting ahead, I take my time, calmed by the perfectly spaced words, the order in which this section of my life still is. This entire file cabinet is dedicated to household items. Appliances, warranties, manuals, and replacement parts. I still have the wiring diagram from when our thermostat was installed. I have filter sizes and EPA reports and inspection records on our fire extinguishers. I open the file on smoke detectors, a moment of worry flaring. Had we purchased carbon monoxide detectors? Did our smoke alarms perform double duty? It only takes a few seconds, and the manuals are out, spread over the open drawer. Whew. No carbon monoxide detection. If I'd been the one to purchase them, our butts would have been covered nine ways to Sunday. Thank God I wasn't. I return everything to the folder and continue. I flip through four more labels, and then my heart stops, a sudden freeze of action, every muscle stiffening as my gaze darts over the label again and again, again and again.

SPARE KEYS

I reach forward, and am almost afraid to breathe.

chapter 59

In the file is a complete duplicate of our key center—a plastic organizer of hooks that hangs on the inside of the coat closet. I've forgotten this version, any need for a missing key satisfied by the handy version we see every other day. There are two white pages, each mounted on half of a manila folder to give the paper strength. Five years ago, I found adhesive pockets online and put one beneath each label, the gold and silver keys shining out like rare coins.

I run my hand across the grid, nine keys on the page. There is one for our safe deposit box, another for Mother's house, for her office, Simon's school, and the exterior shed. I turned to the second page, forcing myself to read carefully, in case I miss it. There is a key to my desk drawer, the storage unit padlock and... my finger stops on the two most beautiful words in the world. UTILITY ROOM. I carefully slide the key out, my palms damp, my fingers delicately holding the simple metal piece as if it might break. I can be free. I can run. I turn to the door and take a step forward, holding the key out like a dagger. Another step, and the metal kisses against the knob. I pinch my eyelids closed and say a quick, furtive prayer, one that begs for forgiveness from my sins and asks for one moment of grace. I open my eyes and push the key. It slides in easily. I turn the key to the right and almost cry when the lock clicks open.

I stop. I haven't even considered the possibility of escape. Now, with this giant new possibility before me, I need to think. I need to be intelligent. I need a plan.

Once out of the room, I will be in the garage. Opening the garage door will be too loud, and I need Simon to stay inside the house, oblivious to my escape. I close my eyes and try to remember the interior of the garage. There is a window, one above his workstation. I could crawl out of it, and run to the closest house. Someone might be home, or there will be a car, someone I can flag down. I can use their phone and call the police. I can—

I stop that line of thinking. My home is a ticking death trap, one that… if I am not home, I could be innocent of. I look at the hot water heaters, at the simple malfunction that I have caused. No one ever has to know that I engineered it. I could get out of the garage, get to Bethany, and come home in a few hours. "Discover" Simon's body then. I could hide the tapes and Bethany would never need to know of her father's crimes. I could avoid a trial and jail time. I could keep my daughter and move on with our lives.

Hope surges through me, and I look around the room for anything I might need. I open the dryer and dig through the clothes. I pull out a pair of stretchy pants and a t-shirt, stripping out of my pajamas and stuffing the dirty items into the washer. My socks also come off, a clean pair snagged and put on. I work through the first step of the plan—getting to Bethany. It's over two miles to my Mother's house, which is certainly in walking distance. I need shoes. Just outside of the utility room is a basket, a place to put muddy items before coming into the house. It will have something, anything better than bare feet.

Before I open the door, I return the folder to its file and shut the cabinet. I run a disinfecting wipe over everything and survey the space, satisfied that any hint of my presence is gone.

I glance back at the hot water heaters and give myself one last opportunity to stop everything, to go back and repair the heater. I could save Simon's life and then run. Maybe I'll get to Mom's before he does? But maybe I won't. Maybe I'll step out of this utility room and he'll be waiting. Maybe, once I get free and to the cops, all of the evidence will be gone and I'll be charged with attempted murder.

The hot water quiets, the run of water stopping. Simon's shower is done. I leave my conscience behind and reach for the knob.

The garage is dark and I reach out, flipping off the utility room switch and halting its spill of light into the space. The dark settles, and I pause halfway through the doorway, and listen. Nothing moves. I step out of the room and slide the door shut. I carefully work my way through the dark and find the mud basket, pushing aside a windbreaker jacket before finding the only other item—a pair of Simon's running shoes.

The garage's window is obscured by a giant political sign, something that Simon agreed to put in our yard and never did. I carefully set it on the ground and push it beneath my car, the slide of cardboard against concrete too loud for my sensitive ears. I work the tennis shoe on my left foot, then pick up the right, not bothering with laces, my feet easily slipping into the size eleven Adidas. Gripping the edge of the counter, I heft myself up, my butt working its way onto the wooden surface. I swing my feet up and kneel, fumbling at the window's lock. I get it undone and grip the sill, struggling to get the window up, the open rectangle barely enough to fit through.

It is enough. I push my feet through, then work my hips out, my body awkwardly bending back as I slide out of the window, my back scraping painfully against the metal sill. I land awkwardly, one tennis shoe stumbling over a rolled up hose, and I hold out my hands in an ungraceful attempt to find my footing. There. I straighten and step toward the brick, hugging the side of the garage, and staying out of sight. Looking up at the open window, I realize it's too high for me to close. It doesn't matter. I move forward, my back brushing against the brick, and round the side of the house. I consider the road, then discard it, my alibi dependent on no one seeing my guilty dash from the house.

I turn and run, as quickly and as quietly as I can, into the woods behind our home.

I am not an athlete, never have been. Now, I stagger through backyards and side roads, my arms as exhausted as my legs, the mere act of swinging them somehow tiring. When the first cramp comes, it feels like a knife and I stop, pressing a hand into the spot, my chest heaving, legs shaky with fatigue. I start again and, at some point, realize I've gone the wrong way, my shortcut leading me into a gated community I can't get out of, and I attempt to scale a fence before I realize that I will have to backtrack, just to get around the brick fence.

Bethany is the only thing that gets me through it. Soon, I will have her in my arms. Soon, everything will be okay.

I jog when I can, and walk the rest of the time, moving as fast as I can manage, my feet flopping around in Simon's big shoes, a blister forming on the bridge of my foot. I practice the lines of my story, the tone of my voice, the look on my face when I see my mother. "You're always telling me to exercise more. I decided to jog over. Do you feel up to an early dinner? You could drop Bethany and me at the house afterward." She will ask questions, she always does. She will smile and agree but there will be an edge of irritation. She will get on to me for forgetting my wallet and my cell. She will go into all of the things that could have happened, and how I can't, I just simply can't, be so absentminded. Not when I am a mother, and have Bethany to think of. She will rattle on and on about stupid possibilities, her voice growing more superior, more condescending, more frustrating. None of it will matter. I'll have Bethany back and be just days away from a new life, one far away from her judgments and admonishments. I inhale deeply and imagine the smell of Bethany, the soft skin of her cheek, the curl of her hair. I am almost there, just blocks away from never letting her out of my sight.

Just ahead of me, Mom's house, the edge of her white picket fence. Maybe Bethany will be in the front yard. I force myself forward, the ache in my side flaring, and round the street corner, rising on my toes to see as much of Mother's house as possible.

Yes. There is a light on in the kitchen, a glow of gold in the fall of dusk. I manage to jog, my feet dragging along the concrete, a squirrel darting across my path. A car approaches, and I wait for it, cutting across the road as soon as it rolls past. I let myself in the gate and climb the front steps, trying the door. It is locked, and I reach out, pressing on the doorbell. She has to be home. I try to calculate how much time has passed since she picked Bethany up. An hour and a half? Two?

I press the bell again, more urgently, and listen to the faint buzz. Where could she be? I leave the front porch and move down her driveway and around to the back. If only I had my cell. Maybe they are at the park. Maybe she texted or called. Maybe they went to the library, or for ice cream. Maybe. Maybe. Maybe. I should have grabbed the spare key to her house. I'd had the key, right there among the others. Stupid me.

Her back door is also locked and I almost scream in frustration. Her garage is locked, and I can't tell if her car is in there. But she wouldn't not answer the doorbell. I slump into one of her front rockers, and wait.

CHARLOTTE

Her cell phone rings, a steady pulse of attention that Charlotte ignores. Something about this story will help, she can feel it in her bones. She waits for the older woman to collect herself.

"When I pulled into their driveway, Simon's car was there." She inhales as if she needs the air to continue. "I was surprised, but also pleased. Before I had stopped by Helena's..." she pulls at the neck of her sweater. "I had been planning on running some errands. I brought Bethany inside and spoke to Simon briefly." Her mouth tightens, a hundred tiny lines in her skin coming to life. "He was fresh out of the shower, and distracted, and I was—" she lifts a hand and covers her face, too overcome to speak. "I was thinking about my *dry cleaning.* I told him that Helena had asked me to watch Bethany, but that she'd given me mismatched shoes. He told me to just leave Bethany there, that he could watch her." Her hand falls away from her mouth for a moment, and she lets out a brittle sob. "So I did. I left them both there." She lifts her eyes and meets Charlotte's. "I don't know if I'll ever forgive myself for that."

"The article says that Helena drove your car to the scene." Charlotte fights the urge to pull out the newspaper clipping and reconfirm the facts. "How did she end up with—"

"I got my dry-cleaning after I dropped off Bethany." Her face flushes, embarrassment tangling with the guilt. "I didn't know Helena was at my house, waiting." She looks back down at the page. "And there was traffic, and the cleaners couldn't find my shirt, this silk shirt that I was going to wear to a wedding..." her voice drops off and she swallows. "When I got home, Helena was on the steps of the front porch. She looked so… so *happy* to see me." Her eyes search Charlotte's for understanding. "When she opened the car door and didn't see Bethany…" she rests her knuckles against the bright coral color of her lips. "I don't think I've ever seen that look on her face before. The way she looked at me—as if I had committed a crime. As if returning a child to her home was criminal."

Returning a child to Simon Park's home. Charlotte feels a stab of dread that doesn't even factor in the carbon monoxide. "So, Helena asked to borrow your car?"

"Oh no." Janice shakes her head sadly. "There was *no* asking."

chapter 62

"You did what?" With each breath, the panic grows, the fire fanned, my psyche closer to the very thin edge of hysteria.

"I dropped her back off at the house. With Simon." My mother shifts the strap of her purse higher on her shoulder, and her keys glint at me from her hand. "What's wrong?"

I can't see through the panic. I can't think through my fear. At some point, I step forward. Somehow, I have her keys. She is holding her hand, her face twisted in anger, her mouth moving, yelling, but I can't even hear her. I only hear my heartbeat, the dull thud, the crack of my steps against the gravel, the creak of leather seats as I shove myself into the driver's seat and shut the door.

I drive. There is the blow of a horn, and a car swerves. The pedal won't go further, and my legs are stretched out too far, the seat way back, the mirrors on the car all wrong. Something clips against my bumper, and I grip the wheel tightly, holding it through the turn.

All I can see is her face. Her tiny hand lifting to those lips, the blowing of a distracted kiss.

When I turn down my street, I see the ambulances, the police cars. I stop in the middle of it and get out, tripping over something in my haste, my palms skinning on the rough asphalt, the skin burning. I move, stumble. I shove at a body and my foot hits the curb, climbs up the driveway.

I am stopped by arms around my waist, the black chest of a uniform bumping against me, strange hands on my shoulders. Yelling. The whip of wind and hair across my face. I scream at them that this is my house, and they don't care. I tell them that my child is inside, and something on the man's face... I will never forget that look, the way that his face hardened and softened, all at once. I see that look, and I understand what it means.

I love her. Even when I left her, even when I was happily writing in that psych ward or slamming dishes onto the floor in frustration—I loved her. I loved her. I love her. I need her. I need... need...

I can't see through the tears, I can't hear through my own screams. His chest won't break, I pound on it until my fists sag, until he lifts me against his chest and carries me to an ambulance.

I beg him to see my daughter, but he says nothing.

MARK

After six hours of silence, she leaves the room and walks past the office door, heading to the other end of the hall. He looks up from his spot at the desk, watching her slowly trudge by, the notepad in hand, her head not turning to him. There is the quiet sound of the door closing, and he waits for a moment.

Silence.

He rises and goes to the room that she left, the door wide open, and he glances in, surprised to see a fully furnished space—a theater room that Maggie would fall in love with. Flipping off the light switch, he closes the door, a key still stuck in the lock. Returning to the office, he settles onto the couch, propping his feet on the end of it and folding his arms across his chest. Staring up at the ceiling, he wonders what she is doing.

"I'll write it. But I need you to leave me alone to do it."

There is a fine line between leaving her alone and neglect. At some point, she'll need food. Medicine. Sleep. He glances at the clock, and considers an interruption. Considers telling her about Charlotte Blanton, and her mention of an article.

He'll give her a few more hours. But then, if she is still awake, he'll bring her something to eat. He closes his eyes, and relaxes against the leather cushion.

Three hours later, there is no response to his knock, and he quietly turns the knob and cracks open the door, tilting his head inside. The light from the hall first illuminates a child's light switch, Beauty and the Beast dancing around the edge. The walls are a pale pink, the carpet cream. He sees the edge of a dollhouse and instantly, soberly, understands. He carefully steps inside and stops, looking down at her. A nightlight plays gently over the scene—her body curled around the notebook, her hand possessively over the top of the page, words half filling the space. Her eyes are closed, her body slack, and he bends over to pick her up, and then stops. In two months, it is the first time she has looked at peace, the lines in her forehead slack, her expression calm, her fists uncurled. His eyes move to the page, where a dozen lines repeat the same thing.

I love you.
I love you.
I love you.
I love you.
I love you.

He ignores the other pages, a sea of them across the floor, underneath her elbow and head, pages upon pages of story. Instead, he grabs a blanket from the floor, stretching it over her body, then steps backwards, gently closing the door. Returning to the office, he stretches back out on the couch and closes his eyes.

chapter 64

A love story has a series of requirements, an equation for success. Love + Loyalty = Happily Ever After. I've written and read enough in this life to understand that an equation for success rarely produces it, but that breaking the rules typically guarantees failure. I think marriage is the same way.

Can you love a monster? I did. I loved him, and I hated him, both for the entirely wrong reasons.

Did we have loyalty? No. I was more loyal to my books, to my words, to my characters, than I was to him. He was more loyal to his secrets, his crimes, his perversions, than to me.

Was there a Happily Ever After? I told you, early on in this book, the chances of that.

I wake up on Bethany's floor, my neck sore, a page sticking to my palm when I lift it. I assemble the loose papers, turn to the last chapter, and write the book's final scene. I have written a lot of The Ends in my lifetime. This one is both the hardest, and the easiest, I have ever written. I print the letters in a neat script, then slide the page off my lap, letting it flutter to the floor with the others.

Done. My story, start to finish. I've spent the last six weeks thinking that I wouldn't be able to tell it, wouldn't be able to walk back through that day, through those terrible moments. Now that I have, I feel lighter, as if I've physically stripped the moments from my heart and transferred them to the page. They say confession cleans the soul. I should have confessed a long time ago.

I close my eyes and sit back against the wall, stretching out my legs and flexing my fingers. Now that I am finished, there is only one thing I want to do.

I move slowly to my feet, my back protesting, my chest tight from the hours of constriction. I crack the wrists of each hand as I move quietly out to the hall, passing the office, Mark's snores coming quietly through the open door, and continue to my old bedroom. Going inside, I use the restroom, then stand at the sink, meeting my eyes in the reflection as I wash my hands.

Am I ready?

I turn off the water and lean forward, examining myself. I look like death. I feel even worse. At the moment, the only thing that doesn't hurt is my mind. I reach down and open the center drawer of the vanity, pulling out the only thing in there, a small white vial of liquid. Four ounces of peace. Four ounces of surrender.

Am I ready?

I pull it out and set it on the table.

MARK

The hand is soft but insistent, pushing against his shoulder, and he jerks awake, his back wrenching painfully as he sits up.

"Shit." Helena's voice moves, and there is the stumble of feet across the rug. "You scared me."

He blinks, trying to see in the dark. "What time is it?"

"Late. I finished. Can you read it?"

He moves a foot onto the floor, pressing on his lower back as he sits fully upright. "Now?"

"No, Steinbeck. In the morning. I just woke you up to ask you the question."

He can see more now. The hang of her dark hair, the outline of her glasses. She stands in the middle of the room, clutching a stack of pages. A ghost, that's what she looks like, the pajamas hanging off her frame, her long fingers skeleton-like in their clutch. "You're being sarcastic."

"God, you're dense when you first wake up. Yes. I'd like you to read them now."

He rubs at his eyes, the fuzz of sleep dropping off. "Fine. Let me get some coffee."

He stands up and stretches, something in his neck popping.

She assembles a fire, her hands moving quickly and without hesitation, kindling crackling, the amber glow smoldering, then expanding, the hearth soon full of flames. "Impressive," he remarks, carrying in two mugs and passing her one.

"Thanks." She cups the ceramic with both hands, bringing it to her face and inhaling the scent deeply, her hair auburn in the fire's glow. She doesn't look ghost-like in this light. She doesn't even look sick. She looks beautiful. Beautiful and healthy, the fire working magic across her features. He settles into the couch and reaches for the stack of pages. She sits back, and lifts the mug, taking a long sip. She hums out a small sound of satisfaction, but it's already lost in the room, his eyes on the page, her voice clear in the words, as if she is reading them aloud. He settles in, the coffee forgotten, and reads.

When he finishes, Helena's eyes are closed, her head resting on the leather, the coffee cup gone, a blanket now wrapped around her. The fire is low, gentle light coming from it, a pop coming as a log shifts. Her eyes open and she looks at him. "Are you done?"

He nods. For the first time in a long time, words escape him. "I'm sorry," he manages.

She lifts one shoulder in a half shrug, her hands smoothing over the front of the blanket. "How was the writing?"

He looks down at the final page, trying to sort through his feelings, to separate his emotions from the content. "Very strong. Better than I ever could have done."

"Oh God, don't get humble on me *now*." One corner of her mouth lifts, and it's almost like a different person, a new Helena, one free of the burdens that lay in these pages.

"No, really." He looks at her. "It's…" he tries to find the right word, a way to discuss the way the words had gripped him, gutted him. "It's difficult to read, it's so vivid. It's painful. I can't imagine going through that. Discovering that. Reacting to it. It's heartbreaking,

Helena."

She smiles thinly, her lips pressed together tightly, and looks towards the fire, her eyes glistening with unshed tears. She takes a deep breath, and he can see the containment of emotion, the moment that she regains control. She wipes a hand across her cheek and glances back at him. "Did you speak to Charlotte Blanton? Did you find out if she is from Virginia?"

"She is." He nods, remembering the stiff phone call, his mind suddenly connecting the dots between this manuscript and their conversation. "She'd like to speak with you. She's writing an article. Probably about Simon."

Helena twists her mouth in a gesture he knows well, one somewhere between a grimace and a frown, the same expression she gives when he asks if she needed to rest. "I don't want to speak to her. I know I should…" she kicks one foot out from underneath the blanket, stretching towards the fire.

A minute stretches into two, and when she opens her eyes, her expression has changed. "The book doesn't have much of a resolution." She looks at him, and the Charlotte Blanton conversation appears to be over. "Will you write an epilogue?"

He picks up the coffee cup, then sets it down, the ceramic cool. "An epilogue?" He considers the idea. "What would you want it to say?"

"I'm not sure." She picks at her bottom lip. "I guess whatever you think, you feel."

"That's a little ambiguous." He sets the pages down beside him. "It's the final note of your book. It's not something I can take lightly."

"It's not going to be authentic if I tell you what to write. Just wait, until after all of the edits and proofs are completed, and then just see what's in your heart." She drops her hand from her lips and looks up at him.

"You mean, after you've passed away."

She doesn't flinch. "Yes. You can tell them who you are, or what your job in the book was. I don't mind if they know I've had help."

They. The gods in their world, the eyes on which the axis rotated. The readers. The critics. What would they think? Was his reading of the content skewed by his relationship with her? Would they vilify or martyr her?

"Please do it. It would mean a lot to me."

She watches him with eyes too wise for such a young woman. Eyes that know his inability to say no. Six weeks ago, those eyes begged him to accept her job proposal. Too much has happened since then. A lifetime worth, literally *her* lifetime worth. Each chapter he wrote had felt like experiences lived. Watching her now, seeing her struggle… he's surprised she's made it this far. "Of course I'll do it."

Her shoulders relax. "Thank you."

Silence falls, and he thinks through the chapters he just read, through everything that happened in this house. He glances at her, at the thin pallor of her face, the hollows under her eyes. "What you did—it was to protect your child. Any mother would have done the same thing."

Her fingers twitch atop the blanket. "Not all mothers," she says quietly, and she's right. Would Ellen have? It is difficult to know. On that day, so many minute changes would have led to a hundred different scenarios, the majority of which could have avoided death. "I was selfish, standard practice for me."

"You loved her." He says firmly. "You fought for her. What happened, her being there, was an accident."

"I know." She tilts her head against the recliner, bringing up one knee and hugging it to her chest. "I know."

She doesn't. Any parent who loses a child holds themselves responsible, even if the act is completely unrelated to them. And in this case, she lit the match that caused the fire. She'll never forgive herself for that, she's carried that weight for four years. She'll continue to carry it until she dies. That is how life is, it gives us burdens to carry and doesn't give a damn about the weight. We shoulder it or we break.

"Do you believe in Heaven?" She doesn't look at him, she pulls at her shirt sleeves, pulling the material over her fists.

"I do. Ellen's there now, waiting on my ugly ass." He smiles, leaning forward and resting his elbows on his knees. "I imagine she has a list of things to yell at me about." The DUI for one. He'd spent a night in the county jail for that, and had heard her voice the entire night, a steady barrage of disappointment. The shame alone had been enough for him to set down the bottle and get help.

"You think I'll see Bethany again?" Her voice is as soft as he's ever heard it.

"I know you will. You'll have eternity with her." He speaks firmly, believing every syllable with his entire heart. She turns her head slightly and meets his gaze, and the edge of her mouth trembles, just a fraction. On her, it is as good as an ear-splitting beam. He smiles back.

MARK

He waits until late morning, after the sun has finished its climb over the oak tree, the home warming, the heater switching off, light flooding through the front windows, before he goes to her. Her bed is empty, and he returns to the child's room at the end of the hall, rapping gently on the door before pushing it open.

The sleeping bag he overlooked the first time is in use, her thin body on its side, her jet black hair splayed over the pillow, eyes closed, both hands tucked under her pillow. She looks so peaceful that he steps back, not wanting to wake her. Reaching for the door, he sees the envelope, propped up on a stack of pages, his name written on its front. He glances at Helena and steps forward, crouching and lifting up the thin envelope, turning it over, the seal undone, the hand-written page sliding easily out. He reads the first sentence and falls to his knees, crawling forward across the floor, pulling at the blanket, his breath coming out in gasps. The fleece pulls away from her, revealing her striped pajamas, her body not reacting to the exposure, nothing moving in her face, in her chest, everything too peaceful, too still. He slides his hands underneath her and lifts her into his chest, burying his face into her, choking out her name as she falls, limp, against him.

Closing his eyes, he grips her tightly, her skin cool and unresponsive, and sobs.

Dear Mark,

I'm sorry you had to be the one to find me. I'm sorry that I didn't warn you. Please don't mourn my death. Please celebrate my life, the tiny stretch of happiness that you brought to it. You made my final months mean something. You gave me the greatest gift anyone could give to another person: peace. I am the happiest I've been since she died. I'm finally ready to forgive myself. There has never been a better time for me to leave.

The drug I took is a heavy sedative, one prescribed to me by two Vermont doctors who specialize in assisted deaths. I will die in my sleep, and won't feel a thing. When you read this, my pain and grief will be over, and I will be with Bethany. I can't wait to touch her face. I can't wait to hug her to me and tell her all about you, and Mater's baby, and that night you kidnapped me and forced me to watch Matthew McConaughey and eat contraband candy.

I can't bear to see Charlotte Blanton's face; I'm too selfish to hear her story. I assume she is looking for closure, and wanting to better understand the man who took her innocence. I don't know that man. I know my husband. I know the things that I loved about him. I know the things I hated. Neither of them gave me any hint to his secrets. In the media room is a duffel bag with all of the tapes. Please give them to her, along with the letter I've placed on top of it, and a copy of the manuscript.

I could not have picked a better writer to tell my story. You are truly talented, one of the best I have ever read. In all of your novels, I found inspiration. In our novel, I found truth and self-forgiveness.

Underneath this letter are the final scenes of our story. Aside from proofs, I'd like you to keep it as original as possible. In my desk, you'll find a few more chapters, random memories that I've written down and held back until now. I'm sorry that I didn't tell you earlier about Simon. It was important to me that you wrote my impressions of him in a naive way. I didn't want those memories tainted by what I later discovered. I wanted the reader to understand how I was so stupid. I wanted them to understand why I did and reacted and failed—the way I did.

Please don't be sad for me. Please don't, for one moment, mourn. We all knew it was coming. I just needed to hurry it along. I needed to go out on my terms. I needed to find peace with myself, and then not lose that feeling.

In this moment, I can feel her smile. In this moment, I can almost remember her hugs. I want to go to her. I want to be done with whatever this life is. If there is a heaven, I am ready for it. If there is a hell, I believe that I am not destined for it. And if there is nothing but oblivion, I am ready to close my eyes and sink into that emptiness. I am ready for nothing. I am ready to say goodbye to this world and die.

You are a good man. I wish I'd had a father like you. I wish I'd married a man like you. I wish, all of those years ago, we had become friends and not enemies. I wish Bethany could have met and known you. I wish I could have known you for longer than I did.

Thank you for your friendship. Thank you for your words. Thank you for helping me with the most important task of my life. And thank you for picking up the pieces, once I am gone. I look forward to reading your next book in heaven.

Your friend,

Helena

Kate

Kate shifts into park and slowly opens the door, stepping from the car and meeting the eyes of the man who stands at the end of the driveway, his hands in his pockets. She steps toward him and Mark opens his arms, crushing her against his chest. She grips him around the waist, her face turned against his shirt, and breaks, her chest heaving with the sobs, the tears flooding her eyes, dampening the flannel of his shirt. He squeezes her tightly, his cheek against the top of her head, the warmth of his embrace the only thing keeping her together.

"She didn't have any pain," he said gruffly. "I asked the EMTs about it. She just went to sleep last night and didn't wake up."

She nods, swallowing hard. "Can I see her?"

"If you'd like." He nods toward the ambulance. "She's in there."

Until she sees her, she almost doesn't believe it. Death had seemed too weak of a path for Helena. The thought of a world without her, without more Helena Ross stories, without her weekly emails and rules, and opinions… in one quick moment, it is as if Kate has lost her entire reason for existing. Helena, simply put, can't be dead. She can't be gone. She can't.

Yet there she is, her pale face slack against a cheap hospital cot.

Kate blinks quickly, the tears leaking out of the corners of her eyes, her fingers reaching forward and gripping the rails of the gurney. Too much emotion pushes forward, her heart not prepared for it. This isn't supposed to happen yet. She is supposed to have more time to prepare, she is supposed to be calm and cool and able to handle this. She isn't supposed to break in half. Her mouth trembles, and she presses her lips tightly together.

"She left you a letter," Mark says, from outside the ambulance. "Reading it might help. It did for me."

"A letter?" Kate turns to look at him, surprised. "For me?"

He reaches back, pulling an envelope from his pocket and holding it out to her. "Here." He steps back. "I'll be in the kitchen, whenever you're done.

She carefully takes the envelope, moving out of the way as the EMTs crowd the space, Helena's gurney locked into place as they prepare to leave. Walking down the driveway a bit, she sits down on the concrete drive and works the page out of the envelope.

> *Dear Kate,*
>
> *I gave you rules because I was afraid. Don't ever second-guess your ability. Don't ever think of me in any way except as a pain. I have been terrible to you. Please forgive me. It came from a place of guilt and self-hatred. Please, in this final letter, allow me a few more moments of bossiness.*
>
> *1. In the file cabinet in the utility room is my will. My attorney is my executor and his information is listed on the inside flap of the folder. Please give him a call. I'll save you the drama of wondering at its contents. I'm leaving all of my assets to the victims of Simon Parks. I'm asking Charlotte Blanton to track them down based on the contents of video tapes that Mark is giving her. I am hoping, given her history in Wilmont, that she will recognize most of them.*
>
> *2. Also in the utility room is a stack of unpublished manuscripts. They are works that I never felt comfortable enough to publish. Feel free to read through them and see what you think. You have always been honest with me about my writing. Please read them in the same critical manner. If you think that there are any quality pieces there, feel free to pitch them. If there is rewriting to be done, please ask Mark to co-write on those titles. I understand that this is more than your standard duties. Please let this letter act as authorization for my estate to pay you a forty percent commission on those titles. You are one of the few individuals that I trust to not let the economic benefits*

outweigh your judgment of the content.

3. As far as this novel, I have been editing and rewriting it as we have gone, so I believe that it is fairly polished in its current state. Please pitch it to Tricia Pridgen, and have any sales proceeds put into an escrow account for future victims that Charlotte may find.

I'm certain that I'm forgetting something. I'm also certain in your ability to make the best decisions on my behalf. Don't hesitate if faced with a question. You know the answer, especially where I am concerned.

Thank you. I never said it enough, and it is too weak here. But it is sincere. Thank you for everything that you did for my writing and my career. Thank you for making me into one of the biggest names in our business. Thank you for your guidance and wisdom and for making it possible to spend so much of my life doing what I love. I appreciate you, and I never showed that enough.

With love,

Helena Ross

She reads the letter twice, then slowly leans back, laying back on the cement drive, looking up into the branches of the tree, fresh tears leaking out of her eyes.

I appreciate you, and I never showed that enough.

She chokes out a laugh. Damn Helena. Becoming a human in her final moments of life.

CHARLOTTE

The phone rings and she ignores it, her pen in motion, Janice Ross's strained voice coming through the mini-recorder. She creates a new bullet point and grabs the police report, underlining the time of Simon Parks' 911 call, his report of his daughter's fainting, his inability to get her to wake up. She pauses the tape and stares at the page, her eyes darting across the facts, trying to piece the circumstances together. Five months of work. Five months of sorting through every Simon Parks, dead and alive, in the country. Five months of digging through reported molestations and trying to find other victims. Five months of nothing, and now—a bunch of pieces that she can't assemble into anything. There is the rap of knuckles against wood and she turns to see her editor, a woman whose patience in the area of Simon Parks is beginning to run thin. Today, however, her face is friendly. "Shipping and Receiving just called. There's something for you at the front desk."

She pushes away from the desk slowly, making a final note on the page before sliding her bare feet into her sandals and standing, her walk to the reception area unhurried. She rounds the corner and slows when she sees the neat stack of boxes, stacked high on the counter. "These all for me?" she asks the receptionist, reaching forward and signing the release form.

"Yep. This envelope goes with it." The woman passes over a thick manila envelope. Eyeing the sender's name, Charlotte's heart picks up pace.

Snagging the envelope, she glances toward the boxes. "Can you have someone bring these to my office?"

She doesn't wait for a response. Instead, she heads back to her desk, her hands hurriedly prying open the envelope and pulling out a thick stack of pages.

> *Dear Charlotte,*
>
> *I didn't know who you were. If I had, maybe I wouldn't have avoided you. Then again, maybe I would have. I don't know. I saw a video of Simon four years ago, and have tried to forget it ever since. I've hidden when I could have been helping. Please forgive me for that. I was mourning the death of my daughter, and struggling with guilt. I was convincing myself that I was both the villain and the victim, and completely lost sight of the children and women like yourself.*
>
> *I can't fix the last four years. I can't go back twenty, to before he became a monster. The only thing I can do is move forward and ask you to help me. With this letter should be several things. One is a manuscript—it is the story of my relationship with Simon, and the truth about his death. I'm sorry for not sharing that story with you in person, and for not listening to your own. In addition to the manuscript, there will be several boxes. They contain every videotape that Simon had. I haven't watched them. I hope most of them are innocent recordings, but fear that a majority of them will be documented instances of pedophilia and molestation. There is also Simon's laptop, and the hard drive to his computer. I don't know his passwords, but my estate will pay for the forensic analysis necessary to pull whatever incriminating files may exist.*
>
> *If you are receiving this letter, and these items, I have passed away from a combination of terminal cancer and pharmaceutical assistance. In death, I hope to be a better person than I was in life. I hope to right some of Simon's wrongs, and am writing to ask for your help in doing so.*
>
> *I understand that you are an investigative journalist. Your job is to find and uncover secrets, to research. I would like you to track down Simon's victims, using the tapes and his computer files. I have appointed an executor, an attorney who will equally compensate each documented victim that you find. There isn't a way to reimburse a child's innocence, but money is the only thing I have to give them. Money, and the peace of knowing that he is dead. I hope this will, in*

some small way, help their struggle. You will, of course, be the first compensated victim. My attorney will also reimburse you for any travel or expenses incurred in finding and confirming the victims. If you need additional compensation for your time, please request that from him.

Words are how I have made my living, but I am at a loss of what to say to you. I will never understand what you went through. I will never understand how I fell in love with a man who would do such terrible things.

Thank you for reaching out to me. I'm sorry that I was too afraid to speak to you. I'm sorry that, right now, I am taking the coward's way out, and writing you instead of speaking to you in person.

Thank you, in advance, for your help.

Sincerely,

Helena Ross

She has passed her office. She turns back, stepping into the small room, and sinking into her chair, rereading the last lines of the letter, her hands careful as she sets the stack of pages onto her desk. She moves the letter to the side, the next item giving her pause, a check clipped onto the top of a letter, one from an Antonio Sacco, an estate attorney in New York. She ignores the letter, her eyes skimming across the check, over and over, the sounds of the office, the chill in the air, everything fading at the pale green check with the neat, cramped writing. Her name so clearly stated. The amount stuttering across the page. One million dollars.

Funny how, in a single moment, your entire life can change.

She moves the check with careful precision, hiding it underneath Helena's letter, then picks up the manuscript. It's the first she has ever held, hundreds of pages clipped together, the title page simple, with only the title and Helena's maiden name.

DIFFICULT WORDS
by Helena Ross

She leans back in her chair, tucking a foot beneath her, and flips over the title page.

DIFFICULT WORDS EPILOGUE

Dear Reader,

Helena Ross died four years after the death of her husband and child. She was laid to rest in New London Cemetery, alongside her daughter. Her gravestone was simple, picked out shortly after her terminal diagnosis, the marble imprinted with only her name, years of life, and two words: I'm sorry.

Before she passed, she wrote me a letter, one now framed in my study, right next to the first letter from her that I ever received. Helena was not an easy woman to love, but she touched my life in a way that few people ever have. I will miss her in my life. I will miss her stories. I will miss her rare and hard-earned smiles.

I wish you could have known the woman behind her stories. This novel gives you a glimpse, but it doesn't show you the person that she became after this story ends. When I met Helena, she was a tightly-wound ball of grief and guilt, her focus on one thing: telling this story. She wanted to confess her crimes and explain her motivations. For many of you, especially for faithful Helena Ross readers, this book will be a disappointment. There is no happy ending hidden in this epilogue. There is no solution for the sadness that you may be feeling. Most of Helena's novels were written to entertain. This book was written for an entirely different reason. This book was for her. It was both her punishment and her absolution.

Since her death, I have delivered several messages from Helena, final words that she never had the chance to say.

This message, by far, is her most important. You, the reader, are the most important recipient of all. Thank you for listening to her story. Thank you for supporting her work, even if you don't support her final decisions.

We are authors, and our lives are not the ones we live, but rather the characters that we create. This character was her truest to date. Whether you love or hate her, I hope that she made you feel. I hope that she touched your heart. I hope that, when closing this book, you will appreciate the life in these pages.

Helena, when you read these words in Heaven, know that you are loved and deeply missed.

Your friend,

Mark Fortune

THE END

Helena Ross (1984 - 2017)

< < < < < > > > > >

Want to be notified when Alessandra Torre's next book releases?

Visit www.NextNovel.com to stay informed!

NOTE FROM THE AUTHOR:

The Ghostwriter is my fourteenth book, and it's been my hardest to date. It's interesting, the development of this novel. Initially, I started the novel much earlier—before Helena was diagnosed, and the book included her receipt of the terminal diagnosis, and her reaction to it. That really stretched out and weighed down the front of the novel, and on one rainy Tuesday afternoon, I deleted 15,000 words and a month's worth of work in one reluctant tap of the DELETE key. Poof. Gone.

That wasn't the only major change I made. While every novel requires a heavy hand of edits, this one had a full-body makeover, four times over. I hope you enjoyed the final product. I hope you felt the love, sweat, and emotions that went into each of these chapters.

I love Helena. She's one of the most enjoyable minds I've ever visited. My heart hurts for her and her struggles. Thank you for picking up this novel, and reading her story. If you enjoyed it, please leave a review online, or recommend it to a friend.

If you enjoyed my writing, you may like my other works, which are mostly romance, though I do have a suspense line (The Deanna Madden series). On the following page is a list of those novels, their genre, and a one-line description of them.

If you've ever considered writing your own book, you may want to check out my series of online courses. My How to Write Your First Novel course is a great, step-by-step tutorial of how to write a book, and takes you through the entire process, from idea conception to The End. You can view my courses at AlessandraTorreInk.com.

A giant 'thank you' goes out to Maura Kye-Casella, my agent, for her unrelenting support of my novels, and your patience with my unending rollercoaster of events. Also, my appreciation to Susan Barnes, Madison Seidler, and Perla Calas—your thoughts, insights, and suggestions on this novel were so valuable—I don't know where this story would be without you all! Tricia Crouch—I'd be lost without your friendship, support, and organizational skills. Thank you for all that you do for me, at all hours of the night, and without ever complaining. Most of all, I appreciate my family. To my incredible husband—thank you for being the love of my life and so supportive of this crazy job and all that it entails.

Until the next story…

Alessandra

Looking for your next read? Check out these other Alessandra Torre novels.

The Girl in 6E. (Deanna Madden, #1) A sexy internet superstar hides a dark secret: she's a reclusive psychopath.

Do Not Disturb. (Deanna Madden, #2) Fresh from prison, an online client's casual interest quickly turns the corner into obsession.

If You Dare. (Deanna Madden, #3) Love turns deadly in this cat and mouse game where police grow closer to the internet's biggest star.

Hollywood Dirt. (Contemporary Romance) When Hollywood comes to a small town, sparks fly between its biggest star and a small-town outcast.

Sexier Reads:

Love in Lingerie. When two best friends run a lingerie company, the only thing hotter than their product is their chemistry.

Blindfolded Innocence. (First in a series) A college student catches the eye of Brad DeLuca, a divorce attorney with a sexy reputation that screams trouble.

Black Lies, the New York Times Bestseller. A love triangle with a twist that readers couldn't stop talking about. You'll hate this heroine until the moment you love her.

Moonshot, the New York Times Bestseller. Baseball's hottest player has his eye on only one thing—his team's 18-year-old ballgirl.

Tight. A small-town girl falls for a sexy stranger on vacation. Lives intersect and secrets are unveiled in this dark romance.

Trophy Wife. When a stripper marries a rich stranger, life as a trophy wife is not anything like she expects.

Love, Chloe. (First featured on Cosmpolitan.com) A fallen socialite works for an heiress, dodges an ex, and juggles single life in the city that never sleeps.